PRINCE OF WOLVES

THE GREY WOLVES SERIES, BOOK 1

QUINN LOFTIS

Quinn Loftis Books, LLC

PO Box 1308

Benton, AR 72018

lovetoread@quinnloftisbooks.com

Cover design by Marianne at Pre-Made Book Cover Shop

❀ Created with Vellum

READING ORDER FOR THE GREY WOLVES AND GYPSY HEALER SERIES

For anyone new to the Grey Wolves Series and the spin-off, Gypsy Healer Series, I've created a list showing the **best order to read the books in**.

GWS - Grey Wolves Series; GHS - Gypsy Healer Series
    GWS: Book 1, Prince of Wolves
    GWS: Book 2, Blood Rites
    GWS: Book 3, Just One Drop
    GWS: Book 4, Out of the Dark
    GWS: Book 5, Beyond the Veil
    GWS: Book 6, Fate and Fury
    GWS: Book 7, Sacrifice of Love
    GWS: Novella 4, Sacred Silence
    GWS: Novella 2, Resounding Silence
    GWS: Book 8, Luna Mine
    GHS: Book 1, Into the Fae
    GHS: Book 2, Wolf of Stone
    GWS: Novella 1, Piercing Silence
    GHS: Book 3, Jewel of Darkness
    GWS: Book 9, Den of Sorrows

GWS: Book 10, The Burning Claw
GHS: Book 4, Wolves of Wrath
GWS: Novella 3, Forgotten Silence
GWS: Book 11, Tears of the Moon
GHS: Book 5, Wolf of Sight

If you want to read them in the order of release:

GWS: Book 1, Prince of Wolves
GWS: Book 2, Blood Rites
GWS: Book 3, Just One Drop
GWS: Book 4, Out of the Dark
GWS: Book 5, Beyond the Veil
GWS: Book 6, Fate and Fury
GWS: Book 7, Sacrifice of Love
GHS: Book 1, Into the Fae
GWS: Book 8, Luna Mine
GHS: Book 2, Wolf of Stone
GWS: Novella 1, Piercing Silence
GHS: Book 3, Jewel of Darkness
GWS: Book 9, Den of Sorrows
GWS: Book 10, The Burning Claw
GWS: Novella 2, Resounding Silence
GHS: Book 4, Wolves of Wrath
GWS: Novella 3, Forgotten Silence
GWS: Novella 4, Sacred Silence
GWS: Book 11, Tears of the Moon
GHS: Book 5, Wolf of Sight

$\mathcal{J}$acque Pierce sat in the window seat of her bedroom looking across the street at her neighbors' house. The golden light from the moon cascaded across the lawn, casting long shadows from the trees. The night was silent other than the sounds of crickets and the rustling of the leaves. *I'm not being nosy, just curious.* "Yeah"— she snorted—"because it's only curiosity that would have me sitting with my eyes glued to someone else's house like some pervert preteen getting a glimpse of his first girly bits. But, whatevs'. I can deal with my dirty little conscience tomorrow."

The Henrys were hosting a foreign exchange student this year. According to Mrs. Henry, he was due any minute. Jacque had promised Sally and Jen she would get deets on the situation and call her friends with an update. She wasn't about to let them down because of some little pre-stalking jitters.

So here she sat, scoping out the Henrys' house, with her bedroom lights off and the blinds cracked just enough to see out into the night. And to top off her *James Bond* experience, she even had binoculars. Jacque was nothing if not thorough. Now, she just needed a little bit of spy music playing in the background and she would be totally golden. She'd been sitting there for an hour already and was just about to give up when a black limo pulled to the curb.

Interesting.

Jacque wondered why a foreign exchange student would travel from the airport in a limo.

Daddy must have money.

She put the binoculars to her face and adjusted them, giving her a clearer view. She settled her focus on the rear passenger door. Maybe the binoculars were a bit much but, honestly. She could see without them. But, in a town with a population of only seven hundred people, there just wasn't a whole lot of excitement, and a girl had to take her kicks where she could get them.

The driver climbed out of the limo and headed around to the rear passenger door, but it opened before he could get there.

"Well…" She released the breath she hadn't realized she'd been holding. "Slap me stupid and call me silly." Jacque licked her lips as her eyes wandered over the long drink of water that emerged from the car. She could easily see through her binoculars the boy was well over six feet tall. His hair was jet black, longer on top with bangs that fell across his face, sweeping to the left and partially covering that eye. He had broad shoulders and, from what she could see of his profile, high cheekbones, a straight nose, and full lips. She realized her mouth had dropped open, and she was all but drooling.

I should so be ashamed. She tilted her head to the other side as if that would give her a better view. *But I can't be because I would be stupid to miss seeing that.* She groaned inwardly as she watched him stretch his arms over his head and move his head side to side as though working out kinks in his neck.

"Come to mama, foreign boy," Jacque whispered. "I'll take care of those kinks." Yes, she really should be ashamed of *that* comment. She laughed quietly as if the two men across the road could somehow hear her.

Jacque watched as he and his driver conversed. She got the impression of stiffness and formality until the driver suddenly hugged the boy with obvious deep affection.

Odd, wonder if they're related or something.

Suddenly, the boy turned as if he had heard what she was thinking and looked straight at her window. Straight at *her.* Jacque froze, unable to look away from the mesmerizing blue eyes that held her in place. All her thoughts seemed to fade into the distance and she heard, or thought she heard, she wasn't quite sure which, the words, *"At last, my Jacquelyn."* Jacque shook her head, trying to clear the sudden fog that filled her mind. Her eyes still pressed into the binoculars, roamed over the features of the male specimen that had her undivided attention.

She had been right about the cheekbones, nose, and lips. What she wasn't prepared for was how his crystal blue eyes seemed to almost glow in the moonlight. The hair that fell across his forehead and over his left eye only added to his mysteriousness. Overall, he had a very masculine, beautiful face. The black shirt he was wearing fit closely to his form and showed off a muscular chest and flat stomach. He wore a black leather biker jacket, but past that, she couldn't see because the car blocked her view. She imagined his legs were every bit as nice as the rest of him. She pulled back from the window, attempting to catch her breath.

"Holy bonanza, Batman," Jacque said as she set the binoculars down. Her hands were shaking. She rubbed them together as if they were cold, though she was pretty sure the temperature in her room had risen several degrees, and at any moment she would need to start discarding clothing to keep from having a heatstroke.

When she looked back at the street the mysterious guy was walking into the Henrys' house. As the door closed, she heard the voice again say, *"Soon."*

Jacque sat there for a few minutes trying to get her brain back online. Like a computer that had suddenly crashed, she found herself having to reboot.

Hearing on? Check. Eyes no longer bugging out of my head? Check. Mouth no longer dripping saliva? Check. Heart not attempting to climb out of my throat? Check. She mentally ticked things off. After several deep breaths, she picked up the phone and dialed Jen's number.

Three rings later, Jen answered. "What's the word?"

Jacque took a slow breath and said, "I think you better come over."

"I'm there, chick. See ya in five," Jen responded and then hung up.

Jacque grinned as she thought about how great it was to have a friend like Jen whom you could always depend on to be there when you needed her.

Jacque picked up the phone again and called Sally, who answered after one ring. She must have been diligently manning the phone waiting for Jacque to call with details to the latest small-town drama.

"Jen is on her way over," Jacque said. "I need you to come too. We need to talk."

"Okay," was all Sally said before she hung up.

Fifteen minutes later, the three friends were gathered on Jacque's bedroom floor, hot chocolate in hand, naturally, because how can you have a girl powwow without hot chocolate?

"So, fill it and spill it," Jen said.

"Okay," Jacque said taking a deep breath, "so I'm sitting in my window seat, shades cracked, lights off, binoculars in hand..."

Sally interrupted. "Binoculars? Really? You were honestly using binoculars?"

"Well, you said you wanted details, so I was gathering you details," Jacque defended.

"Oooh, did you have the *Mission Impossible* soundtrack playing in the background? Cuz that would have been spy-tastic," Jen said enthusiastically.

"Actually," Jacque said, "I was thinking more James Bond-ish. You know, with the whole stakeout thing..."

"No, uh-uh, that would be more like *Dog the Bounty Hunter* type stuff. But you couldn't be Beth 'cause you're not stacked enough on top, so you would have to be Baby Lisa, the daughter." Jen rattled on.

"Are you really comparing me to Dog the Bounty Hunter's daughter right now? And why are we talking about this anyway because it is sooooo NOT the point!" Jacque growled in frustration.

"Spy analogies aside, I was sitting there about an hour when, finally, a black limo pulls up to the curb in front of the Henrys' house."

"A limo? What foreign exchange student shows up in a limo?" Jen asked.

"I know, right? That's what I was thinking," Jacque stated. "I assure you the limo was of no consequence once the person inside stepped out. Ladies, I saw the most gorgeous guy to ever grace my line of sight."

"When you say gorgeous," Jen started, "are we talking Brad-Pitt-boyish good looks or Johnny-Depp-make-ya-want-to-slap-somebody?"

"No, we're talking Brad and Johnny need to bow down and recognize," Jacque answered.

"Aside from him being dropped off in a limo, and besides

the fact that he is a walking Calvin Klein ad, it begins to get strange at this point in our story, boys and girls," Jacque says in a spooky narrative voice.

"Like it wasn't strange already?" Sally asked.

"Well, okay, *stranger*. Just as he is about to walk up the path, he suddenly turns and looks straight at me, right into my eyes, like he could sense I was watching him. I literally couldn't move. It was like I was mesmerized by him or something. Man, when did I start using the word like so freaking much?" Jacque said in exasperation. "So, up until now it was strange, but at this point, we are entering the world of *what the hell*. As he is staring at me, I hear a voice in my head, and it says, 'At last, my Jacquelyn,' then he turns to go in the house, and I hear the voice again say, 'Soon.'"

Jacque stared expectantly at her two best friends, waiting for them to tell her she's finally jumped off the deep end, but they just looked at her. "Well?" Jacque asks. Finally, Jen shifted while sucking in a deep breath. She looked down at her empty hot chocolate mug, and said, "We're gonna need more hot chocolate."

"Agreed," Sally and Jacque said at the same time.

Once they each had three fresh mugs of hot chocolate and Oreo cookies Jen said, "So let me see if I'm catching what you're throwing. Hottie exchange student drives up in a limo, steps out, rocks your world, looks into your eyes, and speaks to you in your head? Am I getting the gist of it here?"

Jacque nodded her head sheepishly, looking at the floor. "I mean, I guess it was his voice in my head. It could be a long-lost dead relative who's been searching for me since they died and happened to find me the moment that hottie looked into my eyes."

Jen and Sally both gave Jacque their get-a-larger-spoon-if-you're-going-to-shovel-it-in-that-big look.

"What? "I'm just saying," Jacque threw her hands up in

frustration before flopping back onto the floor. She groaned loudly and covered her eyes with the back of her hand. "Am I going crazy, y'all?"

"No sweetie, you've been gone a long time now. We just didn't want you to know we knew," Sally said with a smile.

"Seriously, I know it sounds crazy, but I promise you guys I heard a voice. A beautiful, deep, masculine voice in my head … and it knew my name! That is crazy, jacked-up, put-her-in-a straight-jacket, totally insane!" Jacque looked at them both with fear in her eyes. She truly did wonder if she had finally cracked. There were, after all, people in her family of questionable sanity, her mother being one of them. Jacque loved her mom, and they had a good relationship, but the woman didn't always have her feet firmly planted on the ground. And Jacque couldn't vouch for her father's mental state. He wasn't in the picture and never had been. He had bailed before he had ever known Jacque's mom was pregnant. Thankfully, Jacque had two best friends who kept her head out of the clouds, which is why she so fervently sought their opinion on this matter.

Sally finally spoke up. "I don't think you're crazy, Jac. Really, you're not. There has to be some sort of explanation. We'll figure it out. We always do."

"Yeah," Jen added. "It's two weeks until school starts. From now until then we are on scout detail." Sally nodded her agreement.

The three were quiet for a few minutes, each pondering ways to "run into" the new exchange student without seeming too obvious. Jen was laying on the floor looking up at the ceiling fan when she said, "We need to find a way to introduce ourselves to him so that we can each get a good look and see if Sally or I hear a voice in our head."

"My mom was planning on taking over a good ol' Southern meal for him since he isn't from here. You know how she feels it's her duty to feed up anyone who comes within a five-mile radius of her. We could ask if we can go over with her, or would that be too lame?" Jacque asked.

"No, I think that's perfect," Jen stated.

By midnight, the girls had crafted an, admittedly, weak game plan, the whole of it revolving around going with Jacque's mom to the Henry's to give their new exchange student some fried chicken, 'taters, and corn on the cob. *Seriously, how lame can you get?* Jen and Sally had quickly fallen asleep on the other side of her room, each wrapped in a blanket.

Jacque sat up and looked around her room, a place she felt safe and comfortable. The twin-size bed with the new deep green bedspread her mom had bought for her birthday and the stained-glass lamp with absolutely no theme whatsoever that sat on her small wood desk where she, Sally, and Jen had carved various things on its surface. Jacque looked at her dresser mirror which had pictures lining both sides, mostly of Jen, Sally, and her in various places and poses. A *few hours ago, I was just another seventeen-year-old getting ready to start my senior year ... so normal.*

She had three homecoming mums hanging on the wall next to her bed, and on the other side was the window with the seat where she sat tonight, where something in her life— she wasn't quite sure of what just yet—had changed. Jacque lay back down and watched her ceiling fan go around in a circle, the motor lulling her to sleep. Her last thought as she drifted off was of a pair of piercing blue eyes.

FANE STOOD in the bedroom that would be his for the next year. He stared out the window, his eyes were drawn to the house across the street. He looked across to the second-story window where Fane had first seen her … his true mate. *Impossible.* But he knew what he had felt. He had heard her thoughts, and there was only one woman in the world who would be able to share such an intimacy with him. Fane thought hard about what had happened when he had arrived less than an hour ago.

As his limo pulled up to the house belonging to his host family, Fane couldn't shake a peculiar sensation. The feeling wasn't one of foreboding, but something was causing him to be tense and restless.

Fane's trepidation could certainly be because he was more than a thousand miles away from home, he knew absolutely no one, it was his senior year in high school, *and he was going to be spending it in a country he had never been to before. Yes, I imagine that might make a person tense.*

He looked at the host family's house and noticed it was quite large. It boasted two stories and a wraparound porch. It looked to Fane like a house one might see out in the country, on a large farm, rather in a suburban neighborhood. The front lawn was nicely manicured. A tall, full tree stood to the right of the walkway and a bench rested underneath. On the porch, sat two rocking chairs with a little table in between them. Overall it was a charming home—a home in which a person would feel comfortable—a normal home.

Fane hoped this was the case because normal was not usually in his vocabulary. He was, after all, from a family of werewolves, specifically a grey wolf—a *Canis lupus.* Not only that, but he just happened to be the son of the current Alpha. His name, Fane Lupei, literally meant "Crown Wolf." How fitting for the prince of the Romanian Greys.

You made this choice, now you have to live with it. So, get your butt out of the car.

Fane wasn't entirely sure why he had even decided to apply to the foreign exchange program. He'd left his home,

Romania, located in a region containing the highest number of Greys in the world. Fane just knew he felt a pull, as unexplainable as moths drawn to a flame, to come to the United States. And not just any city in the States. Fane knew he was meant to come here, to Coldspring, Texas. *Why here?* There were no *Canis lupus* in Coldspring. Very few in all of Texas, in fact. Had something told him he should go to a different territory such as Ireland, the Balkans, Poland, Italy, or Spain, places that boasted considerable numbers of his kind, he would understand. *But Coldspring?*

Okay, no more stalling. He looked up at Sorin, his driver and friend, and said, "I guess this is it. *Mulțumesc*, thank you, my friend, for coming all this way to drop me off. I appreciate it."

"Think nothing of it, my prince. It is always an honor to serve you."

"Oh, come now, don't go getting all formal on me. Here in Coldspring, I'm just a high school student, not a prince," Fane told him.

Fane knew this was hard for his friend, though Sorin's title was actually "Guard to the Prince," and Sorin had been in that position since Fane was a child. Sorin had wanted to stay in the US with Fane, but Fane insisted he go home and let him be on his own for a while. There were no other Greys in this area which meant there was no danger to him.

Sorin got out of the car to open Fane's door, but Fane let himself out before Sorin could get there. Fane stood six feet, two inches tall, which was a good five inches taller than Sorin. Fane looked his longtime friend in the eye. Sorin bowed only slightly, a show of respect and love for the prince, and then broke formality and hugged him. Fane took comfort in the touch. As a *Canis lupus*, touch was as much in their nature as breathing. Even in human form, packmates tended to touch more than other humans. Fane patted Sorin on the back and stepped away.

Out of nowhere, Fane caught a passing thought in his mind that caused his wolf to perk up.

"Wonder if they're related or something."

Fane turned his head. He heard the thought in his mind, but he knew it was coming from a second-story bedroom in the house across the street. He looked upward and locked eyes with a girl peering out of a window.

Fane phased slightly, just enough to use his wolf sight, but not enough so that any other physical manifestations of his wolf would show. As a grey wolf, his eyesight and hearing were second to very few and his night vision was the best of all the breeds. He found himself looking into eyes the color of emeralds.

At that moment, Fane realized he had *heard* the girl's thoughts. His heart began to beat rapidly. There was only one person in the world from whom a Grey could hear thoughts—their mate. His wolf growled possessively, and it took Fane several deep breaths to keep from phasing completely.

"Are you okay, sire?" It was Sorin. The man was watching Fane intently.

Fane didn't answer right away. He discovered for the first time what it was like to not be in complete harmony with his wolf. The wolf wanted out. It wanted to go to his mate ... his other half. And Fane wanted to let it. But he knew it probably wasn't a good idea to phase into his wolf and go pining at her bedroom window like a love-sick pup.

Fane turned his attention back to Sorin, careful not to allow his emotions to show on his face. "I'm fine, Sorin. I thought I scented something weird for a second. You don't smell anything, do you?"

Sorin cocked his own head and drew in a large breath.

11

After a few seconds, he said, "No, nothing out of the ordinary. Just the typical human smells. There's a stray dog a block over. No … two … scrounging for scraps in a trash can."

"Yea, that must be it. No big deal. Well, I guess this is goodbye, old friend. Give my love to my mother and father. Tell the Alpha female she needn't worry about her only son. I'll be fine for a semester."

Sorin nodded. "Farewell, Prince. Call if you need anything. See you in a few months." Sorin got back in the limo and drove away, leaving Fane standing, alone, staring up at a second-story window across the street.

Reflexively, he sent her a thought as he picked her name out of her mind. *"At last, my Jacquelyn."* But even as he sent the thought, he wondered how such a thing could be possible? There weren't any *Canis lupus* within a hundred miles of here. How could she be his mate? Could a human be the true mate of a werewolf? Fane had never heard of such a thing.

Fane felt distress and confusion come through the bond. This was complete confirmation the woman was indeed his mate. She'd heard the thought he'd sent her. She clearly didn't understand what was happening. But what did that mean? A female *Canis lupus* would know and understand the mating signs as surely as he did. He needed to find out what was going on.

Though it took all his strength to ignore his wolf instincts to go to her, Fane turned, breaking the gaze that locked them together and walked up to the house. As he knocked on the door, he once again lost the battle of wills with his wolf and sent her another thought, one to assure her this encounter wasn't their last. *"Soon."* Once again, he felt her confusion.

. . .

THE HENRYS WOULD BE his host family for the next year. This was the first time he had ever seen them and was surprised at how young they were. They both looked to be in their early thirties. There was a welcoming eagerness radiating from them that made Fane feel accepted even before he'd stepped foot inside their home.

"Welcome to our home, Fane," Mrs. Henry said, reaching out to hug him.

Fane was a little surprised at the show of affection, but he found comfort in the touch and allowed it to soothe his unease about being somewhere new.

Mr. Henry held out his hand, and Fane responded by shaking it. "We are very glad to have you here with us."

"Thank you for allowing me to stay in your home. I greatly appreciate your generosity," Fane said sincerely.

"You must be tired from your long trip, so why don't we show you your room and let you get settled for the night. If you're hungry, the kitchen is right through there, and you're welcome to help yourself to anything you find. We can visit more tomorrow and get better acquainted once you have rested," Mrs. Henry stated.

Fane followed them both upstairs. They went down a long hall, passing several doors along the way. "We will give you the full tour tomorrow," Mr. Henry told Fane.

That was fine with Fane. He was very tired, but his brain was going ninety to nothing thinking about what he had just discovered. The wolf inside was restless knowing his mate, whom he could possibly have had to wait an eternity for, was just across the street.

Finally, at the last door on the left, Mrs. Henry stepped aside and said, "Here is your room. We took the liberty of decorating it a bit, but you are welcome to change it any way you would like. We will leave you to it. Sleep tight."

"Mulţumesc," he stated formally in his native tongue. The

Henrys looked at him quizzically. "Oh, that means thank you in Romanian. Sometimes I forget and start speaking my native language. Forgive me."

"Oh, no, that's great, Fane," Mrs. Henry said. "I would love to learn your language and culture, so please feel free to use it anytime you want."

"Well, again *mulţumesc* and *noapte bună*, which means good night,"

With that, the Henrys turned and walked away, leaving Fane to explore his new territory.

His mind returned to the present, letting the memories of the eventful night fade away. As Fane turned away from the window, he glanced around his room. He was struck again by how comfortable he felt now in this room, a stark departure from the earlier tensions he'd experienced before he arrived. The Henrys had inadvertently decorated his bedroom in winter tones, with wolves as the dominant theme. *How fitting.* The walls were painted a white that glistened like snow, and one wall contained a mural of a winter forest. In the distance, a solitary wolf stood on a snowy hill, his head tilted to the sky, posed in a lonely howl. The scene caused an ache in Fane for the pack he'd left behind. But regardless of the desire to be with his pack mates and family, Fane knew he'd made the right decision in coming here.

The bed was full size with a thick blue comforter and lots of pillows. To the left of the bedroom door was a huge closet with built-in drawers all along one wall. Fane stepped through another door and into a spacious bathroom with a glassed-in shower and separate bathtub.

After the quick run-through of his room, he decided to take a shower and wash off the smell of crowded airports and unfamiliar people. The hot water cascading over his tired muscles felt good. His wolf didn't seem to care about the shower. All he was concerned about was the female across the street. Fane chuckled to himself. "Impatient, aren't you?" His wolf ignored him. He was pouting, and Fane knew there was nothing he could do to ease his ire.

He finally climbed into the plush bed and pulled the warm comforter up around him. His eyes drifted closed, and his final thought before he fell asleep was of striking emerald eyes.

CHAPTER 2

*T*he morning sunlight shone into Jacque's room as she yawned noisily. She glanced over to where Sally and Jen had fallen asleep and saw they were both snoozing soundly. Jacque decided to let them sleep while she went ahead and took a shower. Jacque still had to process her encounter with the hottie across the street.

"Thanks, Jen," she muttered under her breath. Now she couldn't think of him as the foreign exchange student because Jen had so eloquently named him the 'hottie across the street'. Jacque would have to watch herself and make sure not to introduce herself by saying, "Hi, hottie, I'm Jacque. It's nice to meet you." Yeah, that wouldn't be embarrassing at all.

She gathered some clean clothes and realized, as she stared into her closet, she was taking longer than usual to pick an outfit to wear to meet the hottie, grr, the exchange student. *Jac, say it to yourself, ex-ch-an-ge student.*

After a ridiculously-longer-than-necessary amount of time, she chose a pair of her jeans that had holes in various places along the legs. Of course, they weren't there through any fault of hers. They were $75 jeans ... which she paid to have holes in. Go figure. She had a little bit of a jeans fetish. It was so bad she even worked over the summer to earn money to afford the jeans she wanted. Jacque picked a baby doll tee that said, "I'm not stubborn. My way is just better." Stress brought out the sarcasm in her. Okay, so maybe most things brought out the sarcasm in her, and what better way to handle it than with a sarcastic tee? Jacque wasn't sure why she felt the need to bare her personality, so to speak, on her person for him to see. It wasn't like she was planning on them being more than friends. She tapped her lips thoughtfully. Maybe she had considered the whole more-than-friends scenario just a few … hundred times. Shoot her. She wasn't immune to an Adonis-like face or a male body that looked to be sculpted from stone. Slightly disgusted with herself, she shook her head at her outrageous thoughts and headed to the bathroom, seeking refuge in the form of a steaming shower and her favorite cucumber body wash.

Jacque took her time in the shower, only getting out when the water started to get cold, forcing her to seek shelter in one of the huge warm towels her mom had splurged on. She dried off and got dressed, then took her time fixing her hair. Jacque couldn't decide if she should wear it up or down. *Good grief, you never have this much trouble getting ready. It's just hair, you freak.* She paused, pursing her lips at her reflection. "Nor do you usually talk to yourself so much." Her nerves were getting the best of her. But try as she might to brush the encounter off, she just couldn't shake the feeling that something major had happened last night when she locked eyes with the handsome stranger.

With an exasperated sigh, she finally settled on wearing her hair up. It was summer in south Texas, after all, which basically meant frying-eggs-on-the-sidewalk hot. Morning routine accomplished, complete with talking to herself and obsessing over her looks, she headed back to her room to see if Sally and Jen had decided to join the rest of the living.

Sure enough, they were both sitting on the floor, each with bedhead and looking a little dazed.

"You're up bright and early ... and dressed," said Jen, sounding surprised. "And perky. Wait. Who the hell are you, and what have you done with Jacque?" Jen's brow rose as she looked up.

Jacque rolled her eyes at her blonde friend's exaggeration. Okay, so maybe Jacque wasn't usually a morning person, and maybe she walked around with a frown on her face until lunchtime, but she wasn't that bad. Right?

"I woke up with just a few things on my mind and knew it would be impossible to go back to sleep. Also, I need to go talk to my mom about us going over with her to greet the hot — I mean, exchange student. Thanks to you, Jen, I will probably introduce myself to him and say, 'Hi hottie.'"

"Well, if you do, I will be sure to do you the honor of laughing my ass off," Jen said.

"Oh, thanks for that," Jacque retorted.

"Okay, kids, let's play nice. We have plans to make. We don't have time for your usual petty arguments and overall need to degrade one another," said Sally.

"But we love degrading one another," Jen whined.

Jacque nodded in agreement. "It's like our version of coffee in the morning."

Sally ignored them, which she often did when Jacque and Jen were being childish.

"Okay, why don't y'all take turns getting a shower, and I'll go talk to my mom about when she plans to head over to the Henrys?" Jacque asked as she headed toward her door.

"Sounds good," Sally answered.

"Go, team," Jen said dryly.

"Loving that enthusiasm, Jennifer Adams," Jacque said with a freakishly big grin on her face. "Keep it up!"

As Jacque ducked out of the room, Jen mouthed some words to her that would definitely get the blonde's mouth washed out with soap.

Jacque went downstairs and found her mom already in the kitchen cooking up a storm. Lilly Pierce was not your average woman. She had a sketchy background growing up in a foster home. She often had these "feelings" about things that were going to happen, and the scary thing was, she was usually right. Jacque and her mom never really talked about it, though Jacque sometimes showed signs of a similar nature. Only Jacque didn't know things, she could *feel* things, such as the emotions of others. It didn't happen often, and it was very subtle at times. She might be in a room with her mom and without Lilly ever saying anything, Jacque knew her mother was sad or worried or confused. Jacque wasn't sure how or why it happened, it just did. It wasn't reliable because she could go weeks, and sometimes months, without feeling another's emotions. Jacque didn't want to know things, or feel things, she just wanted to be normal. Jen was always happy to point out that normal was overrated.

As Jacque looked around the kitchen, she saw a pan of fried chicken on the stove and corn on the cob in a pot of boiling water. Lilly was steadily mixing a bowl of mashed potatoes, adding milk and butter as she saw fit.

"Hey, Mom, how goes the gut-busting Southern meal prep?" Jacque asked.

"I'm almost done. I just need to drop some rolls in the oven. Would you mind getting them and putting them on a pan? They aren't homemade, just those store-bought, Hawaiian ones, but they're really good. I'm sure he won't mind"

"Yeah, I can do that. Uh, Mom." Jacque hesitated for a

moment. "Sally, Jen, and I were wondering if you needed help carrying all this over to the Henrys." Jacque tried to sound casual. Lilly paused in her tater stirring and glanced at her daughter. The narrowed eyes told Jacque she hadn't come anywhere close to casual.

"Are you really wanting to help, or is this just a perfect opportunity to meet the new exchange student? It is a *guy*, after all, right?" Lilly asked.

"Can't a girl just help out her mother every once in a while?"

Lilly grunted.

"Okay, *maybe* we would like to see who the guy is," said Jacque, "but we do also genuinely want to help you. I don't think you can carry all this over on your own."

"Well, I was going to ask you to help me anyway, and I thought you and the girls would be interested in meeting the new young man, especially since you and Trent have split up."

"Do not go there, Mom." Jacque's shoulders tensed at the mention of her ex. "This has nothing to do with him. It's only natural to want to meet a new neighbor, especially since he's not from our country," Jacque told her, not sure who she was really trying to convince.

"Okay, okay, you don't have to be defensive. I will be ready just as soon as those rolls are done warming. I'm going to call the Henrys now to make sure they are okay with us coming over in about ten minutes."

Jacque grabbed the rolls and shoved them in the oven. Lilly was stepping out of the room to call the Henrys when Jacque caught the briefest hint of worry coming off her mom in subtle waves. It had been a while since she had picked anything up from her mom, so it made the girl take a step back. Lilly was a single parent who ran her own business. It wasn't like there was a shortage of things to worry about. But still, Jacque got the feeling this worry had nothing to do with her mother's normal concerns. This was something else. Jacque rolled her eyes in frustration because, seriously, what was the point of feeling someone's emotions if you didn't know their cause? Irritated and confused, Jacque headed back upstairs.

She forced herself to set the thought aside. It was time to inform her two partners in crime the plan had been set in motion. She paused in mid-step. Man, she felt ridiculous as she thought about how it sounded to have a plan to meet a guy. And not to meet him like "Hey, what's up?", but meet him like "Hey, are you a weirdo or something?" What was her world coming to? Oh well, it could be worse. She could be hearing voices... Oh, wait, she was. Well, crap.

Sally was finished with her shower and doing her hair when Jacque reached her bedroom. The beautiful brunette could be very efficient when she needed to be, and she wasn't one to be overly fussy about her looks. That was a perk when one could be pretty even with a paper bag over her head. Her long coffee-colored hair was striking against her naturally tan skin, and her big brown eyes gave her an easy pouty look. She honestly didn't look like a 'Sally', but whatever. *I didn't pick her name.*

Jen was still in the shower, and when Jacque went to the bathroom door, she could hear Martina McBride's "Independence Day." Jen was belting it out proudly, albeit out of tune, and in classic Jen style, she was adding her own words because she could never remember the actual lyrics of a song. Jacque banged on the door and hollered, "Yeah, yeah, you're strong, free, and independent. We get it. Hurry up! We're rolling out ten minutes ago." Jen just sang louder. Jacque rolled her eyes and went back to her room.

"If she's planning on blow-drying that blonde mess on

her head then we're leaving her here," Jacque told Sally, who was putting on her shoes.

"Well, I'm ready when you are, Sherlock. Let's go check hottie out," Sally said with a wink.

"How lucky I am to have you, my dear Watson," Jacque said smiling.

A few minutes later, Jen stepped into Jacque's room fully clothed, hair up in a French twist.

"What's taking you two so long? I've been ready for two minutes," Jen said with an exaggerated sigh.

"Oh, a whole two minutes? How dare we make you wait. Please don't have us flogged, your majesty," Jacque retorted.

"It's about time you realized who is queen in this outfit." Jen smirked.

"Girls, I'm ready if you all are," Jacque's mom yelled.

Well, here we go, off to Never-never Land. Jacque felt at that moment she was jumping into a rabbit hole complete with a Cheshire Cat and Mad Hatter at her side. Just what was she getting herself into?

"I think I am officially going to be sick," Jacque said with a slight moan.

"Take slow, deep breaths. If at any time you feel as though you're going to pass out, please lean to the left so you don't fall on me," Jen said.

"Then she would fall on me," Sally pointed out.

Jen shrugged. "You're built from sturdy stuff. You'd be fine."

"Well, your butt is big enough that you would just bounce," Sally snipped back.

Jacque let out a huff. "Um, guys, remember me? I'm the one who is hearing voices and is about to hurl."

Both girls stopped their bickering to look at her. Neither seemed as concerned as Jacque felt they should be.

Jen shrugged. "Screw it. If you pass out, I'll just push you so you face-plant. Then neither of us will have to worry about ending up underneath your bushy red hair."

"Man, you are just a ball of warm fuzzies, aren't you?" Jacque asked, glaring at Jen.

"I'm just saying." Jen laughed. "It's important to be prepared for these situations."

Jacque took several deep breaths and then stood up straight. She held her arms out and turned in a quick circle, feeling very much like a rotisserie chicken. "How do I look? Is this shirt a little much?"

"No, I think it's perfect. It makes a statement, like 'Hey, I'm not scared of your little mind gibberish,'" Sally said.

"But I am scared of his mind gibberish, if it is really his mind gibberish and not something else entirely."

"Oh, come on, pull yourself together, man. He's just a guy, okay? Nothing more and nothing less," Jen said as she took Jacque's shoulders in her hands and gave her a none-too-gentle shake. Jacque's teeth jarred together, causing a slight buzzing in her head. Great, she could just add that to her list of growing discomforts.

There was a problem with Jen's logic. Jacque didn't believe mystery guy was just a guy, no, he was more, much more, she just didn't know what yet. As they began to descend the stairs, a thought touched her mind, one that was not her own. *Good morning, my Luna.* The deep voice resonated with her soul and, despite her confusion, brought her a measure of comfort. Not strange at all.

She stumbled a few steps on the stairs. Jen reached out to steady her. "Are you okay?" she whispered, her playful demeanor forgotten.

"I just heard the voice again," Jacque said shakily.

"What did it say?" Sally asked.

"Good morning, my loona," Jacque answered. "I keep waiting for the *Twilight Zone* music to start playing in the background," she said. Then with a childish whine that Jacque wasn't proud of she said, "I can't believe I thought it was a good idea to go over there."

Sally pursed her lips as she nodded. "Mm-hm." She hummed. "We do tend to do desperate and out-of-character things when stress wraps us in its ugly grasp."

Jen looked away from Jacque and narrowed her gaze on Sally. "Who the hell are you? Dr. Phil?"

Sally simply shrugged.

Jacque's mom was standing at the bottom of the stairs watching them closely. She had that look that Jacque knew all too well. The woman knew something was up. Jacque could feel her mother's emotions very strongly. Lilly was concerned.

"Are you girls coming?" her mom asked, but her eyes were on Jacque.

"Lead the way, Ms. Pierce," Jen said as she finished descending the stairs.

Each of the girls carried a dish. Jacque's mom had even made sweet tea. After all, what's a Southern meal without sweet tea?

As they stepped out of the house and onto the walkway, the sun shone brightly down on them, and at 10:00 a.m. it was already blisteringly hot. Although the grass in some of the lawns was still healthy and green, Jacque's lawn was brown and dead. Of course, that could be because her mom mowed it way too short last time in hopes she could go longer than a week between yard work, which inadvertently killed the grass. *Oh, well*. It's not like they were going out for a prettiest lawn competition. Goodness knows both she and her mother would rather pull their toenails out than work in the yard in the ridiculous south Texas heat.

As they crossed the street, Jacque saw the curtains parting in the right, second-story window. Briefly, she saw the handsome face looking back at her. She glanced away to get the attention of Sally and Jen, and then she looked back to point him out, but the curtains had closed.

"Maybe he's just shy," Jen suggested as Jacque stared up at the now-empty window. "He probably has that sexy, mysterious vibe going on."

"You got all that because he walked away from the window?" Sally asked.

Jen shrugged. "What can I say? I'm freaking awesome."

Jacque laughed. Leave it to her friends to keep her mind from dwelling obsessively on the mysterious boy who might or might not be able to speak to her through her thoughts. *Yep, my life isn't weird at all.*

FANE WOKE UP AND, without thinking, sought out Jacquelyn's mind. It was second nature for him, even though he had just met her. Well, he hadn't really *met* her, more like found her.

He spoke to her mind effortlessly, the link between them growing stronger. *"Good morning, my Luna."* Her panic and confusion nearly knocked the breath out of him. He bolted up, pressing his hand to his chest where his heart was beating out a rapid-fire rhythm Fane knew matched Jacquelyn's. His wolf was not happy with him at that moment. It didn't like to be the cause of their mate's fear. *It's going to get worse before it gets better,* Fane told the beast inside him.

He picked up Jacque's conversation with her friends as she explained she had heard his voice, or rather *a* voice she wasn't completely convinced was his. And she wanted to know what Luna meant. He also caught a passing thought that the girls were on their way over to the Henry's house … now.

Fane looked at himself in the mirror and quickly decided

a shower was in order, if nothing else, just to help calm his nerves. He hopped in and was out in a record five minutes. He stood in front of the bathroom mirror brushing his teeth. Then he noticed something different on his chest and shoulder. Fane's eyes widened at the markings that ran along his skin.

Like every male *Canis lupus*, Fane had markings that looked like tattoos which appeared of their own accord once he entered puberty. These markings revealed where in the pack order a wolf belonged. The more elaborate the marking, the higher a wolf was in rank. The tattoos varied in size, shape, and placement on the side of the body. His were on his right side, which indicated he was a dominant. The design started on his right shoulder blade and came over the top of his shoulder before descending onto his bicep and across the right side of his chest. The fact that the markings came around to the front of his body, and weren't confined to his back, indicated he was an Alpha. Only Alphas boasted markings on the front and back of their bodies so that, no matter what direction they were facing, all could see the markings. The marks were dark black with curves and points at the ends of the lines. Now the markings had climbed up the right side of his neck. They looked like flames, only black in color. He honestly didn't know what it meant, as he had never heard of the markings spreading. Fane decided he would have to call his father later today to find out what was going on. Meanwhile, Fane hoped the Henrys hadn't paid much attention to his neck the previous evening. It might be a bit hard to explain the sudden appearance of dark tattoos. He'd just have to claim they'd been there all along and hope they wouldn't press the issue.

Fane moved on and quickly ran a razor across his face and threw on some aftershave. He walked over to his suitcase to pick out some clothes. He hadn't bothered to unpack anything last night because he had been so tired. There wasn't a whole lot of variety in his wardrobe—black, grey, and dark blue shirts mostly. He decided on a dark grey short-sleeved T-shirt and his Lucky brand jeans. He wore biker boots and a wallet with a chain attached to it. Motorcycles were a little bit of an obsession for him, and he owned a Honda. He tried to ride as much as he could, even during the winter months. Of course, he was completely covered in leather when he did ride because it helped keep out the cold. He found himself hoping that Jacque would like to ride with him, and then his mind wandered to the idea of her on a motorcycle. Hot didn't begin to describe how he felt about her on his bike. He let out a low growl and pushed the thought aside. He'd never felt desire like that for a female and knew it might be a problem if he didn't learn to control it, very quickly.

Fane had wanted to bring his motorcycle with him, but his parents told him they would buy him a used bike once he arrived. He was planning on talking to Mr. Henry about that later today, and Fane hoped his host would be willing to take him to a motorcycle dealership to let him pick one out. His parents had given him a credit card with a decent limit, enough to purchase a pretty nice bike. Royalty occasionally had its perks.

His wolf perked up at the sound of footsteps in the street. He walked over to the window and parted the curtains. On the street below, he saw three teenage girls walking with a woman that must be Jacquelyn's mother. The similarities in their features were a dead giveaway. His gaze shifted to the only one who mattered, and she looked up straight into his face.

She is beautiful. Now that he could get a good look at her, he saw she had wild, unruly, auburn curls, freckles dusting her fair skin, and thin lips. She was on the short side and slender. Jacque wore faded, holey jeans and a green shirt that said "I'm not stubborn. My way is just better." So, his Luna had attitude. Of course, she would. A meek woman could not be Alpha to female Greys. The pack would tear a timid Alpha female apart. She turned to talk to her friends. He stepped away from the window to head downstairs. He was tired of only seeing her from a distance. Fane wanted her close to him, where she belonged.

The prince had never been nervous around girls, but he was now. Fane had not dated all that much. No one seemed to catch his eye, and it was discouraged for the males of his race to waste time with females that were not their true mates. The few girls he had dated, in an attempt to find his true mate, had never produced even a quarter of the attraction he felt for Jacquelyn.

Fane, feeling unsettled and wobbly like a fawn taking its first steps, wished he had gotten up earlier and called his father to talk to him about this whole mate thing. The prince had learned a little growing up, but he still felt very unprepared. Especially since his mate was a human and knew nothing of his world.

As Fane reached the bottom of the stairs, the doorbell rang. Mrs. Henry came around the corner. She saw him and smiled warmly.

"Good morning, Fane. Did you sleep well?" she asked.

"*Bună dimineața*," Fane said gracefully. "I slept very well, thank you."

"I take it that *Bună dimineața* means good morning?" Mrs. Henry asked.

"That was a very good pronunciation, and yes," Fane agreed.

"Oh, I guess I better get the door," she said as the doorbell rang again.

Fane felt his stomach tighten in anticipation. What was he

going to say to her? He had a feeling starting the conversation with "Hi, I'm Fane and you are my mate" might not go over too well.

So, he would settle with a simple "Hello, I'm Fane." Yes, he thought that was a very normal thing to say, and normalcy was what he wanted, right? *Right.*

The four ladies were standing at the threshold of the door as Mrs. Henry greeted them.

"Lilly, how sweet of you to come over to meet our guest," Mrs. Henry announced sweetly. Fane was pretty sure the woman didn't have a rude bone in her body.

"We come bearing a home-cooked Southern meal for the newcomer," Lilly responded.

"Come in. Let me introduce you to Fane. He is from Rom —well, here, I'll let him tell you. He can speak for himself, after all," Mrs. Henry said as they filed into the entryway.

"Sara, why don't we set this food in the kitchen and then sit in the living room to make our introductions, if that suits you okay?" Lilly asked.

"Oh, of course. You all can't stand here in the front door holding all that food. You would think I've never had company before. Come on, girls, let's set it on the counter in the kitchen,"

"*Sara.*" So that was Mrs. Henry's first name. He hadn't thought to ask when he met them last night, though it might have been on his paperwork for the exchange program and he just hadn't paid attention.

When the food was deposited on the counter in the kitchen, they filed into the living room, each taking a seat. Lilly sat on the rocking chair by the fireplace, while the three girls sat on the couch to the left of the rocking chair. Mrs. Henry and Fane both sat on the loveseat across from the couch.

Fane realized the five ladies were all silently looking

directly at him. Jacquelyn's gaze lingered on the markings on his neck. His wolf liked that she noticed, even though she had no idea they might have something to do with her. Once again, he found himself wanting to strut around in front of her like a proud peacock. *Good grief.* He growled inwardly.

He cleared his throat and started speaking. "Good morning, *doamnelor*. My name is Fane Lupei. I am from Romania, I am seventeen, and I will be a senior this year." Fane looked at each of the women, pausing briefly on Jacquelyn. "Should I say more?" he asked.

Lilly looked at him quizzically and asked, "What does dome-na-ler mean exactly?"

Fane tried not to grin too much at her poor pronunciation. Romanian, after all, was a very difficult language to learn.

"It means ladies. I was saying 'Good morning, ladies.' I have a bad habit of mixing my native language with English. I beg your pardon," Fane said to Lilly.

"I don't mind. It's actually pretty neat to hear you speak Romanian. It's not a language one hears very often, if ever," Lilly assured him.

"And by pretty neat she means it was hot." The blonde girl sitting next to Jacquelyn spoke up. Fane nearly laughed when his redheaded mate stomped on her friend's toe.

There was an awkward pause for a moment, and then the blonde-haired friend spoke up again. "So, why Coldspring, Texas?"

Fane cocked his head to the side. He could feel his wolf just beneath his skin itching to get out because of the nearness of their mate. "*Scuzaţi-mă?*" he asked. "I do not understand the question."

"Why did you choose to come to our little blink-of-an-eye town?" she reiterated, speaking slowly as if Fane was a child.

Jacquelyn elbowed her. Fane bit back the laugh that nearly erupted out of him at his mate's audacity.

"Oh, I see. Well, honestly, I'm not sure. When I applied for the exchange program, they sent me several candidates for my host family. I read about them, and something about the Henrys felt right. Perhaps that doesn't make much sense, but that is only how I know to say it," Fane answered.

"Your English is very good," Jacquelyn's other friend, the brunette, stated.

"My parents have always spoken both Romanian and English to me. They thought it foolish to think I would only need to know the Romanian language and culture," Fane explained to her.

"So, you have studied American culture as well?" Mrs. Henry asked.

"Yes, American culture is quite different from mine. What I have been taught by teachers has not always stood true in real life."

"Okay," Lilly said, "enough of the Spanish inquisition. Girls, let's briefly introduce ourselves, and then we will be on our way so Fane can get settled."

Fane wanted to tell her that the only place he wanted to get settled was next to her daughter's side, but he imagined that might come across as a little strange and a lot stalker-ish.

Making no move to stand up, Lilly simply introduced herself from where she sat. "Fane, my name is Lilly Pierce, and I'm Jacque's mom. I own a bookstore on the square downtown to which you are most welcome any time to study or chat. Please call me Lilly. It makes me feel less old. I am so glad to know you."

"*Doamna mea, este o onoare*," Fane said, bowing ever so slightly. "In your language, I said, 'My lady, it is an honor.'"

"So hot," the blonde muttered as she stood up and held

out her hand. "I'm Jennifer Adams, AKA Jen. I am also seventeen and a senior. By all means, please speak in your native tongue all you'd like. We don't care if we can understand you or not," she said as he took her hand. There were groans from the other girls, but Jen ignored them.

By the wide eyes that met his, Fane knew he surprised her when he did not shake it. He simply brought the back of her hand to his lips, just barely laying them against it.

Fane looked up at Jen after lightly kissing her hand and said, "*Este o placere sa te intalnesc.*"

Jen looked slightly dazed and confused.

"It is a pleasure to meet you," Fane translated.

The brunette stood up, gently pushing the hazy-looking Jen back down to the couch, and also held out her hand. "I'm Sally Morgan, seventeen, senior, and it's nice to meet you. Let me be the first to apologize for Jen. She lacks any sort of social couth," the girl said with natural cheeriness. Fane liked her immediately. It was obvious to him she was the level-headed one of the trio.

Again, Fane took her hand and lifted it to his lips, placing a feather-soft kiss on the top of it, repeating what he had said to Jen, "*Este o placere sa te intalnesc.*"

Sally sat down next to Jen, and when Jacquelyn made no move to stand up, Jen reached over and pinched the back of her arm.

"Oww," Jacque yelped.

She shot Jen a reproving glare as she rubbed the offended arm and finally caught on to what the blonde was trying to silently tell her. Standing up to introduce herself, Jacque began to speak but she stumbled over her words. She grimaced and looked to Fane as if she were in pain. "Oh, um, I, um, I'm Jacque, seventeen, and a senior as well. Lilly is my mom." Jacque made no move to give Fane her hand.

But he took it regardless. Fane loved the way her breath

caught as his skin touched hers. He bowed over it as he brought it to his lips, and this time they lingered. Her flesh was warm against his and as soft as silk. As he held her hand to his mouth, he took in her scent and found, to his delight, she smelled of cotton candy and fresh snow, an odd but strangely comforting combination. He tried not to growl possessively, but he didn't quite suppress the urge completely and knew Jacquelyn had heard him because she tensed even more.

He lifted his eyes to look at her, and just as he had to Sally and Jen, he said, *"Este o placere sa te intalnesc."*

But unlike with the other two, Fane sent her a message with his thoughts as he spoke to her with his mouth.

"I am so honored to finally meet you my Luna. We have much to learn about each other."

CHAPTER 3

*J*acque stepped into the Henry's house and her nerves instantly began to jangle like an out of tune brass band. And when she locked eyes with Fane, standing at the bottom of the stairs, she felt a weird tingling sensation across the top of her shoulders and behind her neck. She reached up and placed her hand on her neck, tilting it a bit as if it were stiff. The sensation had not been a painful one, but it had been strange.

Jacque tried, unsuccessfully she was sure, to take in as many details of the boy as she could. He wore a dark grey short-sleeved T-shirt, jeans, and motorcycle boots, and the wallet in his back pocket was attached with a metal chain. He took the bad boy look to a whole new level.

The look on Fane's face was one of curiosity. *And could that be...nervousness as well?* The thought surprised Jacque. He didn't seem the nervous type.

In the few moments it took to make their introductions, Jacque became thoroughly smitten. *Was she in love?* Of course not, but she dared any hot-blooded female to stand in the presence of Fane Lupei and not drool. And if they could, well, then bully to them. They certainly must swing for the other team.

A voice suddenly rebounded off the walls of her mind as Fane held her hand to his lips. Deep, deep, way deep down, Jacque knew it was Fane doing the whole mind-talking mojo. But part of her just didn't want to accept it. After all, how could anyone speak to another person through their thoughts? Not possible, right? And if they could...well...she'd seen the Shining. It didn't turn out too good.

Jacque blinked a few times to clear her thoughts. *What on earth could he possibly mean by "finally" meet me? Did this voice know it was waiting for me?* Again, she chose to forgo the option that the voice she was indeed panicking over could be Fane's. There was no reason to think he was a nut job until it was absolutely necessary and without doubt. *Okay, time to go home.*

Jacque needed to talk to Sally and Jen about Fane. And she had to decide whether or not to confide this secret to her mother, and, most importantly, she needed to have a good, cleansing, panic attack. Not necessarily in that order.

Jacque pulled her hand from Fane's grasp, and he didn't try to keep her from doing so. She turned to look at her mom, raised her eyebrows, and asked, "Okay, are you ready? Food delivered. Mission accomplished. I'm good to go," Before her mom could respond, Jacque turned to her two friends. "Sally, Jen, y'all ready to go?"

"And leave this hunk of meat all alone? I couldn't do that. It just wouldn't be neighborly. Ow!" She yelped as Sally now slammed her foot down onto Jen's toes. "What is with you two?"

"Jennifer," said Sally through gritted teeth. She raised her eyebrows and twitched her head toward the door. "We really need to be going. We have that thing we don't want to be late for."

"What thing?"

"Another stomp from the redhead. "Ow, son of a bit—"

"The thing!" snapped Jacque. "At the place." She reached down and grabbed Jen by the arm, jerking her up. Sally followed suit.

"Oh! That thing!" Jen's face brightened. "Yes, terribly important. The thing. Can't be late for it. So sorry, Fane." Sally and Jacque both rolled their eyes and shook their heads.

Lilly looked at her daughter with narrowed eyes. After a moment, she nodded and rose from her seat. "Thank you, Sara, for having us over. Sorry, we have to leave so soon. It was nice to meet you, Fane. Don't make yourself a stranger. You're welcome at our house anytime."

Fane bowed slightly, placing his hand over his heart, "As we say in my country when parting, *Până data viitoare, luna vă poate lumina calea*, which means, 'Until next time, may the moon light your path.'"

Jen looked at Fane with a brow raised, and her lips quirked in a sexy smirk all her own. "How do we know you aren't really saying, 'Ladies, you have nice boo...'"

Sally slapped her hand over Jen's mouth. Jacque pushed the blonde, filter-less flirt while Sally kept her words from bursting forth.

"What she meant to say was 'Back atcha'," Sally called over her shoulder.

Jacque continued to push Jen toward the door, trying very hard not to look and see if Fane was watching her but somehow sensing he was. She could feel his blue eyes boring into her back, and Jacque hoped she didn't have sweat stains. She lost the battle of self-dignity at the last moment and tentatively looked over her shoulder. Sure enough, Fane's crystal blue eyes were glued to her. He had a knowing smile on his face, and his eyes were narrowed ever so slightly. Jacque felt as if Fane knew something she did not, and he found it highly amusing. That thought made her shudder for more reasons than she cared to consider at that moment.

"We're going, Jacque. Good grief." She heard Jen grunt. Jacque had started to push a little harder after having met the gaze of the male in question.

"Well, go a little quicker please!" Jacque whispered through tight lips.

"Calm down," growled Jen. "And I'm going to kill you two for stomping my toes."

"It was necessary," said Jacque.

"Why?"

"I'll explain later. Come on."

The girls walked briskly down the walkway and across the street, not even bothering to see if Jacque's mom was behind them. All Jacque could think was she needed to put some space between her and that hottie. Okay, so she still couldn't help calling him hottie. "Well, crap, it's true, so go jump in a lake already." She grumbled to herself as the Texas heat bore down on her. The blacktop reflecting the sun only made it hotter, and Jacque found her feet moving quicker for more reasons than just a foreign exchange student that had her flustered.

Once inside the house, the three girls double-timed it up the stairs and into Jacque's bedroom. Sally shut the door firmly and turned, pressing her back against it and pinning her eyes on Jacque. Sally's lips were pinched tight, and her big brown eyes were narrowed like an eagle zeroing in on its prey.

"What the hell, Jac." Jen huffed before Sally could speak what was so obviously plastered across her accusing face.

Okay, so maybe she had freaked out just a little there at the end, but what did they expect? She was hearing voices! Jacque took slow, deep breaths. She seemed to be doing that a lot lately. "First impressions?" Jacque prompted.

"Oh, I don't know, maybe something like OH MY, stutter, drool, FREAKING, pant, deep breath, GOSH," Jen spat out.

Sally's head nodded in true bobblehead fashion. "Yeah, what she said, but more panting and deep breathing from my completely and totally inappropriately turned-on body."

"What about you?" Jen asked. "You didn't seem as mesmerized as us. Why is that?"

"Oh, I don't know." Jacque breathed out airily. "Maybe because I was, ya know, a little distracted by THE VOICE IN MY HEAD!" Jacque realized she was yelling. She ran her hands over her face and squeezed her eyes closed tightly. "I'm sorry, I shouldn't take my stress out on you two. I'm just, just … I don't know … freaking out, I guess." She wasn't ready to discuss the fact that she was pretty sure the voice was Fane's. That would just open a whole other can of worms, and she hadn't even figured out what to do with the worms they were already dealing with.

"Have you tried talking back to the voice? You know, like answering it through your thoughts?" Sally asked tentatively.

Jacque shook her head. "I feel like if I do then I am just solidifying the fact that I'm losing it."

"You're NOT losing it. Something is definitely up with this Fane guy. No one, and I mean no one, can look that good, make you want to curl up and purr when he talks to you, and not have some sort of unearthly mojo magic. Something's fishy, and it's not your mom's fried chicken," Jen told her.

Jacque turned to her window and opened the blinds. She looked across the street at the Henrys' house and wondered what to do about Fane Lu-whatever his last name was. Jacque heard her two best friends walk up beside her. They put their arms around her.

"I know I've said it before, and I will keep saying it until it sinks into that unruly, curly head of yours. It will be alright. You are not alone in this, okay?" Sally told her firmly.

"Yeah, chick, you got us no matter what," Jen agreed. "Besides, we're too nosy not to stick around and see what happens."

Sally pulled a strand of Jen's hair as if to scold her. "Ow! Crap, I'm just saying!" Jen scowled.

Jacque turned away from the window, wiped away the tears she hadn't even realized were there, and hugged her friends. "Okay, I know you guys need to go home and assure your parents that you're still alive and haven't been abducted or anything. But do y'all think you can come back later?"

Both girls nodded.

"I will have to do laundry and pick up my room to pacify my mom, you know how it is, but then I can come back over and stay the night again if your mom is cool with it," Jen explained.

Sally spoke up as well. "Yeah, I can be back around 7:00 tonight. I just need to take care of some chores as well."

"Okay, that sounds good. I'll let my mom know. I'm sure she won't care."

Jacque walked them downstairs to the front door and watched as they each walked to their cars. She stood in the doorway looking after them until she couldn't see them any longer.

Jacque stood in the entryway looking at nothing. Her eyes had lost focus on the world around her, and her mind was running amok. She was trying to decipher the thoughts, but it was no use since she was tired, emotional, and beginning to realize that since she had walked out of the Henrys' house and away from Fane, it was taking all she had in her not to turn around and run, not walk, but run like a cat with a firecracker tied to its tail, back to him. What the hell was wrong with her?

Jacque's head snapped up when she heard her mom hollering from upstairs.

"Jacque? I need to go to the store for a little while. I have some new inventory I need to take care of, and since I was able to hire extra staff, I can finally catch up." Her mom came to the top of the stairs and looked down at her. Tilting her head, she asked, "Are you okay, sweetie? You look a little frayed around the edges."

"Naw, I'm good, just a little tired. I didn't sleep well last night," Jacque fibbed. Then she thought of how she had been feeling her mom's emotions so strongly earlier and decided to say something. "What about you, Mom? You okay?"

"I'm fine, just have a lot on my mind, that's all. Nothing to worry about. Why don't you lie down for a little bit? Are you gonna be okay while I'm gone? Need me to get you anything while I'm out?"

"No, I'll be fine. Thanks though. Oh, yeah, I did want to check and see if you are okay with Sally and Jen spending the night again tonight."

"As long as their parents are okay with it. Y'all can order pizza if I'm not home by dinner," she answered.

Jacque hugged her mom and told her goodbye before heading up to her room. She shut the door, turned off the lights, and put her Evanescence CD in her CD player oddly, the music calmed her. Then she lay down on her bed and closed her eyes.

FANE WATCHED AS JACQUELYN, with her two friends in tow, hurried back to her house. He felt a twinge of pain because she was so eager to get away from him, but he reminded himself it was only because she was scared, not because she didn't want to accept him as her mate. After all, she didn't even know him, or anything about his world. He had a feeling she would be doing a whole lot more running before things were said and done. His wolf perked up at this thought. It liked a good chase, and if the hunt happened to be his true mate, then he would like it all the more. Fane chuckled to himself as he chastised the beast. He found it so odd to feel his usually broody, grumpy beast suddenly playful and giddy. He was just as excited as Fane about finding their mate, though his wolf felt none of the apprehension the human did. His wolf wasn't worried about Jacque rejecting them because, in his mind, that simply wasn't an option. She was their mate. She could no more live without them than they could her.

Mrs. Henry called to him from the kitchen. "Are you ready for this delicious lunch Lilly brought you?"

"Yes, I'm hungry, and it all smells really good." Fane's wolf rumbled appreciatively at the smell of the chicken, and his stomach growled. He hadn't realized he was so hungry until his mind was given something besides Jacquelyn to think about.

"The plates are in the cabinet to the left of the stove, and the silverware is in the drawer to the right of the sink," Mrs. Henry pointed out. "Eat all you want. Oh, and she made sweet tea as well. It's in the fridge. The glasses are in the cabinet next to the plates."

"Thank you," Fane told her.

"I'm off to the grocery store. I didn't get a chance to go yesterday. Is there anything in particular that you like?" she asked.

"I'm not picky, and I like to try new things, so whatever you usually buy will be fine with me. I can give you some money as well since you will be feeding another mouth," Fane answered.

"There is no way I'm taking any of your money, Fane, so

you can just get that notion out of your head. You are our guest, and we are more than pleased to feed you," she said firmly but not unkindly.

"*Mulțumesc*, Mrs. Henry. I am most grateful."

"You're welcome. And I keep meaning to tell you, no more Mrs. Henry. Call me Sara, and you can call Mr. Henry Brian. Okay, well, I will see you later. My cell phone number is on the front of the fridge, so put it in your phone in case you need me. Bye," she said with a wave.

Taking his phone out of his pocket to put both numbers in his contacts, Fane found himself thinking it was kind of odd that he would never need Jacquelyn's cell phone number. Instead, he would always have a direct line to her, designated just for him. And she would have the same access to his mind. *That's a bit unsettling*.

When Jacquelyn realized the mental connection went both ways, she'd have the ability to read his thoughts ... all his thoughts. There was a way to put up what one might call a *wall* in his mind if he needed a break from his mate, but it was difficult for mates to be cut off entirely from each other for any length of time—not that he knew from experience. That's just what his father had told him about the mate bond.

Fane slipped his phone back into his pocket and tried not to worry about it. He wanted to keep his thoughts about Jacquelyn appropriate and under control, but she was incredibly hot. It was easier said than done. What was she going to think about his unbridled attraction to her?

Despite the fact that mates were supposed to be uncomfortable when separated, and Jacquelyn had yet to respond to him when he spoke through her thoughts, Fane didn't feel any ill effects from her lack of reciprocation. Once again, he was going to need to talk to his father about this. Everything Fane thought to be true about the mate bond was slipping through his fingers like water, and it left him feeling very unsure of himself. That was not a feeling any dominant male relished having.

He prepared himself a plate and a glass of sweet tea. After taking his first sip, he deduced the concoction should actually be called tea-flavored sugar water. Fane decided to eat up in his room since Sara was gone, and he hadn't yet seen Brian this morning.

Fane sat at the desk that was conveniently located next to the window facing Jacquelyn's house. He pulled the blinds up, giving him a clear view of Jacque's house and yard. He took a bite of chicken and thought about his mate for the millionth time since he had set eyes on her. He imagined her unruly auburn hair, her green eyes, her soft skin dusted with freckles, and, most of all, he thought of her scent. Cotton candy and fresh snow. What an odd thing to smell like, but he supposed maybe it had something to do with her personality—sweet and pure—perhaps?

Fane continued to eat his lunch, his wolf thoroughly enjoying the protein ... even if it was cooked. The beast in him preferred his meat fresh, the reward for a successful hunt. Still, the meal was excellent.

Fane finished his lunch and laid down on his bed. He wanted to see Jacquelyn, and if he couldn't, then he would settle for talking to her. He put his hands behind his head, eyes focused on nothing in particular, and reached out to her. The bond opened between them as if he'd done it a thousand times before. It was as natural to him as breathing. The minute his mind collided with hers, an instant measure of peace rushed over him. It wrapped him up like a warm blanket on a cold night. Perhaps he had been suffering some effects from their separation after all.

"Have I scared you, my Luna? I promise that has not been my intention."

Fane didn't have a clue why he knew how to connect so

easily with his mate. He would simply think of her, and he could visualize a cord that connected him to her, and through that cord, he could communicate with her.

Fane realized it had been several minutes and she had not responded. She was either asleep or ignoring him. He was just about to speak again when she answered.

"Who are you? Are you real, or am I just imagining you?"

Fane frowned slightly. Jacque's voice sounded strained and desperate. He hated she had to go through this. She knew nothing of his world, and he was going to have to explain it to her somehow without her thinking he was some crazy, foreign stalker.

"I am very real," he answered. "And you know who I am. Your human mind just does not want to accept it as reality."

Fane felt he needed to push her gently in a direction that would allow Jacque to come to the truth on her own. He feared if he outright told her he was the voice in her head, then she might not be able to believe it. It was human nature to want to deny anything that couldn't be explained. He listened to her as she wrestled with what he told her—her mind was so interesting and comical at times.

"What on earth did it mean by 'human mind'? Was the voice, whoever it was, implying that it was not human? Oh, wouldn't that be the icing on the cake? I can see the headline now: Small-Town Girl Claims She was Mind Probed by a Nonhuman. Yep, that would be my luck. I'm not just hearing a voice now. Nope, that would still be in the realm of just plain crazy. But I passed crazy a few exits back. No, I'm now entering crackpot-ville and I don't think I like it here."

Fane couldn't help himself, and he let out a small laugh. Where did she come up with phrases like crackpot-ville? He just had to ask. He wanted to know her, all of her, and to understand her. He found himself using the term of endearment "my heart" without even thinking. It was simply a verbal reflection of how he saw her. She *was* his heart. Her existence is what kept it beating, pushing the blood through his body to keep his organs healthy. Jacque was the only thing that would keep him alive and well. He had never considered himself to be the type for pet names, but Fane realized that when it came to his Luna, many of the notions he had about himself were going to be proven false.

"Inima mea...my heart..., you are not crazy, and where do you get your odd way of speaking? Crackpot-ville? What does that mean exactly?" Fane asked her.

Without realizing it, by using his native language, he had not just given her a little push in the right direction—he had pretty much shoved her off the cliff. So much for subtle. It never was his strong suit anyway, according to his mother.

Fane felt her distress rise. He could feel her need for disbelief, and yet there was a small spark of ... relief? *Didn't see that one coming.* Fane closed his eyes and focused on her completely, listening to her mind come to terms with this revelation.

"Well, there was the clincher. I mean, really, if you're going to hear a voice, what are the chances it would have a Romanian accent?"

To Fane's, and evidently her, surprise, she started to laugh —not just a giggle but a full, body-shaking laugh. For some reason, unbeknownst to Fane, it just suddenly struck her as funny that the voice in her head had a Romanian accent. Of course, she now knew it wasn't just a voice. It was Fane. After all, she didn't know any other Romanians, but just to put the nail in the proverbial coffin, she asked in a voice that sounded as small as he sensed she felt at that moment.

"Fane?"

His heart stuttered at the sound of his name. Even though it wasn't from her lips, she had said his name, and it sounded so good coming from her. A small amount of triumph settled over him as his wolf growled in contentment, knowing his mate was thinking of him. Fane answered her honestly, wanting her to believe him without a doubt.

"*Da, inima mea, eu sunt eu.* Yes, my heart, it is I."

Fane held his breath, waiting for her response. His fists clenched at his sides as he wondered if she would continue to try and pass this off as her lack of sanity. What would he do if she refused to take her place at his side? Though his wolf hadn't considered it, the man had briefly let the idea creep into his mind, but he rejected it. He growled in response to the thought. Mates were bound to each other. There would never be another for either one of them. Jacque could date hundreds of men but wouldn't find contentment with any of them. There would always be something lacking, some void she couldn't fill with their inadequate love, and that *something* would be Fane.

To Fane's knowledge, there had never been one who rejected his or her mate. It would be a devastating action to both, and neither would ever be whole again. That just wasn't acceptable, he decided. He would just drag her back to Romania with him where she belonged. *Right, Fane. That would earn her trust. You can't just hit her over the head and drag her around by her hair, even though that actually would be the easier road.* No, he was going to have to do this the honorable way and court her. She deserved that, after all, she was his Luna and would be the Alpha female of the *Canis lupus* one day. She merited his unwavering love and devotion. She would get nothing less.

Fane continued to wait for her response, but so far, she hadn't said anything more. He thought about reaching out to her to find out what she was thinking, but up until now, he had given her privacy, only intruding into her thoughts when he spoke to her. He felt it would be a violation to listen to her when she didn't know he could do so at any time. He could also "see" the things she thought in her head. And as a gentle-man, he would not violate his Luna's privacy, mate or not. Not until she welcomed the intrusion, which he sincerely hoped she would do one day.

Fane decided to let her be for now. She needed time to process things. After all, it wasn't every day that she met a guy who was somehow able to talk to her through her thoughts. That was a lot to absorb. He would wait to see if she would seek him out. He only hoped he and his wolf would be patient. The mate bond called to him and demanded an answer.

CHAPTER 4

*J*acque's eyes snapped open. She slapped her hand against her chest as she attempted to fill her empty lungs with air. But the more she tried, the more futile it became. She sat up and folded herself in half so her head was between her legs. Her mind screamed at the revelation that had brought on the panic. Fane! The voice was Fane! He had actually answered the mental question she had asked him.

What...the...hell?

Jacque had been certain she had only been hearing a voice made up by her own subconscious. Or even a dead relative trying to haunt her. Either was more believable than what was actually happening. The voice was someone real, tangible, and, well ... hot. *Not that him being hot is important, but seriously it doesn't hurt, right?*

No longer able to lie still, Jacque got up and went over to her window. She opened the blinds and looked across the street at the Henrys' house wondering what Fane was doing. *Is he wondering what I am doing?* "Oh, good grief," she told herself, "you just met him, you don't even know him, and you're worried about whether he is thinking about you? Do yourself a favor, Jac. Get a Kit Kat and give yourself a break."

She closed the blinds, turned around, and leaned back against the wall squeezing her eyes closed. Taking a deep breath, she decided she needed to do something to keep herself occupied until Sally and Jen came back over. When in doubt, distraction was always a safe bet. There was a pile of dirty clothes on the floor next to her closet. She loathed laundry as if it were her worst enemy, but at the moment, it appeared like a savior from the barrage of thoughts racing around her mind. She grabbed the clothes basket and headed downstairs. Still not operating on all four cylinders, she didn't even bother to sort them. She threw everything in and tossed some detergent on top of them. She shut the washer lid and went back into the living room.

"Okay, what next?" Jacque turned in a complete circle, letting her eyes roam the room. "Dust. That's it. This house is terribly dusty. It's everywhere. I simply cannot abide this dust." *Who cares that I've never dusted a day in my life without being forced? Cleanliness is next to godliness, right?* "Uh-huh, sure, Jac. Just keep telling yourself that," she muttered. She grabbed a dust cloth and spray from the kitchen. Trying to drag things out, she sprayed each item, and carefully wiped them with the dusting cloth. By the time she was done, Jacque was sure the living room had never been so dust-free since the house had been built.

She moaned when she finally looked at the clock. It had only been an hour since she had come downstairs. Why couldn't they be sloppier? Of all the times for her to appreciate her mother's ability to keep a pretty neat home, this wasn't one of those times. What was she going to do now? "I could go over to the Henrys' and see if they're done with mom's dishes. Yeah, Sherlock..." She snorted. "That wouldn't be obvious at all."

Jacque headed back up to her room, wracking her brain for things to keep her mind off "he who must not be named.", She knew Sally and Jen would appreciate that reference. When she shut her bedroom door, her hand brushed up against the bathing suit that was hanging on the doorknob. "Okay, suntanning it is," she told herself.

Jacque changed into the bathing suit and ran a hand down her legs and decided they were smooth enough for just laying on a towel in the backyard. It wasn't like she was going to have a hot Romanian guy rubbing suntan lotion on her or anything. *Where did that idea come from?* She raised her eyebrows. But it did have some merit.

She looked in the mirror, pleased enough with how she looked, she supposed. She was a little on the short side at 5 feet, 1 ½ inches tall, slender, and muscular from playing on the girls' tennis team. Her figure was curvy, though not quite as curvy as Jen's. Jacque's C cup didn't rival her blonde friend's ample bosom, as Sally liked to call it. Jacque had helpfully pointed out that bosom was not a term used to describe a female's chest in this day and age. Sally's response had been a simple, "I prefer bosom to all the other derogatory terms that refer to the female anatomy." Jen had, of course, added her two cents and told Sally, "So are you telling me that in the throes of passion you want your man to say something like, 'Oh, Sally, you have the nicest bosom'? No thanks. I would prefer my man to be a little more creative in his description of my assets." It had taken every ounce of self-control for Jacque not to make a joke about Jen's assets. She'd long ago learned, with Jen, you sometimes had to surrender a battle so that you had the energy to fight the war. Jacque brought herself back to the present as she pulled her hair up into a ponytail. Her red locks were her favorite attribute and the only thing that kept her from being plain.

The bathing suit was a bikini she had let Sally and Jen talk her into, though she did get her two cents in by buying a mismatched bottom and top. She figured if she liked two different bathing suits, why not buy half of each? With that reasoning, it was no wonder she was hearing voices.

"Could be worse," Jacque told the mirror as she turned this way and that, making sure the bathing suit covered the essentials. She slipped on her pink flip-flops, grabbed her cell phone, earbuds, a towel, and her sunglasses, and she was out the back door.

Her backyard was very simple, just a square, and it didn't even have a fence around it. There was a single tree growing smack dab in the middle of the yard, so depending on the time of day Jacque either had to lie on the left side or the right.

She noticed the direction of the tree's shadow and nodded. "The right side it is."

Jacque laid her towel in the grass. She had already put her earbuds in and set her music player to shuffle. Nineties alternative rock playing at the moment. She put her sunglasses on and turned to sit down on her towel. When she turned, she realized that choosing the right side of the backyard, since there wasn't a fence, put her directly in front of the Henrys' house. "Wait, folks, it gets even better." She grumbled as she glared at the window where Fane had stood staring at her earlier that morning. She was about to plop her half-clad self down for Fane's viewing pleasure. She was basically giving him his own live centerfold. Okay, so he would have to actually be in his room and looking out the window for that to be the case. What were the chances he would look out at the exact time she was tanning … in a bikini … in front of his window? Jacque slammed her palm against her forehead. "Could I look any more desperate than this?" she asked herself through gritted teeth.

Bad. This is very, very bad. I can get up and go lay on the left side of the backyard ... in the shade ... which makes no sense, or I can lay here and look like I totally planned this. "For the love of pigtails, could someone please throw me a bone?" Jacque groaned.

She sat there debating for a minute or two then threw her hands up and said, "To hell with it. I'm already down here. He can get an eyeful if he wants, and if he wants to know if I did it for his benefit, he can just ask me." *Humph.* Jacque laid back on the towel, arms by her side, feet flat on the ground, and knees slightly bent.

As she closed her eyes, she began to feel the warmth of the sun seep into her skin and calm her. She took some deep breaths and focused on the lyrics to the song now playing in her ears. The song was a contemporary love song she had heard a couple of times before but had never really listened to the words. Now, as she heard the lyrics, which were about a distant, unreachable, love causing the singer to 'come undone', something inside Jacque awoke.

The words reached deep inside, penetrating through the confusion and disbelief. Jacque didn't understand how she knew it, she just did. Her future was with Fane. Jacque had no idea what that meant, couldn't fathom what that would even look like, she just knew she had met him for a reason. It wasn't by chance he ended up across the street from her house. Regardless of the revelation, the lyrics also described exactly what Fane was at that moment. He was untouchable, and she sure as hell was coming undone.

The song stopped and her phone started vibrating, and for a moment, she was a little disoriented until she realized she was getting a phone call. She looked at the screen and saw it was Jen calling.

"Hello?"

"Got good news, got bad news. Won't charge you for either, so which do you want first?" Jen answered.

"Slap me first, then pat me on the back," Jacque told her.

"Oh, Jac, so decisive and sure. You know men like a woman who knows what she wants." Jen cooed.

Jacque rolled her eyes. "Spare me your commentary, Jennifer, and spill."

"Fine, I won't attempt to help you bag the Romanian beast that has currently claimed his lair across the street from you."

"Did you just call him a beast? What's with the animal analogies, Jen?"

Jen clucked her tongue at her. "Seriously, you didn't get an animalistic vibe from him? Jacque, he looked at you like he wanted to hunt you down and feast on your body, and not in a masticating way either. I'm talking pure, carnal—"

Jacque interrupted her before she could finish. "Okay, okay I get it. And no, I didn't get that vibe from him."

"Fine, be in denial if you must. We'll move on to the bad news. I won't be back over to your house until 9:00 at the earliest. My mom and dad are in one of their 'We're a family. We need to eat at the table together, blah, blah blah' moods. So naturally, being the sweet, little thing I am, I didn't argue with them for twenty minutes or slam my door and tell them how 1950's they were being. Nope, not me. I smiled sweetly."

"Jen, you don't do anything sweetly. How did you manage a smile?"

"Oh, shut up. The good news is I get to come over, even after the little fit I didn't throw," Jen said with smug satisfaction in her voice.

"Try to keep your mouth shut between now and then so you don't have to call me later to inform me you've been put in lock up," Jacque told her.

"Okay, okay, geez. Who spit in your pizza?" Jen asked.

"I'll give you the full details tonight, but suffice it to say at least one piece made its way into the puzzle." Jacque thought about her words for a moment and then remembered a question Fane asked her when he was 'talking' to her. He had asked where she got her odd way of speaking. Did she speak oddly?

"Hey, Jen, do you think I speak oddly?" Jacque asked her.

There was silence for a moment from the other end of the line. Jacque assumed either Jen was thinking or she had found something more interesting to pay attention to. She was just about to ask again when Jen answered, "You do realize who you are asking, right? 'Cause I just say things like stomp a mudhole in you and walk it dry and you totally get my drift. So, I'm just saying, I might not be the best judge of any oddities you have."

"True dat," Jacque responded.

"I'll see you tonight. Try not to do anything too crazy without me. You know how I like to watch," Jen said, cackling at her own humor as she hung up.

Jacque shook her head, laughing to herself about her friend's sick, twisted sense of humor. She didn't bother to turn her music back on. She just listened to the sounds around her. For the most part, the only noises she heard were the occasional bird or a barking dog. Other than that, it was a quiet summer day. She knew if she opened her eyes, she'd be able to see the heat waves in the sweltering Texas air. Summers in the South could be brutal. As she felt beads of sweat run down her collarbone she thought of the times she and her mom had fried eggs on the sidewalk, and that's not something you could do just anywhere.

Jacque rolled over onto her stomach and closed her eyes. As the warmth from the air and ground seeped into her, she grew drowsy and slipped into a dreamless sleep.

~

IT WAS 12:30. Sara had been gone an hour, and Fane still hadn't heard Brian anywhere. There was an eight-hour time difference between Coldspring and Romania, so it was 8:30 p.m. back home. He decided to call his dad while he had some privacy. Fane had serious questions that should be answered before he had to start explaining things to Jacquelyn and *before* she started asking questions of her own.

He dialed his father's cell phone number. "*Da?*" Vasile said as he answered the phone. This was always the way he answered, with a simple "Yes", no "Hello" or "This is...", just "Yes." Something so small, but it made him homesick.

"*Tată*, Father," Fane answered.

"Fane? *Cum te simți?*" his father asked him.

"English please, father. I'm trying to get in a better habit of not switching back and forth in conversation. I am good. How is *Mamă*? How is the pack?" Fane asked.

"Your mother is good, other than missing her pup. The pack is good," his father responded.

As the future Alpha, Fane had been taught to care for the needs of the pack before his own. So, in keeping with his training and in anticipation of his future duties, Fane made it a habit to inquire about his packmates as a matter of course.

"Good," Fane said. "I'm calling because I need to ask you some questions about the mate bond."

"Okay." Fane heard a note of suspicious intrigue in his father's voice.

"Does the mate have to be a *Canis lupus*, or can she be human? What does it mean when you suddenly have more markings on you than before? What if your mate doesn't know anything about your world and won't accept you?" He'd meant to ask the questions one at a time, but they'd suddenly tumbled out on their own accord like rocks cascading down a jagged cliff.

"You're seventeen, you've been in America for less than

twenty-four hours, and you think you've found your mate?" Vasile asked. Fane heard his mother gasp in the background and begin speaking quickly in their native tongue. "Calm down, love. Let me find out,"

"I know how it sounds," Fane told him. "But the signs are unmistakable, and my wolf seems to know with absolute certainty, even though I am unsure of what's going on. The beast is almost clawing its way out to get to her."

"I find when a situation arises that knocks us off balance, it's best to start at the beginning," Vasile said calmly.

Fane told him about how he had heard Jacque's thoughts the night he arrived at the Henrys'. He told his dad about being able to "feel" her emotions and how her scent had called to him in a way nothing had before. He told him Jacquelyn had spoken to his mind as well, and that she figured out he was who she heard and that she was not having some sort of psychosis. Fane didn't go into the intimate details of his attraction for her. He was sure it would be understood, without saying, that he desired Jacquelyn in a way he'd never felt toward another.

After Fane finished there was silence from the other end of the phone. For a second, he thought they might have been disconnected. But then his father spoke.

"A mate cannot be fully human. There must be *Canis lupus* blood somewhere in her line. It can be generations back, but it has to be there for her life to be bound to yours. There is only one exception to this, but their kind has not existed for a very long time. It is more likely your female has wolf blood. You know how long we live, and when you become bonded, she will take on part of your longevity only if she already has lupine in her blood." His father paused, then continued, "As for the markings, I hadn't discussed this with you yet because I didn't think you would find your mate before you graduated from high school. It's very, very rare. I see that I was

56

remiss in my duties as your Alpha and father. I should have explained all aspects of true mates and bonding. I was over a century old when I found your mother. The markings of a male *Canis lupus* only change when he finds a mate. They are a signal to all other wolves you have found that other half of your soul, the light of a female wolf that quiets the darkness that grows in all male *Canis lupus*. It is very important for you, as the next Alpha of our pack, to be mated. Few unmated Alphas last long in the position."

"Even though I haven't bonded with her? Don't you have to perform the Blood Rites before you can be mate bonded? I mean, the markings changed after seeing her through a window," said Fane.

"*Calmeaze-te*, peace, son," Fane's father told him. "This is something to rejoice over, not fret. We will figure out the details. You have a year to woo her and help her understand our world before you must come back to Romania. It will be hard for your wolf not to mark her and claim her, but you are not just an animal. You are a man as well and can control your beast. You *must* control your beast," he reiterated.

Fane breathed a little easier. It was true there was no rush for him to bond with Jacquelyn. Okay, other than the fact his instincts were screaming profanities at him to claim her, protect her, and have her. She was, after all, his true mate. He had a right— Fane stopped that thought before he could finish it. That came from his wolf forcing his will. The beast only understood the instincts of their nature. He did not understand the human etiquette of courtship and falling in love. *I already care for her*, his wolf told him. *Do you care if she loves us?* Fane challenged. His wolf growled at him. *She will learn to love us after we bond and she is under our protection.* For the wolf that is what most of it came down to—his strong need to keep what was his safe. No, it would not be easy to hold off his wolf, especially since she was right across the street where he could see her, smell her, and hear her. The one thing he had in his favor was that wolves are very patient hunters. *I will watch, and I will wait,* his wolf whispered. *Okay, so now my wolf sounds like a creepy stalker.*

Fane was brought out of his thoughts when his father asked, "Did you happen to notice any marks on her body?"

"Marks on her, like the marks I have?" Fane asked.

"Indeed, but you might not have seen them. The female *Canis lupus* markings are not meant to be seen by any other than her mate. So, they show up different places. They are not a declaration to the world like those of the males. But that doesn't necessarily mean they will be on an intimate part of her body. However, they will appear on a place easily covered by clothing. The markings will match your new ones like a puzzle piece even though they might not be in the same location. The marks are simply another confirmation she is your mate. They are also another way for your wolf to stake his claim. But they are for your eyes only. The female mating marks are an extremely personal gift from our Creator, the Great Luna, to her wolves. Every time your mate sees them it is a reminder to her she isn't alone. She will never be alone again, but always loved, protected, and cherished. Each time *you* see them it is a reminder that you have been blessed to have the other half of your soul returned to you. The marks represent the completion she brings to you. She is a gift to be treasured beyond all others."

Fane heard the passion in his father's voice. It was one he'd heard many times throughout his life as Vasile talked about Fane's mother.

Something stirred inside Fane as his father explained the markings. He had to admit he liked the idea of Jacquelyn bearing markings that matched his own. He liked that there would be a visual claiming on her skin that showed they belonged to each other. Fane felt a low growl in his throat as he realized his dislike at the idea of another male seeing Jacquelyn's markings, even if they were on her arm or leg, they were meant for him only.

"Fane, are you alright?" he heard his father ask him.

"I'm just a little … I don't know what. I mean, I'm seventeen, and the thought of another wolf seeing markings on a girl I barely know infuriates me. I'm not even out of high school," Fane said as his jaw clenched and unclenched. There was a growing tightness in his chest as all his father explained bounced around inside Fane's head like loose screws that had yet to be put in their place.

"I know you are only seventeen, son of mine, but you have to remember when your wolf finds his mate, he is no longer a juvenile. He becomes a full-fledged adult overnight. Your wolf expects you to step up and be ready to be the Alpha you are meant to be because you are to protect her at all costs. Yes, you are only seventeen, but you are not a mere human. You are *Canis lupus*, you are prince to your pack, and you are Alpha," Fane's father told him.

Fane took several deep breaths to calm and compose himself. It wasn't like him to get so upset over something he couldn't change. His emotions seemed a little on edge today, and he could only imagine it had everything to do with the sassy redhead across the street. She threw him off balance, and he was sure it was something she would continue to do for the rest of their long lives. Oddly enough, he looked forward to it.

"One more thing," Fane said. "I know mates cannot go long periods without sharing their thoughts or being near one another without feeling discomfort from the separation. I've been restless since I met Jacque but it hasn't been like torture or anything. Why would that be?"

"You won't begin to feel some effects of being mated until after the bond is completed through the Blood Rites, so until then neither one of you should have any problem being apart. Consummation will make the connection stronger and being apart more difficult, though it might be different for the female. If she isn't fully *Canis lupus*, then she might respond differently to the bond."

"I wouldn't say that I won't have *any* problem being apart," Fane mumbled.

Fane's dad continued without acknowledging his comment. "There is a reason this has happened to you so young. She is part human which means she can't phase and is weaker for that, so maybe she will need your protection in some way. Keep your eyes and ears open. Nothing happens by chance. There is purpose in everything."

"What could possibly be a threat to her in this little, insignificant town?" Fane asked.

"Lesser words have preceded many a war, Fane," his father answered. "All will be well. Get to know her, be her friend. Keep your wolf in check and call me to keep me updated or ask more questions. *Te iubesc, miul meu.* I love you." And with that, Fane's father and Alpha hung up.

"Be her friend," Fane scoffed. "How am I supposed to be her friend when what I really want to do to her goes way beyond the realm of friendship?" His voice was guttural with his wolf as his need for her threatened to suffocate him.

Fane sat there for a while longer going over in his head the things his father had told him. Jacquelyn had to have *Canis lupus* in her bloodline somewhere, and it was either very distant or perhaps came from a relative she did not know ... or didn't know was *Canis lupus*.

He heard the door open downstairs and caught Brian's scent. Fane decided he needed to get some fresh air, preferably behind the handlebars of a motorcycle. He went in search of Brian to see if he would take him to a dealership to look at some used motorcycles. Fane found his host father whistling an unknown tune in the kitchen while pouring himself some of the sugar with tea in it.

"Hope you like sugar better than tea because that's about all you're going to drink when you take a sip of that," Fane told him with a smile.

Brian chuckled. "Yeah, that's how we do it in the South. It's not really sweet tea. It's tea-flavored sugar."

Fane laughed with him.

"I have a favor to ask if you have time."

"Shoot," Brian said.

"My parents have given me money to buy a motorcycle, but I need a ride to a dealership to look at some. Would you mind taking me?" Fane asked.

Already nodding his head as he took a drink and swallowed before saying, "Yeah, that's not a problem. If you're ready, I don't have anything pressing, so we can go now."

"Okay, let me grab my phone. Give me just a sec," Fane said as he headed toward the stairs.

Fane retrieved what he needed from his room, but before leaving he went to the window, curiosity getting the better of him. He pulled the curtains back and looked across the street to Jacquelyn's house. Fane had to blink several times to get his brain to understand what he was seeing, and then he had to take slow deep breaths to keep his wolf from growling possessively. *What the hell is she wearing?* The question did nothing to calm him. For there, across the street, was his Luna laying out in the sun in a skimpy bikini. And it wasn't enough that she was essentially wearing undergarments. Also revealed, besides her lovely body, there at the top of her back stretching out from shoulder to shoulder and up her neck to just below her hairline, were the markings that would fit his perfectly. Her markings were there on display for any male who came by to see, not to mention her mom if she came out. Without thinking, his mind reached for hers.

"You do realize that they only sold you a quarter of that bathing suit, don't you?" Fane said, trying to sound casual. What he really wanted to say was "Where the hell are your clothes, female?" He figured that wouldn't go over too well.

At first, he didn't get a response. As he was looking at her, he realized she must have fallen asleep, which was not a good thing because in this heat she'd burn terribly. Fane focused his concentration on her and, using a not-so-subtle push of his power, spoke to her. *"Jacquelyn, wake up!"*

Still, she did not move or respond. Fane was deciding whether or not to walk across the street and disturb her when she finally spoke to him.

CHAPTER 5

*J*acquelyn heard Fane's question. "So, he thinks he's a funny guy," she muttered under her breath. Two can play at that game. She'd been asleep, but as soon as Fane had spoken to her, she'd snapped awake. She continued to lie perfectly still, knowing he must be watching her. Jacque didn't want him to know she had heard him. The second time he spoke to her, she felt a push that made her want to obey him. *Did he seriously just command me to wake up?* She was surprised when he didn't respond to that thought.

She made him wait a full minute before she finally answered.

"They only sold me twenty-five percent of the bathing suit, but I still think it covers a bit too much," she retorted as her lips curved up into a wicked smile. He couldn't see the smile, but it still satisfied something inside of her.

Jacque heard him growl at her. *Growling, really?* Was he actually jealous? If so, jealous of what exactly? He didn't know her from Adam.

"I have told you before, you are my Luna," she heard him answer her thought.

"And I'm telling you now I don't know what that means, and I'm not your anything!" She growled back.

"If nothing else, could you at least be mindful of the fact that you are going to burn if you lay out in practically nothing and fall asleep," Fane retorted, sounding very annoyed.

What did he mean if nothing else? Was he implying that she was trying to lie out and show off her body to just any Joe Blow that walked by? Jacque sat up and glared up at Fane's window, and sure enough, he was standing there staring at her. Frustrated with herself for allowing his disapproval to actually bother her, she stood up, and with as much sarcasm as you can put into an action, she curtsied to him then picked up her things and marched back into the house.

"Meu inimă, my heart, did you just curtsy to me?" Fane asked, sounding astonished and amused.

"Well, seeing as how you seem to think you deserve something from me, I thought I would indulge you just a little, but I assure you my intentions were completely rude," she responded. Jacque heard him chuckle at her sass.

As Jacque walked into the house, she set her things on the couch and went to the kitchen to get a drink. She hadn't realized how thirsty laying out in the sun had made her, which didn't make her happy because it only confirmed what Fane said about getting too hot. "I mean seriously, who is he, the bathing suit police?"

"No, puţin foc, small fire, I am simply trying to look out for you. Who knows what wolves lie in wait to pounce on unsuspecting sunbathing beauties?" Fane said.

"And you aren't one of these so-called wolves?" she asked him in exasperation.

Just then she realized that their whole conversation had

been thoughts back and forth to one another. Man, had her life gotten weird…. No, actually, it wasn't just weird, it was bordering on crazy.

"I didn't say that," he told her as his voice dropped to a deep rumble. "But if any wolf is going to be pouncing your way, it will be me."

"Okay, first of all, there will be no pouncing of any kind by anyone, wolf or not, and don't you have something you need to be doing?" she asked him as she went upstairs to take a shower. Although all she had done was lay outside, she smelled like the outdoors and sweat.

"Actually, yes. I am going with Brian to look at motorcycles. My parents gave me the money to purchase one so I will be able to get around on my own," Fane told her.

"Why not a car? And what if it rains? Won't you get soaked?" Jacque asked.

"I won't melt, Luna. A little rain won't cause me any harm. And they make rain gear I can wear when it rains. Why would I want to be cooped up in a car when I could be on a motorcycle with the sun on my face?" Fane explained.

"You might be rethinking that when the Texas heat is beating down on your leather-clad body," she answered and then wanted to kick herself for mentioning leather and his body in the same sentence because all that did was conjure all sorts of thoughts. "Puppies and cute little critters, Jacque. These are the things you must think about. Not hot, Romanian males on motorcycles wearing leather… AGH!" She growled while shaking her head and attempting to purge the tempting thoughts from her mind.

Jacque began gathering clothes for the much-needed shower. As she walked into the bathroom and closed the door, she discovered she was reluctant to undress while they were talking through their thoughts. Somehow that felt way too intimate. As if sensing her discomfort, Fane asked, *"Is something wrong? Did I do something to upset you … besides imply your bathing suit was a bit skimpy?"*

"No, no, I'm fine. Ya know just, um, got things to do is all. People and places, you know how it is," she said awkwardly.

"Jacquelyn, please tell me what is wrong," Fane persisted.

Jacque rolled her eyes. Couldn't he just leave it alone? If she had to spell it out for him, she was going to be mortified. She could just hear herself explaining how she was sweaty from the sun and stank, needed a shower, and the thought of talking to him through their thoughts while she was butt-freaking naked was just a tad beyond her comfort zone. Fane must have caught her passing thoughts. Man, she really needed to learn how to block him out somehow.

"I will leave you alone since you have things to take care of. Just so you know, I may be a teenage guy, with teenage hormones, but I assure you I am not dishonorable, nor would I abuse our thought connection," he said with firm conviction.

"I know you can hear my thoughts, but can you, like, see through my eyes?" she asked apprehensively.

"No, but I can see the things you think. Just as you can see what I think if you want. Also, when your emotions are strong, I feel you and hear your thoughts very loudly, even when you aren't trying to communicate with me. You might want to bear that in mind," Fane told her.

"How do I keep you out of my mind?" Jacque asked.

"All you have to do is imagine a wall in your mind between mine and yours. I will not be able to get past it. The same goes for me if I don't want you to hear my thoughts."

Jacque was surprised to find herself a little hurt at the idea of him not wanting her to hear his thoughts, but then she thought how absurd that was because everyone needed their own private thoughts.

"Okay, I will keep all that in mind, and since we are in

Mind Reading 101, could you answer me this? Who else can you do this with?" Jacque asked not realizing how jealous she sounded.

"No one, meu inimă. Only you, just as you will not be able to do this with anyone else as well," Fane replied. "Talk to you later. Be safe."

And just like that Jacque "felt" him leave her. She pursed her lips and frowned, wondering why there was a sudden emptiness inside her. She undressed and, without looking in the mirror, got into the steamy hot shower letting the water wash the empty sensation away. It was silly to feel so alone without him in her mind, she knew that, and yet she couldn't shake the hollowness that was left behind in his wake. It just seemed so natural to talk to him, like she had done it all her life. She found it so odd she was jealous of the idea of him talking to another girl through his thoughts. She had only known him a day after all, but the thought irked her regardless. "Okay, Jacque," she told herself, "move on to another topic." She hadn't heard from Sally and figured she'd better call her after showering to make sure she was still going to come over.

Jacque got out of the shower. While she was toweling off, she turned and caught a glimpse of herself in the mirror. She froze at what she saw. Without even realizing it, she reached out to Fane. *"Fane, what the hell is on my back?"* she screamed at him mentally.

No answer.

"Fane!"

Still no answer.

Calming down, she examined the design that looked like a tattoo and ran from shoulder to shoulder and up her neck. It was scrolled lines arching and curving, coming to a point at the nape of her neck. It was beautiful and feminine, and it was also very *not* there before she had laid out in her back-

67

yard. Had Fane done some Romanian voodoo on her? 'Cause she would so do some voodoo on his ass if he had.

He still hadn't responded to her after a few minutes, so she got dressed and combed out her wet hair and put mousse in it, pausing every few seconds to check her back. *Yep, tattoo still there.* Her phone rang. For a fleeting moment, she hoped it was Fane, but that would be ridiculous. Not only did he not have her number, apparently, he could just mind magic his thoughts to hers whenever he wanted. He wouldn't call her on the phone. Shaking her head in frustration at her sudden obsession with the new guy across the street, she answered the phone.

"So I'm thinking bikini, towel, tunes, and catching rays, you in?" Sally's cheerful voice came through the phone.

"You're a little late, Charlie Brown. I've already cooked, rotated, and cooked some more. I just got out of the shower. So, am I to assume you are going to be able to come over soon?" Jacque asked, relief in her voice.

"That's the rumor. You free?" Sally asked.

"Free, crazy, completely deranged... Take your pick." Jacque answered.

"I'm on my way over now. Be there in five," Sally hung up.

Jacque looked around her room and decided she needed to pick up from last night's impromptu sleepover. She folded the blankets and laid them on the bed. No sense in putting them away since the girls were staying the night again. Her mind was restless, and she decided she needed to write out her thoughts. Sometimes writing down what was floating around upstairs helped her put things in perspective. She sat down and grabbed a pen and paper.

I'VE MET A GUY. Not just any guy, but a really unusual one. He's from Romania, he is beautiful, he can talk to me through my thoughts, and I can talk to him that way also. It's so unreal. To top it all off, I have these strange markings on my back that appeared out of nowhere. I don't know what to even begin to think about the whole thing. But I know for the sake of my waning sanity I need to talk to him, face to face and see if he will answer any of my questions. My other problem is, I seem to be...

JACQUE'S PHONE BEEPED, indicating she had text message:

SALLY: @ **coffee shop, frap moca?**
Jacque: **def.**

GRATEFUL THAT HER friend could recognize a much-needed caffeine binge when it was called for, Jacque turned back to her writing.

...jealous over a guy I barely know. I feel like we are somehow connected, like we've known one another our whole lives. I also think my mom knows something. She's been acting a little weird, or maybe I should say she's been feeling weird since I can sense her emotions. Funny, I haven't felt Fane's emotions when I've been around him, which has only been one time, but I don't feel them when we've been 'talking' either. I don't know if it can possibly get any stranger, but I know since I just thought that, it likely will.

JACQUE SHUT the notebook and closed her eyes as she took a deep breath and let it out slowly. Fane Lupei arrived less than twenty-four hours ago, and he had managed to tip her world upside down. She felt completely out of control, and she hated feeling that way. Jacque wasn't delusional enough to think she actually had any control in most situations, but she allowed herself to believe she did for the sake of her sanity. Somehow, Fane had ripped the rug right out from under her, and she could hear her butt hit the proverbial ground with a loud thud. Now, she was sitting on the ground after a good tumble, with the air knocked out of her lungs and stars dancing around her head. She was looking up, wondering what in the world had happened.

As Fane got into Brian's car to leave, he felt Jacquelyn's alarm and heard her scream at him, *"Fane, what the hell is on my back?"*

For a brief moment, he received a flash of the picture in her mind of her back. Though everything within him wanted to drink in the sight of his mate's markings, he quickly shut her out. He'd promised not to intrude on her privacy. And though it broke his heart to leave her in a state of confusion and fear, he didn't answer. If he said so much as a word to her right now, his wolf might compel the man to jump from Brian's car, sprint across the street, and go barreling up Jacque's stairs so it could see the markings with its own eyes.

And some things were better said face to face. Especially if you're going to be telling someone they have *Canis lupus* markings on their body because they have found their were-wolf mate they didn't know even existed. You know, the standard, 'Hey, let's get to know each other', stuff. He flinched a bit when she screamed. Brian noticed and asked if he was okay.

"Yeah, I'm good, just had some ringing in my ears for a minute," Fane lied.

"So, where are we headed? I know there's a dealership on

Grand Ave. Are you looking for anything in particular?"
Brian said.

"That will be fine. I'm not picky, and I'm good at working
on them, so it's okay if it needs a little fixing up."

"Alright then, let's roll," said Brian.

As they backed out of the driveway, Fane found himself
staring at Jacque's house and thinking, if he looked hard
enough, he would be able to see past the walls that separated
them. Fighting the urge to slip into her mind, he wondered if
she was alright or if she thought she was having some sort of
mental break. It felt strange when she had called out to him.
It was the first time she had done so without him first
prompting her. His wolf was pleased she was turning to him
for help. He was, after all, her protector. He quickly
reminded the preening-animal part of him that she didn't
exactly have anywhere else to go. That got a growl out of him
he had to disguise as a cough.

Fifteen minutes later, they pulled into the motorcycle
dealership. Several bikes lined the storefront. After only a
few minutes of browsing, Fane's eyes fell on a solid black
cruiser with wide wheels. Even the pipes, normally shiny
chrome, were blacked out. *Perfect.*

The motorcycle was used but still looked to be in good
shape. Fane liked his bikes to be simple, nothing flashy or
fancy. He just wanted to ride, not show off. A salesman
walked out into the heat and went immediately to Brian. He
was, after all, the adult. Brian shook his head and quickly
pointed him in Fane's direction.

"Can I help you?" the salesman asked. In the next instant,
he sucked in a sharp breath. Fane was positive he heard a low
growl as the salesman abruptly stepped back a few steps,
turning his head ever so slightly so that his neck was exposed
to Fane.

Fane looked at him, briefly confused, and then took his

own deep breath. The smell hit him like a freight train and nearly caused him to phase: *Canis lupus.*

Brian, thankfully, had begun to wander around the lot, not paying attention to them, so Fane stepped toward the salesman, Steve, his name tag said. Instinctively, Fane growled as his wolf perked up at the presence of another male Grey in the area that Fane had deemed his territory. And rightfully so since there was no record of a pack residing in Coldspring. Wadim, the Romanian pack historian, had specifically double-checked the area after Fane had informed him where his exchange program would take him.

After a moment, the wolf named Steve asked, "Who are you? Why are you in the Alpha's territory?"

Fane wanted to scoff at the fool's use of *the* in his sentence. As though his Alpha was THE Alpha. Steve had obviously never met Vasile. Fane's head tilted ever so slightly as he took in the wolf before him. Unlike humans, *Canis lupus* could instinctively tell exactly where their opponent stood with them. If they were friend or foe, dominant or submissive, and even if they were mated. Steve was no match for Fane in the dominance battle, but this Alpha he spoke of might be a different story. He would keep his cards close to his chest until he knew more about the situation.

"I wasn't aware there were any Greys in this area," Fane stated vaguely.

"I wasn't aware that I had to cater to a pup who showed up uninvited and unannounced, and with a human no less," he spat at Fane. Steve couldn't meet Fane's eyes—he wasn't dominant enough to do that—and it was obvious he wasn't too bright. Perhaps it was time to show him just who the pup before him was.

Fane's wolf pushed to come out, and Fane let him come forth just a little. His power poured over him, and Steve felt

it instantly and nearly bowed involuntarily as his wolf realized just how dominant Fane truly was.

"I don't have to dignify you with an answer, but just so
you know what you have provoked, I will oblige you. I am
the Prince of the Romanian *Canis lupus*. I am next in line to
be Alpha, and I submit to no one but the Alpha of all the
Romanian *Canis lupus*." Putting as much push in his words as
he dared without unleashing the full power of his line, he
asked, "Who is your Alpha, and how long has there been a
pack of Greys in Coldspring?"

The man whined just a little but answered, "I have heard
of your father. It is said he makes all Alphas bow just by his
presence."

"Answer my question, Steve. Now." Fane glared at him.

"My Alpha is Lucas Steele. I have been a member of this
pack for three years. I don't know how long it has been
active. Why are you here? You're a teenager from another
country? What could you possibly be doing in Coldspring,
Texas?" Steve asked bewildered.

"My business is not yours.

"Okay, okay," the man said holding up his hands. "I don't
want any trouble. What do you want, Prince?"

"That black bike," said Fane pointing. "How much?"

"You want to buy a motorcycle?" Steven asked.

"Is that a problem?"

"No, not at all. Do you want to test drive it?"

"No. How much?" Fane asked again, ready to be done
with Steve so he could speak with his father about the new
developments.

"Two thousand, five hundred dollars, and there is no
warranty left on it. It has five thousand miles on it, the tires
are new, never been in an accident," Steve rattled off his spiel
as if he were reading it from a piece of paper, but his face still
held a look of bewilderment.

Fane pulled out his credit card and handed it to him. As Steve walked off with the card, Fane realized he might have just made a big mistake. Steve now had his father's full name and credit card number. That kind of information could be dangerous in the hands of a rival pack. But ... given that there was not even a record of this pack's existence, they probably wanted to keep a low profile. Stealing from the most powerful Alpha in the world would likely bring attention this mystery pack wouldn't want.

Brian wandered back over to where Fane was waiting.

"So, did you find something to buy?" Brian asked.

"Yeah, actually, I'm going to purchase that black one. It looks to be in pretty good shape. Do you think you could take me to get the license and do whatever else I need to in order to finalize the sale?" Fane asked.

"That's not a problem. Let me know when you are ready," Brian responded.

"Okay, *mulţumesc*, thank you, Brian. I appreciate your help."

"You're welcome." Brian smiled.

Fane turned to see Steve coming across the lot toward him. "Everything looks good," he said. "Could you step inside for a moment to sign these papers?"

Fane simply nodded and started to follow Steve in the direction of the building. They stepped inside and Steve sat down at a table. The stiff set of the salesman's shoulders told Fane that Steve did not like being reminded that a teenager was over him, at least in the world of the *Canis lupus*. Sitting in the presence of one lower on the scale could be a power play. It could send the message that he wasn't threatened by the less-dominant wolf. Fane preferred to remain on his feet where he could move quickly if the need arose. So, he simply leaned down and signed the places Steve had marked. Once done, Steve stood back up and handed Fane the keys. Before

Fane turned to leave Steve said, "I have a message from my Alpha."

Fane turned back and looked Steve in the eyes, and the less-dominate Grey instantly dropped his gaze but continued. "He says don't unpack." And with that, Steve turned and hurried away.

Fane pushed the door open and walked back out to where Brian stood. "Okay, Brian, I'm ready if you are," Fane said, trying very hard to contain his anger. His wolf was not happy. There were other wolves in a territory he had claimed. On top of that, his mate was in the same area and they weren't yet bonded. He would say things couldn't get worse, but that would be a huge mistake when it came to talking about *Canis lupus* unmated males and un-bonded females all in the same vicinity.

Though Fane didn't technically yet have a license, he still drove the motorcycle home. He'd decided if he was stopped by a police officer, Fane would pretend driver's licenses weren't required for motorcycles in Romania and feign ignorance as to the strange American culture. As Fane pulled into the driveway to the Henrys' house, he was pleased with how well the motorcycle ran. Brian had insisted they go straight to a motorcycle shop and buy a helmet since they didn't think to purchase one at the dealership. It felt so good to be on a bike again. He parked behind Brian's car and locked his, and the helmet he had impulsively bought Jacquelyn, on the side of his bike. When he'd bought the extra helmet, he'd seen the questioning look in Brian's eyes. Fane had simply winked at him and Brian didn't press the issue. Fane saw Lilly pulling into her driveway.

Lilly stepped from her Volkswagen convertible and waved at Fane.

"Fane, hey, I wanted to invite you over for dinner tonight," she yelled across the lawns. "The girls are having pizza. You are welcome to come, that is, if you don't mind hanging out with a group of teenage girls," she said with a wink.

Fane was a little surprised at the invitation, but he was not about to miss an opportunity to spend time with Jacquelyn.

"I would be honored," Fane responded.

"Great, we will order the pizza around 5:00, oh, and tell Brian and Sara they are invited as well. We'll make a night of it and play some games," Lilly said enthusiastically.

Fane couldn't put his finger on it, but Lilly seemed a bit edgy. She waved and turned to go into her house as he did the same.

Sara was sitting on the couch reading a book when he entered, and he told her they were invited to Lilly and Jacquelyn's for pizza and games.

"Oh, that sounds great," Sara said excitedly. "I will make some brownies. Do you like brownies, Fane?"

"Yes, I do. I'm going to excuse myself and call my parents to say hello if that is okay," Fane told her.

"Of course, that's fine, you don't have to ask us. You are practically a grown man, Fane. So long as you aren't selling drugs or going to all-night raves orgies, you do what you want. We trust you until you give us a reason not to," Sara said casually.

"What's a rave orgy?" interjected Brian. "You've been reading those smut books again, haven't you, Sara?"

"Brian, enough." She huffed at him.

Fane laughed at the redness that colored Sara's cheeks. "Thank you," he said and turned to go upstairs to call his father and tell him what he discovered that day. Fane was also going to have to explain how he lost his temper and revealed his title and used a little of the power endowed in him to put the wolf in his place. Honestly, he'd been in Coldspring one day and he'd found his mate, met another Grey, found out about a pack that wasn't supposed to be here, and been threatened not to stay. Needless to say, it hadn't been boring since he arrived. He dialed his father's number for the second time that day. His father answered on the first ring, "There's more to your mate than meets the eye," his father said.

CHAPTER 6

"*Y*ou did what?" Jacque sputtered, interrupting her mother just as Lilly was telling her and Sally she had invited Fane and the Henrys over for pizza.

"Hi, Sally," Jacque's mother said, ignoring Jacque's outburst. "You're staying for dinner, right?"

Sally nodded. "And spending the night, if that's okay with you," Sally answered sweetly.

"The more the merrier. We're going to play games too. It'll be fun! Jen is coming too, isn't she?" Lilly asked.

"Yes, mother, now could you please tell me why you are so interested in Fane?" Jacque asked her mom.

"New neighbors are interesting, that's all. What do you have against him that you have such an aversion to getting to know him?"

Jacque just didn't get her mother's behavior. Maybe her mom thought because Jacque and Trent had split up, pushing another guy on her would help Jacque move on. Yes, the breakup had been kind of hard on Jacque. She and Trent dated for almost two years. But she'd moved on now. Hadn't her mom noticed that? It had been two months since Jacque had even seen Trent, and she had barely thought about him. In fact, in the past twenty-four hours, she hadn't thought about him at all. But she wasn't going to argue the point with her mom now. Jacque knew a losing battle when she saw one.

She looked at Sally and motioned for her to go upstairs. "We'll be upstairs, Mom. Jen probably won't be here until later. She said she would have to eat with her parents, but hopefully, she will make if for the game portion of the evening," Jacque said in mock excitement.

"Keep up the attitude Jacquelyn and see where it gets you," Lilly warned.

Lilly rarely got angry with Jacque, so that's when she knew it was best to double-time it up the stairs before her big mouth got her working in the bookstore every Friday and Saturday night for her entire senior year.

The two girls settled in Jacque's room. Sally turned on some music while Jacque flopped across her bed like an ungraceful fish.

"So, let's hear it. What happened when Jen and I left today?" Sally finally asked after situating herself on the floor.

Jacque thought about the moment when she realized the voice she was hearing in her head was actually Fane. When he had spoken to her in Romanian, she had no more doubt. She filled Sally in on the events of the afternoon and couldn't help but laugh at the expressions flitting across Sally's face.

"So it *is* Fane?" Sally's brow rose and she clucked her tongue. "My, my, those Romanian boys are just full of surprises.

Jacque chuckled. "Because you've met so many Romanians and you would know." She paused and then added, "The final nail in the coffin was when he spoke to me in Romanian, and honestly, Sal, if you're going to hear voices, why on earth would you hear one that speaks in Romanian?"

"Well, duh, because you secretly have a fantasy about running away with a gorgeous Romanian noble to his beautiful ice castle," Sally said, a hint of wistfulness in her voice.

"Oh, of course, I completely overlooked that very plausible answer," Jacque said, rolling her eyes.

"So how long did you guys talk?" Sally asked, making air quotes with her fingers when she said the word *talk*.

"After he spoke to me in Romanian, I asked if it was Fane. Ya know, just for clarification purposes."

"Good to be clear on these matters," Sally concurred. "It could have been anyone."

"Well, when he confirmed it, I'm not ashamed to admit that I went into the flight mode of the whole fight or flight scenario. It all just seemed like a lot to absorb, and I'm still not convinced this isn't some weirdly elaborate dream. So, I did the logical thing and cleaned the house." Jacque shrugged.

"All your mom needs to do to get you to clean is find some Romanian foreign exchange student to go all mystic mind reading on your butt. Huh. Who knew?"

"Yeah, yeah, whatever, then I decided to get some sun. So, I laid out in the backyard. I don't know how long I was out there when I heard his voice again. This time he was ... not mad, exactly, but sort of frustrated or something. He had the nerve to point out how skimpy my bikini was by asking me if I knew they only sold me one quarter of my bathing suit." She was sure her face was just as outraged as it had been when Fane had questioned her, even though that had been hours before.

"Oh, Jen is going to love this. A Romanian hottie with a sense of humor. Brilliant and hot to boot," Sally said grinning to herself. Then she paused a minute in thought. "Wait, so he was looking out his window at you?" she asked.

"Yep, so you know what I did?" Jacque asked.

"Please tell me you didn't flip him off, moon him, or some

other terribly twisted suggestion that Jen would have offered," Sally said worriedly.

"No, but I wish I would have. Those all sound like great ideas. I simply stood up, gave him a good ol' Southern curtsy, and marched myself in the house ... after I graciously explained I would have preferred the bathing suit *not* cover so much." Jacque rolled on the bed as her laughter shook the mattress. Okay, so maybe it wasn't *that* funny, but at that moment her brain was tired, and pretty much everything was hilarious.

Sally rolled her eyes at her. "Remind me never to be in a lions' den with you now that I know you like to taunt them."

"Oh, come now, my dear Watson. Are you telling me you are afraid of lions and tigers and bears—"

"Oh my," Sally finished, slapping her hands on her cheeks as her eyes widened.

They both laughed as Jacque pulled her hair up into a ponytail, not thinking about the shirt she was wearing. She climbed awkwardly off the bed because it would have made too much sense to attempt the ponytail after she'd removed herself from the bed. Jacque didn't give a second thought as she turned to grab a hair tie, turning her back to Sally.

Jacque's arm froze in the air when Sally gasped. She turned slowly, looked at her friend, and realized where Sally's gaze was locked. Jacque had forgotten she had purposefully worn a shirt with a low back so she could show Jen and Sally the markings.

"Oh, did I forget to mention those?" she asked casually as she quickly finished putting her hair up.

"What the hell, Jac! When did you get that?" Sally's eyes were wide, and her voice had reached that squeaky point that made Jacque want to stuff cotton balls in her ears.

"Well, let's see. If I remember correctly, after y'all left, I downed a pint of whiskey, ran to the nearest tattoo parlor, had some dude named Snake with piercings in every visible body part, and quite possibly not so visible, give me this awesome ink. I just totally forgot to mention it," Jacque said and then added, suddenly sounding tired, "I don't know where it came from. When I came up to take a shower after lying out in the hot sun it was just there. I kind of had a mini-meltdown. I screamed at Fane, but he never answered me, which tells me he is the guilty party involved."

"So now he's not only doing his mind voodoo, but body voodoo too," Sally said, and then giggled as she realized how it sounded.

"You know what Jen would say..." Jacque started just as her bedroom door flew open and Jen walked in,

"Depends on what is called for, my dear, but do tell, what smart-ass comment am I supposed to be making?" Jen asked as she folded her arms across her chest and tapped her foot.

"Fane has done body voodoo on Jacque," Sally said in a tattletale voice.

"Ooooh, was it good?" Jen asked.

"Good freaking grief, she doesn't mean, like, physical voodoo, pervert." Jacque turned around to show her the markings on her back.

"I guess he decided to forgo the whole 'Hey, will you wear my class ring' and straight into 'Let's get body art together'," Jen said, studying the markings.

"What? You think maybe he has some...". Then she remembered when they were at the Henrys' she had noticed a tattoo that ran up the side of Fane's neck. She had forgotten it because it just sort of went with the whole biker thing he had going on.

"Hey, he did have a tattoo on his neck. I saw it when we were at the Henrys', but that doesn't mean it matches this one," Jacque told them, looking for reassurance.

"No, it most definitely does not mean they match," Sally agreed, but Jacque could hear the doubt in her friend's voice.

Just then Jacque turned her head and narrowed her eyes at Jen "What are you doing here. I thought you said 9:00 at the earliest?"

"Well, I just happened to mention you were a little depressed about the whole Trent thing and needed some girl support, yadda yadda, and my mom totally swallowed it whole. She's all about the hoes before bros," Jen said with a shrug.

"That's just great, Jen. Now your mom thinks I'm all torn up like a kicked puppy about Trent, and I'm not! I'm totally over him ... aren't I?" Jacque asked.

She started thinking back to the two years she and Trent dated. Even though they had only been sophomores and juniors in high school, their relationship had been pretty intense. Then out of nowhere, Trent came over and told her he felt like they needed a "break." Jacque politely told him not to treat her like an idiot and just tell her the truth. The breakup came out of nowhere. Jacque had asked him several times what happened because the day before they had been hanging out on the couch, and he actually told her he thought he might be in love with her. When he left her house, he said he would call her that night but he never did. The next time she heard from him, he came over to call it off. Jacque hadn't seen or heard from him since.

Thinking about him was making her start to miss him. Trent was a great guy, and they'd had a lot of fun together. He was tall, muscular from lifting weights, had messy wavy hair that he wore just long enough to be wild, and he had unusual grey eyes. He liked to goof off, but he was always a gentleman and could be pretty deep sometimes. They dated for quite a while before their relationship got physical, and when she told him sex wasn't on the agenda, he was completely okay with it.

"I don't like where your thoughts are at the moment, Luna." The words blew through Jacque's mind, causing a chill to run down her spine. She had forgotten Fane told her when her emotions were strong, he felt them even if she wasn't broadcasting them to him.

"Well, then I guess you should knock before entering," Jacque snapped back, irritated at how he caught her off guard and that he'd heard her thoughts about Trent.

"Who is this Trent? What does he mean to you? When and why was he kissing you?" Fane asked in quick succession.

"Okay, you listen up, and you listen good, you little Romanian, voodoo-casting, mind-reading, nosy..." Jacque stumbled for a minute looking for a word, and when she didn't find one, she lamely finished with "... person. I am NOT your loona or whatever you call me. You have no right knowing my business, and I don't owe you an explanation. So, so just ... grrrr!" She was beyond frustrated because she wanted to tell him to take a hike, but then a huge part of her rebelled against that because she wanted him with her. She was absolutely nuts.

Acting like he hadn't heard a word she said, Fane asked again, *"So, who did you say Trent was?"*

Jacque huffed in exasperation. He was clearly not phased in the least by her agitation.

"Are you talking to the Romanian hottie?" Jen asked.

Jacque nodded. "He heard me thinking about Trent and wants to know who he is."

"Why does he care ... oooh," Sally said with a thoughtful look, "he's jealous. Exchange boy wants a taste of American cuisine."

"Good one." Jen nodded to Sally and then looked back at Jacque. "Why do you always get the hotties?"

"Hold on, girls, give me a sec," Jacque said.

"Oh, by all means, don't mind us, the non-voodoo freaks. We'll just hang out while y'all make out mentally," Jen smarted off, and Sally burst out laughing.

"That's a good one, Jen," Sally said as they bumped fists.

Jacque just rolled her eyes at them. Turning her attention back to Fane, she had a feeling he wasn't going to drop it. With a resigned sigh, she answered his question.

"Trent is a guy I dated for the past two years. We broke up two months ago."

Fane was quiet for a moment, and then said, "I'm sorry for your pain because of that, but I will not deny my pleasure in knowing I will not have to convince him it was in his best interest to take his intentions elsewhere."

Jacque was a little taken aback by his honest comment. *"And why exactly would you do that?"*

"Because I intend to court you myself, and it would be a tad awkward if you had affections for another, don't you think?" Fane asked her.

Jacque looked at the clock on the wall and realized it was 5:15. The Henrys and Fane were supposed to be coming over in fifteen minutes.

"So, I guess you are going to be over in a few minutes," she said. Jacque wanted to drop the whole Trent conversation. The past was just that, the past and Jacque was not going to sit around dwelling on it.

"Yes, I am looking forward to seeing you again. Is that okay with you, Jacquelyn?" Fane asked her.

His bold question caught her off guard, and she thought about it for a minute. Jacque couldn't deny the rabid butterflies —only rabid ones would make her want to hurl—in her

85

stomach at the anticipation of seeing him again. She heard Fane laugh and assumed he must be listening since she kept forgetting to try and put the wall up, as he had explained to her earlier.

"I have some questions I need to ask you, so yeah, it's okay," Jacque told him honestly.

"I'll see you in a few minutes then, meu inimă, my heart," he told her.

AFTER HIS MOTORCYCLE RIDE, Fane had showered and made himself as presentable as possible. Fane felt something he'd never experienced before—a desire for approval. He'd never been nervous around women, but now he found himself feeling a deep need to gain Jacque's approval, and he could tell his wolf felt the same. He attempted to comb his hair out of his face, but it just fell right back in front of his left eye. He had chosen a crimson, polo-style shirt. It contrasted nicely with the markings on his neck, which he thought looked pretty cool if he did say so himself. He grabbed his phone and wallet, put them in his back pockets, and headed downstairs.

Sara and Brian were waiting in the living room. Sara had the brownie pan in her hands and Brian was carrying some games, only one of which Fane recognized—dominoes. His family back home liked to play dominoes.

He took the brownie pan from Sara. "I will take these for you," he said. Sara smiled.

"Ready?" Brian asked them.

With silent nods, they marched out the door.

Sara knocked on Lilly and Jacquelyn's door, and Fane felt a tingle of awareness on the back of his neck and turned to see a car cruising slowly by. He used his wolf's superior eyesight to see who was driving. Fane was on edge. He now knew there were other Greys in the area and his father had indicated that he had information concerning Jacque's family. Fane had also received an anonymous phone call from a wolf claiming to be the Alpha of the Coldspring pack, stating that Jacque had already been claimed by another wolf and Fane was to leave immediately. Fane hoped the Alpha was used to disappointment because he had no plans of going anywhere.

Jacque was the one who answered the door, and Fane couldn't help the smile that crossed his face. She was, after all, his fiery miracle. Like others before him, he could have waited centuries before he found her, and yet all it had taken was a mere seventeen years. The Great Luna had well and truly blessed him.

"Come in, y'all," Jacque said politely, her Southern drawl as cute as it was sexy.

They entered and Jacque pointed them in the direction of the kitchen where Fane could smell the aroma of the already delivered pizza.

"You look beautiful, Jacquelyn," he told her, walking beside her toward the kitchen.

"Flattery will get you everywhere." Jacque winked at him. His eyes narrowed on her, and the blush that rushed up her neck to her face told him she felt the intensity of his gaze. He wouldn't keep it a secret that he wanted her. This wasn't some high school crush. This was his soulmate, and he wanted no confusion between them. He was here for her and her alone.

"Hi, you guys," Lilly greeted them, effectively saving Jacquelyn from any more of his intense attention. "I'm so glad you could come over!" Lilly and Sara hugged. Jen and Sally were already filling their plates when Lilly looked at them, "What, y'all couldn't wait on the guests?"

"Hey, we were doing you guys a favor," Jen said.

"Oh really," Lilly said, "and just exactly what favor is that?"

"Ya know, testing out the product, making sure it's safe. I would hate to unknowingly poison our Romanian guest, although it would make for a great headline," Jen answered.

"Jen, do you always have to say what you are thinking? Have you ever thought to yourself, 'Hey, self, maybe I should keep my trap shut? Yeah, good idea, self'? Jacquelyn glared at her best friend.

"You're just cranky because you've been thinking about Trent." Jen's eyes gleamed knowingly at Jacquelyn.

Fane couldn't help the low rumble in his chest that escaped at the name of his mate's all-too-recent old flame.

Lilly's head snapped around to look at him. Fane cocked his head to the side as his wolf perked up at her perceptive gaze. *"Interesting. She knows something."*

Jacquelyn must have caught that last thought because he heard her ask, *"She knows something about what?"*

Fane looked away from Lilly and turned to look at his Luna's confused face. He was certain Lilly knew he wasn't human, but Jacque, apparently, wasn't aware of that fact.

"Fane, what are you thinking about?" Jacque asked again.

"We will need to talk later, Jacquelyn, and your mom needs to be present as well," Fane told her.

"Ooookay."

Everyone filled their plates and moved to the dining room. Fane noticed that Jen and Sally managed to maneuver things so he and Jacquelyn had to sit next to each other. He found it amusing. He would have made sure he sat next to her without their feeble efforts.

"So, are you kids looking forward to starting your senior year? Do you know what classes you will be taking?" Brian asked.

Mouths full of pizza, they all nodded simultaneously. Jen

was the first able to talk. "Naturally, I'm taking anatomy and physiology."

"Really, is that because you like—" Brian started to ask.

But Sally and Jacque interrupted quickly. "Don't go there," they both spit out.

"Because I like science?" Jen finished for him. "Nope, 'cause I like boys, silly rabbit."

Lilly rolled her eyes, and Fane almost choked on the pizza he was attempting to swallow. Jacque looked over at Fane, and he noticed her face was red.

Once he'd recovered, Fane winked at her, and that only caused the blush to deepen.

"Just what is your favorite subject, *fetița mea picantă*, my spicy girl?" he asked her.

She was just taking a drink when he sent her the thoughts and she nearly spewed it out of her mouth.

"Are you okay, Jacquelyn?" Fane asked her, his voice sounding a little too innocent.

She glared at him as she answered, "Fine, thank you."

"I will have you know that I prefer contact sports to classes. I find that a little physical violence is good for the soul," Jacque returned with a smirk.

"*Like I said,* you're fetița mea picantă." Fane ran his tongue across his bottom lip as his gaze held hers.

Her eyes widened slightly, and she quickly looked away.

"Lilly, how is the bookstore doing?" Sara asked her.

"Great! Since I hired more staff, I've caught up on inventory and started working on some other ideas I've been brainstorming, like maybe putting in a coffee shop and having a gift section. You know, just more things to help bring in a variety of customers," Lilly told her.

"Mom, I didn't realize you were planning all this." Jacquelyn frowned.

"Well, you've been preoccupied this summer, and I've

been at the store a lot. I was going to tell you about it, but time just seemed to get away from me."

Fane caught the implication when Lilly said Jacque had been preoccupied. She was referring to the breakup with Trent. Apparently, it had been a bigger deal than Jacquelyn let on.

"Does it really matter to you that much?" Jacque asked him.

Wow, he needed to work on blocking his thoughts, or he was going to get himself into trouble.

"Be patient with me, Jacquelyn. I will explain things soon, and then you might be able to understand why I react the way I do," Fane said. He was attempting to keep his voice calm and stifle the biting tone of his impatient wolf, who disliked the distance between them.

After everyone finished eating, they cleared the table and picked out a game Fane had never heard of called "What's Yours Like?"

Jen read the directions.

Fane didn't catch everything, but he got the gist of it. The active player would listen to others describe "what *theirs* was like." For example, someone might say, *Mine is big,* while someone else might say, *My wife likes mine.* The answer in that example was *paycheck.* Fane realized right away this was going to be a game in which Jen would enjoy causing Jacquelyn as much embarrassment as possible. He inwardly grinned, looking forward to seeing his mate squirm.

"Okay, who's going to be in the hot seat first?" Brian asked.

"I'll go first," Lilly answered. "I have a feeling things are going to get inappropriate very quickly, so I might as well start them out rated G."

Fane smiled when Jen let out a low groan. "Come on, Ms.

P, give us a little credit. We are more than mature enough to keep our minds out of the gutter."

Jacquelyn and Sally's eyebrows rose at the same time as they looked at their blonde friend. "We are?" they asked in unison.

Jen growled. "You two aren't helping our case."

Brian spoke up before the girls could continue their banter. "Jacque, you pull out the answer and say your first clue, then pass your card to the next person. Lilly can take a guess whenever she is ready and feels she knows the answer, or she can wait until all the clues are given."

Jacquelyn pulled out the card, and sure enough, her face turned red. *Oh, yes, this is going to be fun.*

"Mine is..." Jacquelyn paused. "Curly," she said simply, but she still couldn't keep from turning red.

Fane saw the answer in her head and winked at her.

Sally was next. "Mine is long."

Sally handed the card to Sara, who said hers was like chocolate, smooth and dark, and Brian said his wife claimed his was the color of sand.

Finally, it was Jen's turn, and Fane could tell everyone was a little nervous about what she would come up with.

"Mine is silky to the touch," Jen said with a wink at Fane.

Fane felt Jacquelyn's wave of jealousy like a tidal wave. His head tilted slightly as he studied her. *Interesting., She doesn't like Jen flirting with me.* Her head snapped around to glare at him, and he realized she had heard what he was thinking.

"Relax, my Luna. I assure you I am all yours," Fane promised, and he meant it down to his marrow. He was hers, and there would never be another. He was careful to block those thoughts from her. Fane had a feeling it might make her a tad nervous if she fully understood just how permanent was their bond.

91

"Oh, this coming from the Romanian who is jealous of a boy I'm no longer dating. Not to mention, you and I are not together, so it's really of no consequence how you feel," Jacquelyn told him in a huff. "It's your turn, by the way," she added.

Fane looked over at Jen, realizing she was holding the card out to him and looking at him knowingly. She must have recognized he and Jacquelyn were conversing.

Fane looked at the answer on the card and debated what to say that wouldn't completely embarrass him. The choices were not good. He could go with straight, or short, or black. All those options could be taken, as Jen would no doubt do, to have very *un*-innocent connotations.

"Mine is"—well if you gotta go down, do it with a bang —"short." And with that, everyone lost their composure. It was obvious Jen knew all his choices were pretty poor, and she had been waiting for him to choose to take it and run with it.

"Nice," Jen said putting her hand up for a fist bump with Sally.

In all the commotion Fane just couldn't help himself and looked up at Jacquelyn, who was giggling wildly. He raised an eyebrow at her. *"Did I amuse you, fetița mea picantă?"* Fane asked her.

All Jacquelyn did was wink at him, but it about did him in. She was a joy to his heart, and she was all his. Now, he just had to convince her of that ... and, quite possibly, her mother as well. Fane had considered whether to talk to Lilly and Jacquelyn tonight, but as the evening carried on, he decided to talk to his father again one more time. Perhaps the Alpha had uncovered more information that would help Fane make the safest decision for his mate.

The evening turned out to be a lot of fun and laughs. Sometimes, the girls laughed so hard they had tears streaming down their faces. At one point, Sally fell out of her chair from laughing so hard because the answer to the question had been tires on your car. Naturally, Jen had not disappointed and said hers were round. And when it was Fane's turn, he realized a little too late that his vehicle only had two wheels, so his response was, "Mine has two," which resulted in Jen laying her head on the table and laughing so hard her whole body shook. It was wonderful, even if they were enjoying making their answers sound like they were talking about certain parts of their anatomy. What did you expect from teenagers with a game called *What's Yours Like?* The whole evening made Fane feel at home because these people were close-knit like his own pack. They often got together and ate and played games or just gathered around the fire to talk.

As the evening came to a close, they began to say their goodbyes. As Fane walked past Jacquelyn to the front door, he turned to her and asked, "Could I talk with you a moment? I won't keep you from your friends long."

Jacquelyn turned to her mom and girlfriends. "I'll be outside for just a minute, okay?"

"Okay." Lilly nodded. She looked like she wanted to say more but refrained.

"Don't hurry on our account. You hate to rush these kinds of things the first time around," Jen commented.

Sally hit her on the arm. "Quit embarrassing her."

Jen shrugged. "It's what I do."

Fane put his hand on Jacquelyn's lower back to gently guide her to the porch. He felt a shudder go through her body as he touched her. "*Mine,*" his wolf told him.

Once outside, Jacquelyn turned to him, looking up into his face with curiosity, and asked, "What's this about?"

It felt so good to be this close to her. She completed him and filled a void he hadn't realized was there. He'd heard other males in his pack talk about the darkness that grew inside them without the light of their true mate. He hadn't reached that point yet because he was still so very young for one of their kind. Now he would never reach that point, as long as Jacquelyn didn't reject him. *Mine.* His wolf growled more sternly than before. Obviously, the beast didn't appreciate the idea of their mate rejecting them. All the wolf wanted to do at that moment was wrap her in his arms and just hold her, take in her scent, mark her as his.

Fane pushed those worries and desires aside so he could answer her question.

"There is much I need to talk with you about, but I don't think tonight is a good time. I'm not trying to be cryptic," he said quickly when he noticed the irritation flitting across her face, "but I need to talk to my father about some things. I would, however, like to take you out on a date, if you would do me the honor," Fane told her.

Jacquelyn looked at him blankly and blinked a few times. Clearly, she'd not been expecting the request.

"So, what I'm hearing you say is you have information that I need to know, but you're not going to tell me just yet, and with all this bizarre stuff going on … well, bizarre to me, you want to go out on a date like everything is just rosy?" she asked as her hands flitted in the air punctuating her irritation.

"Pretty much."

"Well, I can't very well hold a gun to your head and make you tell me, although Jen would think that a perfectly acceptable response. But then again, Jen also thinks going to football practice and lying out in her bikini is amusing so, ya know, gotta keep it all in perspective." She paused and tapped her lips with her fingers. After a few seconds that felt to Fane like an eternity, she continued. "Okay, I'll go out with you.

When is our little adventure, and how should I dress?" she asked.

"Tomorrow, wear something comfortable to ride on the motorcycle, and don't worry, I bought you a helmet."

"You did what?" Her voice rose right along with her forehead. "Presumptuous much?"

Fane stepped closer to her, lowering his face toward hers, and whispered, "I felt my chances you would say yes were pretty good. I can be very persuasive when I need to be."

Fane stayed there a minute longer but decided it best he back away from her a little because he was very tempted to kiss her. She shook her head as if to clear it when she stepped back and looked at him with what he thought might be longing in her eyes.

Time to go. He took her hand and lifted it to his lips, never breaking eye contact, and gently pressed it to his lips. Her scent hit him hard, and he had to grind his teeth together to keep his chest from rumbling in contentment. To his surprise, he also had to fight his wolf for control to keep from licking her skin. Yes, she was temptation in its purest form and would no doubt cause him endless amounts of pain.

"Thank you for a wonderful evening. I truly enjoyed your company, my Luna," Fane said quietly.

Jacquelyn seemed at a loss for words as her mouth opened and closed, resembling a fish out of water and endearingly cute, but she finally spit out, "Me too."

Fane didn't want to leave her. It was against his instincts, and his wolf growled at the thought. She was supposed to be with him where he could take care of her and keep her safe. If she had grown up with his kind, and been raised knowing *what* he was, she would understand their single days were over. She would accept him willingly and eagerly because she would fully grasp the magnitude of finding a true mate. But Jacque didn't know about him or his kind. She didn't know how desperately he needed her. So, he would have to be patient and take advantage of the time they could spend together soaking up her presence. Fane leaned in quickly, took a deep breath, then blew gently next to her ear. She shivered. What Jacquelyn didn't know was that he wasn't trying to be sensual by blowing next to her ear. He was putting his scent on her so other Greys would know she was his. It would only linger a day or two since it was only an external marking and not in her blood. The only permanent way to put his scent on her was to complete the bond, to share his blood, and take hers. Unfortunately, they weren't quite there yet.

With that, Fane forced his feet to move and turned away from his mate. His steps felt as though he walked through quicksand as he trudged back to the Henrys' home. At the door, he turned one last time to find her still standing there watching him, and he lifted his hand to his mouth, blew her a kiss, and sent her a thought. *"Sweet dreams, meu inimă, my heart. Dream of me. I will be dreaming of you."*

CHAPTER 7

*J*acque stood on the front porch, staring after
Fane as he retreated to the Henrys' house. She
wanted to call him back. Something deep within
her, something she didn't understand, was loathe to spend a
second without him. "Get a grip on yourself, woman," she
scolded. In an attempt to clear her head, Jacque sucked in a
few deep breathes. She noticed the subtle scent of woods and
spice. The scent called to her, to a deep and primitive part of
her she hadn't known existed. Something made her want to
claim the scent as *hers* in a primal way. Yet, the smell also
comforted her. But, why? Jacque decided she wasn't going to
touch that with a ten-foot pole. Her bizarre meter had
already reached a critical state. Attempting now to understand the animalistic urges she was suddenly experiencing
would only send her completely over the edge.

She took one last longing look at the Henrys' house
before turning to go in.

"Mom," she hollered, "I'm back in."

"Okay, the girls took some brownies upstairs. Are you
okay? Need to talk about anything?" her mom asked.

"No, I'm good." Jacque waved as she started up the stairs. She stopped in mid-step and turned slightly. "Oh, there is one thing. Fane asked me out on a date for tomorrow night. Is that okay?"

Lilly tried not to let her eyes widen. She pursed her lips and looked at her daughter, trying to decide how to respond. A foreign werewolf in Coldspring who was interested in Jacque? *What the hell did this all mean?* Though Jacque didn't know it, Lilly had been down this road herself. It didn't end well. She could tell by his behavior at dinner, Fane knew Lilly was aware of his true identity, or at least that he wasn't entirely human. But surely Jacque couldn't know. If she did, her daughter should be freaking out right about now.

Lilly couldn't outright forbid Jacque from seeing Fane. That would send up a ton of red flags and require an explanation. Lilly wasn't sure she had one, at least not yet. "Yeah, that's fine. You two know what you're going to do?"

"Not yet," Jacque answered and then continued up the stairs.

Lilly watched her daughter until she was out of sight. She felt a pain deep in her gut as she considered Fane and all the possibilities that came with him. Lilly had never told Jacque about her father and had hoped she'd never have to. She'd hoped the secret of his true nature would never affect Jacque. She had been a fool to think such a thing. Now the day had come, and the wolf was scratching at their door, literally.

"Damn you, Dillon Jacobs," she muttered under her breath, feeling that same old ache she endured anytime she thought of him. It had faded over the years, and, regardless of the pain, she couldn't regret their relationship. After all, it had given her a beautiful daughter. Now she just hoped it didn't end up taking the girl away.

. . .

JACQUE OPENED her bedroom door to find Jen and Sally lying on her bedroom floor happily munching on the brownies.

"Soooo, did he confess his undying love for you and ask you to run away to his Romanian castle?" Sally asked in a wistful voice.

Jacque gasped. "Oh my gosh. How did you know?"

"I'm just good like that, ya know, with the seeing the future and whatnot," Sally answered.

"Yeah, yeah, you're a real gypsy, complete with crystal ball and ridiculous clothes." Jen snorted.

"So, do we have to beat it out of you or are you going to confess willingly? 'Cause you know I'm into the whole torture thing, it's how I roll," Jen said completely unashamed.

"Well, he told me that we had things to talk about but he didn't think tonight was the night to do it, and he wanted to talk to his father first, whatever that means. Then he asked me out on a date, and he leaned in close to me—" Jacque explained but Jen interrupted.

"He kissed you?! Was it good? Were his lips soft? Were his lips closed, or were they slightly parted like he might want to wrestle with—" Jen asked rapidly, not even taking a breath.

"Step back, Don Juan. Don't even finish that sentence." Jacque held up her hand as if that would keep the words from tumbling out of Jen's unfiltered mouth.

"Well, if he didn't kiss you then lie to me so I can live vicariously through your pretend love life." Her blonde friend grumbled.

Jacque ignored that comment. "So, he leaned in close, and at first, I thought he was going to kiss me, but instead he placed his mouth right next to my ear, and he blew on my neck." Jacque shivered at the memory. And it wasn't because she was afraid.

"Why'd he do that?" Sally asked.

"I know, right? I don't know. But I nearly grabbed him by

the shirt and kissed him myself. He must have been blocking his mind from me because I didn't pick up anything."

"Wicked," Jen murmured as her lips turned up slightly. She looked like a wolf about to pounce on an unsuspecting rabbit.

"I assume you said yes to going out on a date with him?" Sally said.

"If she said no, she might not want to go to sleep tonight 'cause I'm going to dye her hair blonde to complement her being a dumb ass," Jen told them.

"Uh, Jen, you're a blonde," Jacque pointed out.

"No, not really, God just got it wrong, and it was too late to change it once He noticed."

Sally shook her head and said, "Sometimes, Jen, I worry about you."

Jen just shrugged.

"Well, put away your hair dye, you overreacting freak. Of course, I said yes. I asked him what I should wear, and he said something to be comfortable riding the motorcycle, and just when I was going to tell him I didn't have a helmet, he said not to worry because he already bought me one!"

"Yummy," Jen said. "Confidence is sooooo smexy."

"You think anything is smexy," Sally retorted.

"Not true. Guys driving those hybrid cars are so not smexy."

"Is she serious?" Sally asked Jacque. "I mean, who thinks of stuff like that?"

"I have found if you just nod your head while she's talking, she eventually wears herself out." Jacque dodged the hairbrush Jen threw at her. She'd gotten used to dodging things Jen threw. It was an hourly occurrence some days.

"Oh, and then when he was walking to the Henrys' he turned and blew me a kiss, told me to have sweet dreams, and said he would be dreaming of me." Jacque would love to say she did not have a swoony look on her face as she relayed this information to her friends, but then she'd be lying, and she tried only to lie when it would embarrass Jen.

"Oh, that is so freaking romantic!" Sally said as she rolled over onto her back, kicking her legs in the air and squealing.

Jacque couldn't disagree, but it also felt surreal. She had to admit Fane had successfully gotten her to stop thinking about Trent. How could she when this gorgeous Romanian hunk was claiming she was his ... whatever it was he called her.

"Yeah, it's romantic," Jacque said, "but there is definitely the proverbial other shoe that is sooner or later going to drop and squish me like a bug."

"Oh, don't be so pessimistic," Jen told her. "Maybe he's the one, you know, like in those romantic movies where a person has one true soul mate. I mean, he can talk to you telepathically. Why couldn't he be your soul mate? And if he's not, when you meet your soul mate, he should be pissed that another man has access to your wicked thoughts."

Jacque couldn't argue with Jen's assessment of the situation. *Anything is possible at this point.* And who was she to complain if her soul mate happened to be tall, dark, and handsome with a yummy accent?

Jacque stretched and yawned. The clock on her phone showed it was 11:30 p.m. Man, she didn't realize how late it had gotten. They had been having such a good time playing the game that time had flown by.

"I'm gonna crash, y'all. Here are your blankets," Jacque told them as she handed them each a pile.

"Yeah, you'd better go to sleep. You need to look your best since bags under your eyes don't say, 'Hey, throw me on the floor and take me,'" Jen told her as she spread out her makeshift bed.

"Yes, and that is so the look I was going for, so how 'bout I just wear fishnet stockings, thigh-high boots, and a sheer bra? Do you think that would look too desperate?" Jacque asked, looking innocently at her.

"No, it would only look desperate if you added nipple tassels. That just says, 'I'm not confident enough to get noticed without fancy trappings.'" The seriousness with which Jen spoke was a testament to just how twisted her little mind was.

Jacque walked out of her bedroom shaking her head. In the bathroom, she took off her shirt she turned around and used the handheld mirror to look at the marks on her back and neck.

She realized as she studied them, the markings on her neck looked like they really would fit into Fane's like a puzzle piece. "Wicked," Jacque muttered. She and the girls had talked about the possibility of getting tattoos one day, but they agreed to wait until they were eighteen so they didn't have to broach the subject with Jen's parents. Jacque supposed she should be a tad thankful she didn't have to go through the pain that came with getting a tattoo. "Nope, I just had to become a freak and start having telepathic conversations with a yummy exchange student."

She felt a shiver go down her spine and quickly shoved on her tank top realizing it wouldn't cover the markings on her shoulders. The last thing she needed was her mom to see them and start asking questions, especially since Jacque didn't have any answers. She brushed her teeth, washed her face quickly, then darted across the hall to her bedroom. Going to her closet to find something more covering, Jen saw the marks for the second time. Almost if talking to herself, Jen said, "This is really happening, isn't it?"

"I'm afraid so, sweet girl. There's nothing to do but go with the flow, or sink trying to fight the current," Sally said using her best Mary Poppins voice.

Jen looked at her and narrowed her eyes. "If you bust out in 'Just a Spoonful of Sugar,' I'm going to duct tape your mouth closed."

"You really should seek help for that temper of yours. You know they have medicine that would help," Jacque told her, trying to sound gentle like she was speaking to an unruly child.

Jen simply flipped them both the bird.

Jacque turned off the lights as they all lay down to sleep. They were quiet for a while, and just as Jacque was drifting off, she could feel the waves of worry coming off Sally.

"Sally," Jacque said, "it's all going to work out. Remember, we're all too stubborn to accept any other outcome."

Sally didn't respond. Then Jacque spoke again. "Jen, seriously, you didn't have some smart-ass comment right when we needed it?"

Jen was quiet, too. Jacque and Sally seemed to be holding their breath waiting for their outspoken friend to work her magic.

"Well," Jen finally answered, "I was thinking about the game we played tonight and about when the answer was tires on your vehicle and Fane said he had two. I so wanted to ask him if they were big."

And just like that, the atmosphere lightened. The three girls laughed until they had tears. Of course, Jen could never stop at just one perverted or smart-ass comment, so when they had all caught their breaths she added, "Jacque, you could always throw your friends a bone or, heck, even just a kibble, and find out for us."

"Is that all you ever think about, Jen?" Sally asked in exasperation.

"About how big Fane's you-know-whats are? Good grief, no, I think about other things," Jen defended.

"Anything not pertaining to the opposite sex or, for that matter, sex itself?" Jacque asked sarcastically.

Jen started to open her mouth then abruptly shut it. Looking at nothing in particular and thinking, she finally answered, "Nope, uh-uh, don't think so."

They all broke out in laughter again and then finally drifted off to sleep.

FANE WOKE up early and decided to go for a run, which always helped him clear his mind. He got up, resisted the urge to reach out to his Luna figuring she was probably still asleep and changed into some workout shorts. He decided against a shirt knowing he wouldn't leave it on long anyway. Brian and Sara were still asleep, so he tried to make as little noise as possible, which was easy for him, being a werewolf and all. Stealth was something they were just born with, like most predators. He went downstairs, grabbed a banana, and ate it quickly before heading out the front door. Being *Canis lupus* had other benefits besides the ability to move quietly. Fane could also run for very long distances without tiring, even in his human form. He didn't have to work out to keep his muscular physique. That was just the way all *Canis lupus* were built. Some were leaner than others, but all very muscular.

He glanced up at Jacquelyn's window, and, giving in to his desire, he reached out to her mind briefly. If she was thinking about something that might embarrass her, he would retreat quickly. But she was still asleep, and her thoughts were scattered. He kept seeing his face then another male face, which he assumed was this Trent she had dated previously. She didn't seem to be interested in him anymore, but it was obvious he had hurt her. Fane and his wolf did not like that.

Now that he had reassured himself she was safe and sound, Fane pulled back from her thoughts and started up the street. He had to restrain himself from running full speed because he was much, much faster than a human. Anyone that happened to be watching would surely notice and think it odd. But the wolf wanted to run, wanted to hunt. Fane pushed down the urge and kept a steady jog.

As he ran, Fane thought about the night before, about the car that had driven by Jacquelyn's house. The men inside were much too interested in his mate's home. There had been two males, one of whom had been the salesman at the motorcycle dealership. The other, Fane didn't recognize, but he could only assume it was a packmate of the salesman. Their presence made it clear they wanted Fane out of their territory—a territory they, being a rogue pack, had no right to.

So far, Fane's Alpha had not commanded him to leave, so Fane wasn't going anywhere. But what would happen if that command came? Fane would have to convince Jacquelyn and her mother to come with him. There was no way he was going to leave his mate there unprotected. The plan had never been for Fane to stay in the United States permanently, even if he did miraculously find his mate. His place was with his pack, and hers would be by his side.

As he continued to run, Fane's thoughts alternated between thinking about Jacquelyn and their date that night to thinking about the local pack he hadn't known existed. When he finally made it back to the Henrys' house, Fane had been running for over two hours and his wolf wasn't any less restless than when he started. *No hunt,* his wolf growled at him. *We can't hunt as we do at home. We need to stay close to Jacquelyn.* Fane responded. His wolf sent him the image of their mate hiding from them while they searched for her—a game, Fane realized. His wolf wanted to play with her, wanted her to join in with them and be a part of their world. *She will. Now.* His wolf growled. Fane ignored him knowing that he couldn't reason with him. His wolf only understood instincts and action, not logic and reasoning.

Fane went through the front door and, as he was walking in, he saw Sara coming down the stairs in workout shorts and shirt with her hair up in a ponytail.

"We're going out to run some trails at the park across town. You're welcome to come, but it looks like you've already been out and about," Sara told him.

"Thank you for the invitation, but I did just finish running, so I will pass for today. I wanted to check with you and make sure this was okay. I asked Jacquelyn out on a date for this evening, so I will be out. Will that be a problem?" Fane asked.

"No problem at all. Jacque is a one-of-a-kind girl, and we all love her, but I don't think I have to tell you to treat her well. You seem to have impeccable manners."

Once the Henrys left and Fane took a shower, he sat down to call his father again and see if they could come up with some sort of plan for how to deal with the unregistered pack.

The phone rang one time, then his father's voice was on the other end.

"*Da*, yes," he said.

"It's me," Fane told him. "I need to know what you want me to do. Do I need to request a meeting with this Alpha and find out who this other wolf is that is laying claim to what is mine?"

"I have been thinking about it and I've decided to send Sorin back to you. I think his experience and age will be of some help, not to mention show them you are not on your own," his father told him.

"As my Alpha, what are you telling me to do?" Fane asked him.

"I want you to protect your mate and her mother, but do not act on anything unless provoked. If it gets out of hand, I don't care how, but you get your mate and her mother on a plane, ... and fast," his father said firmly.

"Okay, so when will Sorin arrive? And where is he going to stay?" Fane asked him.

"He should be there sometime around 8:00 p.m. You might find this interesting, but he is staying with Lilly Pierce."

"That's my mate's mother," Fane said confused.

"I am aware of that. I guess it's time for me to tell you, but you must wait to talk to Jacquelyn until after her mother tells her so she doesn't feel betrayed by her mom," Fane's father explained. "I did a little searching and found out that your mate is indeed part *Canis lupus*. In fact, she is half Grey and half-human. Jacquelyn's father is a Grey. He and Lilly were together for quite a while, although they were never married. At some point in their relationship, he decided to tell her about his origins because she had a special gift and knew there was something different about him. She actually received the news very well. After that, things were good, but one day Jacquelyn's father came home, packed his things, and left Lilly a note. All it said was 'I have to go. I have no choice. I'm sorry.' Jacquelyn's father did not know Lilly was pregnant with his child when he left. I have since located him and found that he is with his true mate in Colorado, and that is why he had to leave Lilly. You see, Lilly was not his true mate, and even though he had feelings for her, they weren't even a pin drop compared to what he feels for his mate. This is exactly why we discourage relationships with humans, even if casual. Someone always gets hurt."

"Lilly has known this Jacquelyn's whole life and never told her?" Fane asked.

"She probably didn't think she would ever have to. For all she knew, Lilly gave birth to a healthy human baby girl. Jacquelyn may have never shown any wolf tendencies whatsoever. Regardless, Lilly knows who and what you are, Fane. I called and spoke with her about what is going on, and she took it well. She agreed to let Sorin stay with them because she realizes he would be added protection," Fane's father explained.

"I know I can trust Sorin, but you know how hard it is for a male wolf to allow another to be so close to his mate, especially when the bond ritual has not been performed," Fane said through gritted teeth.

"I know it is going to be hard for you, but you're going to have to leash your wolf and recognize what will keep her safe. Still, I don't know if Sorin will be enough of a deterrent to keep the other pack from attempting to take Jacquelyn. I have no idea how dominant this Alpha is or how large his pack. How he has managed to hide from us is a mystery to me, not to mention why he has hidden at all."

Fane growled at the idea of his mate in the hands of a pack to which she did not belong.

"How can they possibly want her when she is not a true mate to any of them?" Fane asked.

"I know it is hard for you to understand because you are so young, especially in *Canis lupus* terms. You found your mate quickly, which is rare. Most go decades, if not centuries before they find their mate. Female Greys are not abundant, and after such a long time some males get desperate enough to settle for less and hope that, over time, their wolves will bond. Blinded by the darkness slowly driving them mad, they foolishly believe any female will be the balm to their pain. They forget their true mate is the only one who can bring balance with her light. They disrespect themselves, the one they take, and their own true mate when they do this."

Fane couldn't imagine being with a female that wasn't Jacquelyn. The idea was repulsive to him.

"Will Sorin need me to pick him up?" Fane asked, getting back to matter at hand.

"No, he will rent a car to keep for the duration of his stay," his father answered.

"I will keep you updated as I learn things. You lay low, Fane. I don't want my only son and future Alpha of this pack killed." His father used his Alpha voice that demanded obedience and could not be defied.

"Yes, Alpha," Fane replied, recognizing at that moment he was not speaking as a son to father, but as a pack member to Alpha.

Fane hung up and laid back on his bed, staring up at the ceiling. He decided to wait a couple more days before he confronted Lilly and Jacquelyn, but he was going to have to convince Lilly to tell her daughter first. He would obey his father and not tell Jacquelyn before then.

Because he needed her touch, even if only mind to mind, Fane reached out to his Luna. *"Are you awake, meu inimă, my heart?"* He patiently waited for her response.

"Well, I am now. Is it customary in Romania to wake people at the crack of dawn?" she replied grumpily.

"It is not the crack of dawn, Luna. It is already 10:30 a.m." Fane told her.

"Oh, my bad, it's moved up to still-too-freaking early," Jacquelyn grumbled sleepily.

Fane chuckled at her grumpiness and found it rather endearing.

"So, I take it you are not a morning person?" he asked her.

"I'm not a person at all until after noon so make a note to yourself to keep your thoughts out of mine 'til then."

"Duly noted. I will not seek you out until 12:01 p.m.," Fane said, joking with her.

"Aren't you just so clever?"

Fane wondered what she looked like in the morning, hair a mess, rumpled clothes. He imagined she was adorable.

"I would rather you not see me first thing out of bed, nor imagine what I look like. I assure you 'adorable' would not be the description you would choose," Jacquelyn assured.

"I believe how I see you is not really up to you, my Luna," Fane said gently.

"What exactly does loona mean?"

"I will tell you soon, but not today. Rest assured, it is a high honor to be called that. I was planning to pick you up at 5:30 p.m. Is that too early?" he asked her. Fane hoped not. He'd prefer to pick her up now if he could. He desperately wanted to spend time with and get to know her. Fane wanted her to know him as well, and he hoped she liked what she learned. He wanted to be worthy of her because she brought him balance and control and love. Fane carefully kept those thoughts from her.

"5:30 is good. Are you going to tell me what we are doing?" she asked him.

"I was thinking that golf game Americans play that has all the different obstacles," Fane answered.

Jacquelyn giggled at his description, and Fane grinned, glad he could make her laugh, even if it was at his expense.

"You mean putt-putt. That sounds like fun. So, I will see you at 5:30. Are you going to be in my head anymore today?" she asked him.

Fane's voice was very soft and intimate when he answered, *Do you want me to be in your head, Luna?*

Fane felt Jacquelyn respond to his voice. When she

answered, even her thoughts sounded breathless. *"I, um ... I don't know."*

"I will take that as a yes, and you can tell me to leave at any time, knowing I will obey you. Talk to you later, meu inimă, my heart," Fane said to her sweetly.

"Bye," was all Jacquelyn could manage to get out.

CHAPTER 8

"*H*ello, earth to Jacque," Sally said as she snapped her fingers in front of her friend's face.

Finally, Jacque turned her head to Sally, looking spacey and out of it and said, "I'm in trouble."

"What is that supposed to mean?" Jen asked her as she sat on the floor painting her toenails.

"I was just talking to Fane, and his voice got all sensual on me, and it was like…"

Jacque didn't know how to finish, so Jen offered up, "Phone sex, virtual mind sex, and I would say sex on a stick, but that really only applies to Dove ice cream bars."

"Jen, paint your toenails," Sally ordered.

Jen stuck her tongue out at her but obeyed.

"I could so fall hard for this tasty Romanian," Jacque told them.

"There's nothing wrong with that, just make sure it's not a rebound from the whole Trent thing," Sally told her honestly.

"I hear what you're saying, Tonto," Jacque told her with a smile.

"Are you going to tell us about the upcoming date?" Jen asked.

Jacque thought about Fane's cute description of putt-putt. She hadn't played in a long time, so she was looking forward to it.

"He's picking me up at 5:30 and taking me to play putt-putt. I think it will be interesting to see a Romanian hottie play something he didn't even know the name for," Jacque told them.

"He didn't know what putt-putt was called?" Jen laughed. "That's awesome."

"It's the little things, Jen, the little things," Sally told her.

Jacque spent the day discussing various scenarios for the evening with Fane. Naturally, all Jen's included vivid make-out scenes and somehow always ended with their clothes off. Jen truly was a piece of work. *You can't help but love her.*

At 3:30 p.m. Sally and Jen sat Jacque down on the edge of her bed then began pulling various outfits from her closet. She decided right away that a skirt or sundress was out because of riding the motorcycle. Finally, it came down to a pair of jeans with holes in various places and her "Daisy Duke" shorts that looked worn out, only they weren't because that's how she had bought them. She had already decided on a hunter green, spaghetti-strap shirt with various sparkly designs.

"Just go with the jeans," Jen said. "They're sexy in a badass kind of way, and they will help keep your skin intact if you are in a motorcycle wreck."

Sally glared at Jen.

"What? I'm just saying," Jen defended.

"Yeah, I think I will go with the jeans. They leave something for the imagination, and if it is the slightest bit cool while riding that bike after dark, they will be much more comfortable than the shorts," Jacque decided.

"Okay, hair up or down?" Sally asked.

"I'm thinking down for the motorcycle ride because of the helmet, and then I will take a hairband to put it up once we get there. It's putt-putt, Sal, no need for a French twist," Jacque told her. "I'm just gonna wear my green flip-flops," she told them. Jacque hated wearing shoes, and if they weren't required, she avoided them—just another one of her weird quirks.

She took a shower while her two best friends picked out eye shadow for her. When she returned to her room, they had Jen's phone hooked up to her computer speakers jamming to a Southern rock band. Jacque just shook her head at them. She dressed and Sally pushed her down onto her desk chair to work on her unruly hair while Jen started on her eyes.

By the time they were finished with Jacque, it was 5:00 p.m. Sally and Jen looked at her, spun her in a circle to see their finished product, then looked at each other and bumped fists, saying together, "Damn we're good."

"I would have to agree ladies. Y'all are fantastic. Thank you both so much," Jacque told them.

"Oh, hell no, don't go getting all sentimental on us. If you mess up the work I did on your eyes, I will not hesitate to kick your butt between your shoulders," Jen said sternly.

"I love you, too, Jen," Jacque said sarcastically.

"Are you nervous? Sally asked her.

"If I said I wasn't, I would be lying. But I would also be lying if I didn't say I was absolutely beyond excited," Jacque told them.

"Why do you say that?" Jen asked her in a rare moment of seriousness.

"I wish I could tell you guys this without y'all thinking I'm a total nut, but no matter how I put it, it's still going to sound crazy," Jacque admitted.

"Um, Jac, hate to point this out, but two days ago you told us you were hearing a voice in your head," Sally told her.

Jacque thought for a moment. "Point taken," she agreed.

"Okay, well, I don't know quite how to explain it, but I feel like I belong with him, like I have always belonged with him. Now that I have been close to him, it's like a part of my soul was missing, and now that he's here, I have it back," Jacque explained.

"That is so romantic," Sally said dreamily.

"I guess now you should spend time with him, get to know him, and see if he feels the same way," said Jen.

Jacque and Sally looked at each other in shock. "Jen, did you just suggest something that didn't involve wild making out, clothes coming off, or is comparable to the car scene in *Titanic*?" Sally asked incredulously.

"You didn't let me finish. Then after you get to know one another, seal the deal with a steamy make-out scene on the motorcycle, like in *Top Gun*. Ahhh, see there is always a time and place for lip-locking, hand-roaming, and good ol' fashion clean, or if you're lucky, not so clean, fun," Jen said with a wink.

"As always, Jen, you do not disappoint," Jacque told her.

"I aim to please, my dear," Jen replied completely undaunted.

Jacque looked at her watch and realized it was 5:20 p.m. *Okay, have fun and don't worry about all the other crap going on.* Jacque took one more look in the mirror and caught a glimpse of her neck and shoulders.

"Oh shite, the markings are showing," Jacque exclaimed.

"We know," Sally said.

"Why didn't you remind me?" Jacque asked.

"Because they look cool as Hades, that's why," Jen piped in.

"That statement doesn't even make sense, Jen. Hell is not cool, jeez—"

"Oh, my bad, they look hot as Hades, that's why," Jen interrupted.

Jacque continued undaunted, "And what should I say to my mom? Hey, Mom, going on my date. Oh, don't worry about these handy dandy marks. Ya know how it is with random, mysterious markings and whatnot just popping up when you least expect it," she said with thick sarcasm.

"No, we were going to tell her they are the stick-on type, and that Jen insisted you wear them," Sally said.

"The idea that I am the one to blame was completely involuntary, I will have you know." Jen frowned.

"I doubt she will swallow it, but he is gonna be here—" before Jacque could finish, the doorbell rang.

"I don't have time to change," Jacque finished.

"Look, you're going to be great. Just be yourself," Sally told her in a motherly voice.

"For goodness sake, if you wind up not liking him, kiss him anyway for us, okay? Throw us a bone, Jac," Jen told her.

"And if I like him but I'm not ready to kiss him, what then my little nympho?" Jacque asked her.

"If you like that gorgeous piece of meat out there, and you don't kiss him, I will personally take every bra you own and hang them on all the antennas of the cars on your street. Oh, and I will write your name on them in black magic marker, being sure to hang two on hottie's motorcycle! How'd you like them apples?" Jen told her.

"Where on earth do you come up with these ideas? Is there, like, a website called vindictive.com, or cruel-mean-ideas.org?" Sally asked her sarcastically.

"Nope, I think of them all by my little self," Jen answered.

The girls all turned when they heard a soft knock on Jacque's bedroom door.

"Come in," they said. Jacque looked at the other two as if to say, "Hello? My room," but they just shrugged.

Jacque's mom came in the room looking at the girls like they were guilty of something, because, in truth, they usually were.

"Fane's here. He's brought a helmet. Did you forget to mention you would be riding a motorcycle?" Lilly asked her.

"No, I just assumed you knew," Jacque said.

"Why would I assume that? I figured he'd borrow a car.

"Well, you know what they say about assuming," Jen added.

Both Lilly and Jacque turned their heads to look at Jen, who simply shrugged and said, "I'm—"

"Just saying, yeah, we know," Sally finished for her.

Jacque decided to just go ahead and let her mom see the marks so she wouldn't freak out in front of Fane.

"Mom, what do you think about these fake tattoos Jen put on me?" Jacque asked, turning around so her mom could get a look at her shoulders and neck.

Jacque heard her mother take in a sharp breath. She turned to look at her and saw her mom's hand over her mouth. There was fear, major fear, in her eyes. Once again, Jacque knew her mom knew something she wasn't sharing.

"Are you okay, Lilly?" Sally asked.

It took a minute for Lilly to regain her composure, but as soon as she did, her face went right back to normal.

"Of course, I'm fine, it was just a bit of a shock, and they look so real," her mom told them.

Jacque turned to look at her two best friends. "Are y'all planning to stay here or going home?" she asked them.

"We're going back to Jen's to hang out. If you want to come over after your date and Lilly's okay with it, that's fine," Sally answered.

"That's fine with me," Lilly told Jacque.

Jacque didn't know what to do. Part of her wanted to be with her friends, but the other part wanted to be alone so she could talk to Fane. She would see how the night went and decide then.

"I'll call you guys and let you know if I'm coming. I don't know what time we will be home, so I wouldn't want to come over if it was late and y'all were already in bed," Jacque told them.

Sally and Jen gave her a 'Yeah, what a load of crap super-sized with fries' look. Jacque just tried to look as oblivious as possible to their scrutiny.

Jacque expected her mom to say something about a curfew, but she didn't. She just turned to go back downstairs. "I'll be downstairs with Fane telling him embarrassing stories from your childhood, so you might want to expedite your final preparations," Lilly told her daughter.

Jacque turned back to her friends. "Look, I'm not going to lie. Part of me wants to stay home tonight so I can talk to Fane, but the other part of me wants to be with my girls," Jacque told them.

"We're totally cool with you staying home to get to know him more. There is only one stipulation to this, and that is we get everything in living-color detail. No condensing, no paraphrasing, no in-conclusions, and no summaries—every single detail!" Jen told her adamantly.

Jacque laughed and gave her two friends hugs. "Thanks, *chicas*, you two are the best," Jacque told them. "Okay, I'm ready. I'll see you guys later."

"Have fun!" Sally and Jen said together. "Oh, look, Sal, our little girl is growing up. Where did the time go? From teaching her to cut her Barbie doll's hair, then to cutting her own hair, and now sending her off with a hot piece of Romanian meat. I'm getting all choked up," Jen joked as she faked tears.

Sally looked at Jen and shook her head. "You done?" she asked her.

"Yeah, I'm done. Why you always gotta cramp my style, yo?" Jen asked in her best slang voice.

"Cuz', that's how I roll," Sally answered.

"Are you two sure you can be left unattended and to your own devices?" Jacque asked them smiling.

"Go already," Jen said.

Jacque opened her bedroom door and walked to the top of the stairs. She took a deep breath and let it out through her mouth.

"Luna, I've been waiting to see you all day. Are you rethinking going out with me? Because that's okay. I'll just go back to the Henrys' and let you be with your friends," Fane told her through his thoughts.

"NO!" Jacque responded, realizing a little too late that she had just incriminated herself letting him know how much she wanted to see him as well. *"I'm on my way down now. Quit being so impatient. It's not becoming,"* Jacque told him.

She felt his confusion when he asked, *"Becoming what?"*

Jacque couldn't stop the giggle that escaped, but she regained her composure by the time she was on the last step of the stairs.

"Never mind," she answered as she came around the corner into the living room. Lilly was sitting on the couch, and Fane was sitting across from her on the antique, high wingback chair her mom had inherited from some distant relative. It was a horrible shade of peach, but Lilly loved it, so the ugly lump stayed in their living room. Somehow, with Fane sitting in it, he managed to make it look good. Man, she had it bad, Jacque thought to herself.

Fane must have caught that last thought because he grinned at her knowingly, but he did not speak through her thoughts.

Fane stood up when she entered the room and, without shame, looked her up and down from her toes to her head and back again. Jacque was a tad surprised he would do this in front of her mother, and she supposed because of her nerves she should be excused for having a Jen moment. "Did you get your fill, or would you like me to turn around for you too?" Jacque asked sarcastically.

"Jacque, is that any way to speak to your date?" Lilly asked her.

"Actually," Fane started, "I would love for you to turn around so that I may admire the new addition to your already beautiful skin."

Jacque couldn't help but blush for two reasons: one, he had called her skin beautiful. I mean, come on, who wouldn't blush at that, right? And two, the way he commented about the markings seemed very possessive, like they tied her to him in some way. For some weird, messed up reason, Jacque liked that. *Yeah, they have a padded cell in the insane asylum just waiting for ya, babe.*

Jacque also didn't miss the way her mom responded to Fane noticing the markings. She was glaring daggers at him as if daring him to make further comment about them. Jacque knew that look, and it was one of the looks in her mom's repertoire that meant if you wanted to keep your ass, then you better cover it now.

So, Jacque did a quick turn around and grabbed Fane by the hand—he had great hands. *I mean, seriously, does he have to have great everything?* She nearly burst out laughing because she could just imagine the comeback Jen would have for that question.

"Alright, we're going, Mom. Love you, don't wait up, I'll wake you when I get home, yes I will wear my helmet, no I won't be cold, no I don't need any money, yes I have my house key, and yadda yadda yadda," Jacque answered before her mom could even ask.

They were out the front door before Lilly could get in a word, which had been what Jacque was going for.

"Was that really necessary?" Fane asked her.

"Did you not see the look my mother was giving you when you asked about these marks on my skin? And I know you know something about them, and you will be happily divulging said information tonight," Jacque told him.

Fane acted as if he simply had not heard her. Since he had not let go of her hand once they had made it outside, he pulled her along to his motorcycle. He handed her a black and dark pink helmet which, upon closer inspection, had various designs on it and was actually pretty awesome. She put it on her head, trying not to feel too ridiculous, and waited for his instructions.

Fane turned to look at her and grinned a breathtaking smile, dimples and all. "You ready, Luna?" he asked her, and it felt like he wasn't just asking her about the motorcycle ride. It felt to Jacque like he was giving her a choice—one she had no plausible outcome for.

"Probably not, but what the hell. What's life without a little excitement, or craziness, ya know? Take your pick," Jacque answered.

As FANE DROVE across town on his motorcycle with his mate behind him, her arms wrapped tightly around his waist, he thought about how it had taken every ounce of self-control for him not to reach out and run a finger across the markings on Jacquelyn's shoulders and neck—his markings. It was bad enough Lilly had noticed the possessiveness in his voice when he asked about them, but his wolf just wouldn't ease up now. Thankfully, he hadn't made a total fool of himself by touching them or growling in contentment, but the night was still young and he still had ample time to make a fool of himself yet, so better not count your pups.

Before they got on the motorcycle, Fane asked her if she was ready, and although he meant for the date, he was also pleading to her with his eyes to understand he needed her to be ready for more. He knew she was strong mentally and physically. The moon would not give him a weak mate since he was an Alpha. She would have dominion over the females of his pack. But Fane was not so naive to believe it wouldn't be a shock to anyone to learn werewolves were real, and quite possibly so were other things that go bump in the night.

"How are you, Jacquelyn? Are you cold?" Fane sent her the question.

"I'm great! This is awesome. I've never ridden on a motorcycle before. I can honestly see why you wouldn't want to drive a car after you've been on one of these! Oh, and no I'm not cold," Jacquelyn answered him, sounding excited.

It pleased Fane to know he was able to bring her happiness. He could feel joy pouring off her in ripples and waves, and it was soothing to his wolf. His mate was happy, and that was very important to him.

They reached the restaurant Fane had chosen. Brian had told him about it when he mentioned he was taking Jacquelyn out. It was a little mom and pop diner with a bit of everything.

"This okay with you?" Fane asked her.

"Yeah, this is great," Jacquelyn answered.

Fane looked at her for a moment. He couldn't help it when his eyes lingered on the markings on her shoulders and neck. Those marks told all *Canis lupus* she was his, his to make happy, his to protect, his to... To his astonishment, he realized she was his to love as well. Even though he didn't know her very well yet, he knew without a doubt he would love her.

"Fane, is everything alright?" she asked him.

"Yes, Luna, everything is fine, better than fine actually," Fane told her with a smile.

To Fane's satisfaction, dinner was pleasant, easy, and there was at no time when he felt the conversation was forced or awkward. He smiled over the fact she did not refuse dessert as most girls would on a first date, and she had absolutely no qualms about taking food off his plate without even asking.

After they ate, Fane took Jacquelyn to a nearby park. He had no plan of telling her anything yet. He had told his Alpha he would keep quiet until her mom talked to her, and he planned to keep his word. But he knew she would ask questions, and here in a park, their conversation would not be easily overheard.

"I know you have only been here a few days, but how do you like Coldspring?" Jacquelyn asked him.

"Thus far, it seems like a pleasant place to live, not as formal as the life I am used to, or as cold," Fane told her with a wink.

"No offense, but based on what you wear, your life doesn't seem all that formal," Jacquelyn told him.

Fane hadn't thought about how his appearance might look to her. She probably thought he lived in a little hovel of a house chiseled into the side of a mountain. She would be surprised to find his home was a 7,000 square feet mansion. It had to be, as his father often hosted emissaries from other packs, as well as other supernatural races.

"I guess the clothes would lead you to a different conclusion," Fane responded.

Suddenly, Fane had an intense desire to know her, know

anything and everything. "What's your favorite color? What is your favorite song, book, and movie? What do you like best about being an only child and what is worst?" Fane fired question after question, not giving her a chance to answer. He was so eager to learn all about his mate, his Luna.

"Step back and take a deep breath 'cause any minute now you are going to pass out from lack of oxygen," she told him. "Well, seeing as how I am so shy this will be hard for me to share, so bear with me," Jacquelyn teased him.

Fane rolled his eyes at her sarcasm. Jacquelyn was anything but shy.

"My favorite color depends on the day and my mood. For instance, today it is green," she explained.

"Is that why you are wearing green?" Fane asked.

"Yes, I have to admit I dress very much in accordance with my mood, and the colors I choose reflect that. I know, I'm a conundrum, what can I say? I like to keep things interesting. Favorite song, that changes frequently as well. Right now, I would have to say it's 'Accompany Me' by Bob Seager, but ask me again next week and it will be different. Favorite book, well, you're probably going to laugh if you know what this book is, but it's one I have always loved. It's called *Where the Sidewalk Ends* by Shell Silverstein. It's a children's book of outlandish poetry. Ever heard of it?" she asked him.

"No, actually I have not. Perhaps you will share it with me sometime," Fane told her.

Jacque laughed. "I don't have a copy of it right now. I've somehow misplaced it. It's either somewhere lost at the bottom of my closet or Jen took it and she hasn't 'fessed up," she explained.

Fane made a note of this is in his head. It was something he could get her, something to show her he cared about what she liked.

"Okay, where were we... Oh, my favorite movie, well, it's

not just one. It's a series, the *Harry Potter* movies. You've heard of them, right?" she asked.

"Yes, I have seen them as well. They were good," he told her.

"As far as being an only child, I don't know if I have ever really thought about what it would be like to have a sibling. I have always been so close to Jen and Sally, so it's like I do have sisters," Jacquelyn explained. "What about you? Same questions."

Without repeating the questions, Fane simply answered them in the order he had asked her. "Any shade of black or grey, *Lord of the Rings*, the movie *300*, and I don't like the responsibility that comes with being the only heir in my family."

He realized she wouldn't understand the whole heir reference, but in an effort to be as honest as possible, he would share what he could.

"So, um, I was wondering … ya know, if you…" Jacquelyn stumbled around her words. It was obvious she was uncomfortable with what she wanted to ask. Catching the thought in her mind, he realized she wanted to know if he had a girlfriend in Romania. He was a little shocked she thought he would pursue her if he *did* have a girlfriend, but he had to remember she did not know him yet.

"No, Luna, I do not have a girlfriend, nor am I recently out of a relationship." Fane knew the jab about her ex wasn't necessary, but he couldn't help it. He loved to see her get riled up, and sure enough, if she had hackles, they would be at attention.

"Why does it bother you so much that I had a boyfriend? I mean, it's not like I even knew you existed a week ago, not to mention Trent and I aren't together anymore," She told him firmly.

"I know, Jacquelyn. I'm sorry. I'm not bothered by it

anymore. Well, mostly not bothered by it. I have to admit I don't like the idea of another male touching you, but as long as I know he won't be again, I think Trent is safe," Fane told her honestly.

"You're saying that if I dated another guy, they wouldn't be safe?" she asked him in disbelief.

"Do you want to date another guy?" Fane countered.

Fane felt in her mind the answer was no, she didn't want to date anyone else, and he smiled at that, which was not a smart thing to do at that moment.

Jacquelyn stepped forward and put a finger against his chest, poking him with every word. "Don't dodge my question with a question of your own, you pushy, bossy Romanian butthead!"

She was fuming. Fane imagined if it were possible, there would be smoke rising off that hot-tempered red head of hers, and she wasn't done yet either.

"I can damn well date who I want when I want. There is nothing you can do or say to change that, so if you want to continue with this … this … *thing* between us," she said flinging her hand back and forth to indicate them both, "then you had better just back the hell up, buddy!" By the time she was done, she was panting from her little rant.

"I didn't say you couldn't date another person. I asked if you *wanted* to," Fane told her. "Is that so hard to answer?"

Jacquelyn glared at him, obviously wanting to hit him with something, and he decided to back up just a little. He continued to stare into those deep green eyes, waiting to see if she would admit what he already knew.

Jacquelyn looked down as if something could possibly be interesting on the ground, and in a voice so soft he would have missed it without his wolf hearing, he heard her say, "No, I don't want anyone else."

When she looked up at him there were tears in her eyes, and his heart broke.

"*Meu inimă*, my heart, why the tears? I did not mean to hurt you. Please tell me what I can do. You are breaking my heart," Fane told her with agony in his voice.

Fane wrapped his arms around her and pulled her close. He stroked her hair gently and whispered words of comfort and reassurance in his language. Finally, after several moments, she began to speak. She didn't pull away from him, which was good because he wasn't ready to let her go. He had hurt her. His wolf was not happy and needed the touch of his mate.

"I'm sorry. I'm not usually a blubbering idiot. It's just that I'm so confused. My emotions for you are so freaking intense, and I've known you all of three days. I mean, this isn't a movie where we meet and fall madly in love in a matter of days, Fane—this is my life!"

"I know. I'm sorry I wasn't more considerate. Please, love, forgive me. I won't let my jealousy or pride get in the way of considering your feelings again," Fane told her in all sincerity.

Before she could pull away Fane kissed her lightly on the forehead and took a deep breath, enjoying the way she smelled to him.

She looked at him oddly and said, "I'm not even going to ask why you just sniffed me."

"Because you smell wonderful," Fane told her, completely unashamed he'd been caught.

They were quiet for a few moments, and then the questions he had waited for her to ask finally came.

"So, are you going to fill me in on why we can share thoughts or why I suddenly have markings on my skin that would fit yours like a puzzle?" Jacquelyn asked him.

"You noticed that the markings match?" Fane asked her, surprised.

He had to tell his wolf to chill out because he desperately wanted to preen in front of her, proud that she had noticed his markings. *Good grief, this is ridiculous, wanting to prance in front of my mate and show her I am worthy of her. Act normal, you hairy baboon, or she's going to run from you screaming about what a psycho you are.*

"They are unusual markings, climbing up your neck like that, so, naturally, I noticed them." She tried to sound nonchalant about it.

"Look, Jacquelyn, I want to tell you. You have no idea how badly I want you to know everything. But your mom needs to talk with you first. She has to tell you what she knows and then when I explain how I fit into it, it will make more sense to you," Fane said, imploring her to accept this.

Fane knew, however, that she would never let it go that easily.

"What does my mom have to do with any of this?" she asked him incredulously.

Just as Fane was about to answer her, a car pulled in next to his motorcycle, which was quite a distance away from where they were sitting on a bench. Fane let his wolf out enough to use his eyes and saw, to his displeasure, it was the wolves that had driven past Jacquelyn's house the night before.

Four men got out of the car and began walking toward them. Fane's mind began to race, trying to work out a strategy to keep his mate safe. But what could he do? If he attempted to fight them, she would be left unprotected. If they tried to make a run for it, the Greys would easily overtake them because she could not run faster than them. He could carry her, but Fane had a feeling that would not go over too well with his Luna.

He would just have to wait and see what they wanted.

"Who are these guys? Do you know them?" Fane heard her thoughts, clouded with worry.

"I know very little about them. This is another thing we need to talk about, but we must talk to your mother first," Fane answered.

Fane never took his eyes off the wolves coming toward him and his mate, but out of the corner of his eye, he saw Jacquelyn give him a displeased look, obviously not happy with his answer.

Fane couldn't suppress the low warning growl that escaped from his throat. If he had been in wolf form, his hackles would have been standing, tail down, stance wide and low, ready for any sudden movement they might try.

The wolf from the dealership—Fane remembered his name was Steve—spoke first, "My Alpha wants to know why you are still here."

Fane took a step forward, which had the wolves backing up a step, and they couldn't help but lower their heads just a little because Fane was more dominant.

"I hate to break it to you, Beta, but your Alpha has no authority to order me out of a town that he has not made known to be his territory," Fane replied. "There is no record of this pack existing."

The man looked a little confused by this, which gave Fane pause. Was the wolf somehow unaware that he was in a rogue pack?

Quickly, Steve composed himself. "Regardless, there is only one of you compared to our entire pack. What do you really think you can do against those odds?" he asked.

Fane glared menacingly at the four Greys, and they backed up even more. "You tell your Alpha to back off. There is only so much disregard for pack laws that I will overlook." Fane glared at each wolf, looking directly into their eyes, and they dropped them instantly. Then, in the same voice his father used to make his own wolves obey, Fane told them, "Leave, now."

When a dominant issues a command like that, the submissive can only obey, whether they want to or not.

Steve and the others walked away, but Fane could tell they were fighting against his order. Before he got in his car, the man turned to Fane and said, "Just so you know, pup, she has already been claimed, and if you don't stay away, her true mate is going to challenge you, and, rest assured, he will tear you apart."

At that, Fane snarled furiously. His eyes began to glow, and he felt his canines elongate. The Grey whined and scrambled into his car, squealing his tires as he peeled out.

Fane closed his eyes and took slow deep breaths. *Calm yourself. No one is going to take her from you.* He chanted this to himself over and over until he and his wolf were somewhat in control. Fane turned to face Jacquelyn and saw confusion on her face, but to his relief, there was no fear.

"Okay, you can forget trying to get away with not explaining that little episode of the *Twilight Zone*. I am not an idiot, so don't think I didn't pick up on the whole animal kingdom references, the way you just nearly went postal on their hides or the fact that the 'she' they were talking about was me," Jacquelyn said, arms crossed and brow furrowed in determination.

Fane walked up to her, towering over her short frame. To her credit, after seeing him act like the animal he was, she didn't take a single step back.

"You're right, Luna, it's time to talk, but your mom will start it. Let's go," Fane responded.

And with that, they were on his motorcycle headed back to Jacquelyn's house.

CHAPTER 9

*J*acque held on tight to Fane's waist, laying her cheek against his back, taking in his warmth. She was nervous but glad she was finally going to get some answers. She was still a little shaky after that scene at the park. Jacque could not make sense of anything those guys had said to Fane or vice versa.

Fane and the other men had thrown the term 'Alpha' around a few times. What in the world had that meant? Jacque thought she could remember the term referred to as the first letter of the Greek alphabet, and she had heard it used when mentioning dogs or wolves. And who were those men to tell Fane he had to leave, and what did they mean by she already had a mate? The questions swirled around in her brain over and over, yet she could find no explanation.

"Luna, are you okay?" Fane asked, sounding worried.

She smiled, enjoying the fact he worried about her. It felt good to be cared for, not that she wasn't cared for by others, but it felt good coming from him.

"I guess I'm as good as can be expected. Don't be alarmed

if I freak out or have a meltdown. It will pass," she told him with only a small amount of teasing in her voice.

The truth was, she was already on the verge of a panic attack. When those guys had told Fane he had to leave, the mere idea of him gone actually caused her pain. How messed up was that?

Jacque closed her eyes and concentrated on her breathing. "In and out, in and out," she told herself. "Whatever it is, whatever he tells you, you will not cower in a corner and shake like a frightened puppy," she told herself firmly. "No, but I make no promises that I won't pass out from shock. There is no shame in passing out. It's simply the brain's way of saying 'hold the stink up.' I need to process this mess." Jacque smiled, wondering if other people talked to themselves like that. Probably not, but everyone's got something, right?

Fane pulled into her driveway and turned off the engine. The neighborhood was eerily quiet. Jacque climbed off his bike, taking the helmet off as well, and shook her hair out. She looked up to find Fane watching her.

"What?" she asked him.

To Jacque's surprise, Fane blushed! He turned his head away from her, and she saw the small smile that had appeared.

"Sorry, it's just, um, well, you looked attractive shaking your hair out," Fane stammered.

Jacque tried hard not to laugh but was completely unsuccessful. She looked up at him and saw embarrassment in his eyes.

"Fane, you can't possibly be ashamed by thinking I'm hot. I practically drool all over you every time I see you. I should be the one embarrassed," she confessed to him.

"Are you?" Fane asked.

"I guess maybe I should be, but throw me a bone. You are

freaking hot. I can't change that, so I'm embracing it."

Fane chuckled and told her, "You amaze me, Luna, truly you do."

It was Jacque's turn to blush. "Thanks."

Fane took Jacque's hand and they walked to the front door. Warmth spread up her arm and throughout her body just from holding his hand. Jacque reached her free hand to the doorknob. But just before she grabbed it, the door opened.

"Mom, are you—" Jacque's words froze in her throat. Instead of her mother in the doorway, a man stared back at her. She recognized him. It was Fane's limo driver. The man she'd seen drop Fane off just three nights ago was now standing in her foyer. Jacque froze, not sure what to do. Fane stepped around her, went to the man, and embraced him just like they had done on the night he arrived.

"Okay, I'm about to have a two-year-old moment," she said. "MOM! WHO IN KING ARTHUR'S NAME IS THIS MAN IN OUR HOUSE, WHAT THE CRAP DO YOU KNOW THAT YOU AREN'T TELLING ME, AND FOR THE LOVE OF ALL THINGS THAT KEEP US SANE, WHAT THE HELL IS GOING ON?"

Jacque walked into the living room where she was met by Lilly coming out of the kitchen. "I guess it's time for me to tell you the truth about your father, Jacque," said her mother.

"What truth? What are you talking about?"

Lilly let out a heavy sigh. "Please, everyone, sit down. Jacque, this is Sorin, Fane's bodyguard."

"Bodyguard?"

"Just sit. I'll explain everything," said Lilly.

They all did, Fane taking a place by Jacque on the couch. The strange man was completely silent. He took an armchair and fixed Jacque with an appraising gaze she didn't' appreciate.

Lilly continued. "I hoped this day would never come, my daughter. I truly hoped you would grow up and have a normal life and never be affected by your father's blood. Apparently, that was too much to hope for.

"Again, mom, what are you talking about? My father's blood? That doesn't make sense."

Lilly folded her hands in her lap. "Jacque," Lilly began, "there is no easy way to explain this. It's going to sound insane, but just listen, it's all true."

"If you knew what my life has been like the past few days you wouldn't even have to lead off with that. So, as Jen and I like to say, go ahead and slap me with it."

Her mother took a deep breath, "Your father, Dillon, is not a human. He is a *Canis lupus*."

"A *Canis-whatsit?*" Jacque asked.

"You might know them better as werewolves," came Fane's deep voice. Jacque's head whipped around at Fane. She opened it to ask again what the heck they were talking about, but found herself staring into luminescent blue eyes which rendered her completely speechless. For a moment, all questions fled from her mind. After a few moments, she regained her voice. Instead of speaking to Fane, she turned back to her mother."

"I don't know what you are talking about, but if it has to do with my father, you should have told me a long time ago. Why have you kept this from me?"

"I wasn't planning on telling you as long as it never affected you. I figured there was no reason to add confusion to the pain of your father leaving."

"Did you ever think that wasn't your choice to make?" Jacque was yelling now. "There was nothing in the world she hated worse than being lied to, and her mother hadn't been honest with her.

"*Jacquelyn, calm yourself. She was just trying to protect you,*

134

not hide things from you," Jacque heard Fane's soft, comforting voice tell her. Unfortunately, it just fueled her fire.

Jacque turned on him. "Do not tell me to calm down! Everyone in this room seems to know something about my life that I don't, and frankly, that just ticks me off a teeny, tiny bit, so back off!"

Fane held his hands up in surrender.

Jacque jumped up and began pacing the room.

"I understand why you are angry and that you are hurt, but I need you to hear me out and then judge me," Lilly told her.

Jacque stopped and tried to wipe away the tears that were running freely down her cheeks. She turned to look at her mom and simply nodded her head. Her mom patted the loveseat for her to sit on, but Jacque took one look at Fane and knew she needed to sit back down by him.

"I'm sorry, love. It's just that I see you hurting, and all I want to do is comfort you. It's MY job to comfort you. Please bear with me a little longer. Sit by me. Calm the animal inside, please."

When Jacque didn't say anything else, Lilly said, "I knew there was something different about Dillon when we met. The longer we dated, the more certain I was he was not normal. He was too big, too strong, for a regular man Sometimes, I would catch his eyes glowing unnaturally. It was spooky and alluring all at the same time. So, finally, one night I just asked him, *'What* are you?' And he told me. At first, naturally, I didn't believe him, but then he showed me."

"Showed you?" Jacque asked.

"His wolf," replied her mother. "He phased right in front of me. He showed me his wolf and he was beautiful. Over time, he told me more and more about his culture and his species. Most importantly, he told me about true mates. It was then I realized he would have to leave me one day, for I wasn't his true mate. That, we both knew. Obviously, because I wasn't *Canis lupus*. Your father was open and honest with me about it, and I chose to stay with him anyway because I felt whatever time I could have with him was better than not being with him at all."

Lilly paused for a moment and looked at Jacque, who was just sitting there staring at the table in front of her, saying nothing. Fane took one of her hands in his.

Lilly continued, "Three days before he left, I found out I was pregnant with you. I was going to tell him that very night, but when I got home, he wasn't there. Instead, there was a note waiting for me."

Jacque looked up at her mother when her voice wavered and saw Lilly had tears in her eyes. She realized then her mom still loved her father, even though he was a *Canis lup* —whatever.

"*Canis lupus, meu inimă, my heart,*" Fane told her through her thoughts.

"I was not thinking to you, now was I? No, I was not. I was thinking to myself. So if you don't mind, keep your nosy Romanian brain out of mine," Jacque told him.

Fane simply squeezed her hand, and even this ticked Jacque off because she didn't want anyone's comfort or understanding. She just wanted to be pissed off.

Jacque's mom pulled herself together, and when Jacque still did not say anything, Lilly soldiered on.

"I had no idea what would happen to you since you were half *Canis lupus*. I didn't know if I would come in your room one day and find a wolf puppy in your crib. I guess I could've tried to track down your father and ask him, but the thought of seeing him again, especially now that I knew he was with his true mate, would have hurt too much. Instead, I watched and waited.

"As time went on, you seemed to be completely normal.

You showed no werewolf tendencies, so, I decided to let it go. As you approached puberty, I began to get worried again. I was afraid that might trigger some change in you and your *Canis lupus* side would come out. When it didn't, I thought we were home free. But then..." Lilly looked at Fane, and there was no condemnation when she said, "You came along, and I knew all my hope was in vain."

Fane looked Lilly in the eye and told her, "I am sorry to have brought your fears to pass, but I am not sorry to have found Jacquelyn. She is my mate, and I will claim her, as is my right. You know, Lilly, she will not be complete without me, nor I without her."

Lilly nodded her head. "I know this, Fane. At first, I was angry, then scared. Now that I have spent some time with you, albeit not enough, I can tell you are a good man. I say man because you can no longer be a boy. You have to protect my little girl." Her voice sounded nearly desperate now.

Jacque's head snapped up when she heard her mom's tone and saw the fear in her eyes.

Jacque took a deep breath, "Give me just a moment, okay? Let me process this ... out loud." She turned her head to look at Fane. "You, Casanova, give me some space. You're freaking me out right now."

Fane let go of her hand and moved away from her, although only a tiny bit. Jacque rolled her eyes at him.

"Are you two telling me, my father, a man I've never met, grows fangs and claws and turns all hairy once a month? Is that what you are saying?"

Fane and Sorin both let out a snort of laughter and then pulled it together when Lilly glared at them.

"No, Jacque, all the things you think you know about werewolves are false," said Lilly. "*Canis lupus* can phase—they don't call it changing—whenever they want to. They can phase their whole body to wolf form or just their eyes or teeth or whatever. It has nothing to do with the moon, at least not in that sense."

"I can't phase though, right?" Jacque asked apprehensively.

"I've never seen any evidence of it," her mother replied.

"Well, that's a crappy deal. Here you have a dad who can turn into this cool wolf thingy and you can't even get a sexy bushy tail," Jen said as she and Sally walked into the living room.

"What are you two doing here?" Jacque asked them.

"I asked them to stay and listen in. I knew you would tell them anyway and figured you would need some support after I broke the news," Lilly told her.

"You guys heard everything?" Jacque asked tentatively.

"Every page-turning word. I wanted to pop some popcorn. I figured there might be some tense moments, and you know I eat when I'm tense, but Goody Two-shoes here wouldn't let me," Jen said as she cocked an eye in Sally's direction.

Sally patted Jen's hand in mock sympathy, "We know, sweetie, but, see, since it was Jacque finding out it was her dad who gets hairy, not yours, we didn't really care if you were tense. Okay, honey?"

Jen took Sally's hand off hers and bit into it hard enough to leave teeth marks.

"Hey, what the hell, chick?" Sally exclaimed.

"See, now don't you wish you had given me the popcorn?" Jen retorted.

Jacque couldn't help but laugh. She was so grateful to have Sally and Jen here giving her something normal to grasp onto, which she knew was why her mom had asked them to stay.

Jacque turned and looked at her mom, "My father left because he found his true mate or whatever?"

"Yes, and I want you to know I don't blame him. I knew it would eventually happen," Lilly answered.

"Did he know about me?" Jacque asked, not sure if she wanted to know the answer. Because if he did, and he had never bothered to come meet her, it was going to hurt.

"He has no idea you exist. After he left, I had no way to contact him to tell him. As I said, I might have been able to track him down, I'm not sure. But, if he would have known, he would have wanted to be part of your life. I couldn't have that. The *Canis lupus* world is dangerous. I didn't want you to have any part of it. It tore me up inside to keep him from you. That wasn't fair of me and I knew it, but I felt it was safest for you. Dillon is a good man, Jacque. The only problem is, he isn't really a man. Just my luck, huh?" Lilly said with a smile.

Jacque thought for a moment, and then something Fane said earlier came to the forefront of her mind—he had called her his mate!

She slowly turned to look at him and saw his head was down, his shoulders slumped as if he was deflated. It broke her heart to see him look so broken. Jacque took her finger, placed it under his chin, raised his head so she could see his face, and the look she saw brought tears to her eyes. She didn't talk out loud. She felt like this was just between them. For the next few moments, there was no one else in Jacque's world but Fane.

"What's wrong, Fane?"

"You know what you are to me, yes?" he asked.

Jacque whispered her answer out loud, "Mate."

Fane nodded his head, "Yes, *Meu inimă*, my heart, you are my mate. The other half of my soul and the thought of you not wanting me is more than I can bear," Fane told her honestly.

"No pressure, huh?" Jacque said, trying to lighten the mood.

"I would never ask you to do something you do not want to, Luna, but I will not lie and say that I won't follow you around like a sick puppy," Fane said with a smile, though the tears were not quite gone.

"I just need time, okay, to sort through all this. I'm not saying I don't want you. I mean, now that I've met you, the idea of life without you makes it hard to breathe," Jacque told him.

Fane took her hands in his and said, "Time is one thing I can't give you, love."

FANE HELD the hands of his mate in his. He hated having to tell her he couldn't give her the one thing she wanted, but Fane just couldn't give her time. He needed to complete the bond through the Blood Rites, especially since there was another *Canis lupus* in town claiming Jacque for his own. Once the bond was complete, no other male could dispute whose mate she was.

Fane pulled Jacquelyn up off the floor and returned her to the seat next to him. He continued to hold one of her hands, taking comfort from her touch.

"I'm not trying to rush you, Jacquelyn. Under different circumstances, I would give you all the time you need, but you are not safe unbonded," Fane explained to her.

"Okay, that was clear as mud. Would you mind elaborating on why I am not safe?" Jacquelyn asked him. "And what the hell *unbonded* means?"

"When I came here, my father ... wait, let me back up for a moment and tell you a little about who I really am so everything will fit together better, okay?" Fane asked.

"Whatever gets us to the place we need to be. I'll try not to ask if we're there yet," Jacque answered a little impatiently.

"I am *Canis lupus*, like your father. My lineage is in Romania. There are many types of werewolves, but we are known as grey wolves.

"How can you know my dad is a grey wolf?" Jacquelyn asked.

"My father told me," he answered.

"*Your* father?" Jen asked, enthralled in the conversation. "What's he got to do with this?"

Everyone in the room turned to look at her. She just lifted her shoulders and said, "My bad. That was Jacque's line, wasn't it?"

Sally shook her head and hit Jen in the shoulder. Jen scowled at her.

"My turn," Jacque piped in. "So, who is your father?"

"I'm getting to that. You two jumped the bullet," Fane told them.

The three girls giggled, Sorin coughed, trying to disguise his laughter.

"Jumped the gun, handsome, not bullet," Jen corrected with a grin.

"Oh, well, as you would say, my bad," he told Jen.

"Let me continue. As I said, I am a Grey and my pack is in Romania. Every pack has an Alpha, just like our animal cousins. The Alpha is sort of like the king. He rules the pack. He keeps order so that dominant wolves don't tear each other apart and so that everyone, especially the non-dominant wolves, also called submissives, are protected." Fane was trying to make everything as clear as he could so Jacquelyn would understand where she fell in all this and what her new life would look like.

"My father is the Alpha of the Romanian *Canis lupus*. I am next in line to be Alpha, and so our pack calls me the Prince of the Romanian *Canis lupus*. I am a dominant, which means it is in my nature to want to protect those weaker than me. It is also my nature to be aggressive and very territorial. An Alpha must be a dominant or he cannot maintain order in the pack. Are you with me so far?" Fane asked her.

"You're a Romanian werewolf prince, your dad is the werewolf king, you are bossy, possessive, and territorial by nature which if you were just a wolf would mean you'd pee on what you want to mark as yours."

Jen was nearly rolling on the floor at Jacquelyn's description.

"And why exactly did you bring your royal butt to Texas?" Jacquelyn finished with a question.

Fane was smiling, thankful her sense of humor was still intact, which he took to mean she was handling this news rather well.

"Here is where we get to the *unbonded* part. Every male *Canis lupus* has one mate, only one. Sometimes they are drawn to a certain area where their mate lives. I think it's nature's way of helping us wolves because, you see, it can take years and even centuries to find your mate." Fane let that sink in a minute knowing the inevitable was coming, but Jen beat Jacquelyn to the punch ... again.

"Hold on, put on the brakes, throw it in park, and set the emergency brake while you're at it. Did you just say centuries?" Jen asked dubiously.

This time nobody even paid attention to the fact that it wasn't Jacquelyn who asked. They were all too busy looking at Fane, waiting for an answer. Sorin, however, was just sitting in the ugly, peach chair looking bored. *He could just throw his two cents in at any moment.* Instead, Sorin just sat there.

"Yes, I said centuries. *Canis lupus* live much, much longer lives than humans," Fane answered.

Jacquelyn asked, "How much longer, 'cause you know I'm only good for like seventy-five years, maybe eighty. If I sit longer than that on the shelf I expire," Jacquelyn said.

"Once we complete the Blood Rites, your life is tied to mine, and you will live as long as I do, just as I will live as long as you do. You see, Jacquelyn, once mates are bonded, one cannot live without the other. It is the way of our species that when one mate dies the other follows," Fane told her.

"Oh, my gosh!" Sally exclaimed. "That is so freaking romantic—or depressing. It's all in how you look at it. Do you have any cousins?" she asked him hopefully.

"I'm sorry, Sally, but you must have *Canis lupus* blood somewhere in your lineage to bond with a *Canis lupus*."

"I can check, you know, like do some research, 'cause there is no telling what's in my blood. I could go back generations—" Sally began but was interrupted when Jen covered Sally's mouth with her hand.

"Don't mind her. She is missing that part in her brain that tells her to shut up," Jen said.

"You're one to talk," Jacquelyn said smiling.

"Okay, keep going, I need to get this all out tonight so I can have tomorrow to freak out," Jacquelyn told Fane.

"I came to Texas because my wolf somehow knew you were here and that his mate, our mate, was in danger. Before you ask, I will try to explain this quickly. My wolf and I are one, but at the same time, we are separate. When I am not in wolf form, he is still there. I can call on him for his help and use his attributes. Just as when I am in wolf form, he uses my human attributes. I can still think and reason like a man. That is why we don't call it changing because that implies once we are in our wolf forms, we no longer retain any human attributes, and when we are in our human form, there is no wolf there at all, which is not the case. We always coexist together. Does that make sense?" Fane asked.

"Yeah, I get that, not that it's easy to believe, but I understand the logistics of it," Jacquelyn answered.

Fane let go of her hand and brushed her hair away from her face. *She looks so tired.* He was so grateful she had not thrown him out or told him he was crazy, even though what he was telling her sounded insane. But, he told himself, there is still more, so she might just throw me out yet.

"I realize what you're saying is that I'm your mate. You've mentioned this bond thingy, and blood… What did you say?" Jacquelyn asked.

"Blood Rites. Even though we are mates, we have to perform a ceremony to bond us to each other," Fane began.

"Oh, Sally, get some popcorn now. It's fixing to get rich," Jen interrupted.

Jacquelyn rolled her eyes, and Fane just ignored the comment. He didn't want to be distracted. His Luna needed to know what was coming and that it had to happen very, very soon.

"Okay, back up. When you say 'perform a ceremony,' are you talking behind-closed-doors type stuff?" Jacquelyn asked him through her thoughts, sounding embarrassed and nervous at the same time.

"If you are asking me if we must consummate our relationship to complete the bond, the answer is no, Luna," Fane answered her.

He saw her take a deep breath and let it out in obvious relief.

"Put up the popcorn Sally. Things are staying stale," Jacquelyn announced.

"Can't you ever just drizzle on my parade, or do you always insist on a full monsoon?" Jen asked her with obvious irritation.

"Is the idea really that bad to you, Luna?" Fane asked, honestly wondering.

"We are so, so, so NOT having this conversation right now. I may be your mate or whatever, but I have only known you three stinking days. What kind of girl do you think I am?" Jacquelyn thought back to him.

"Well, in truth, love, it does please me to know that is something you do not take lightly," Fane told her. Then he asked, "You haven't taken it lightly, so to speak, with anyone else, have you?"

Jacquelyn closed her eyes and shook her head. She took a deep breath, and Fane could tell she was trying to reign in her fiery little temper.

"If you absolutely must know, there has not been anyone I wanted to take lightly … ever. So, since you are being so stinking nosy, what about you? Is there a double standard in the Canis lupus world? Is it okay for a guy to take any and every one lightly without repercussions of a bad reputation?" Jacque threw back at him.

"Thank you. To answer your question, it is very uncommon for a male Canis lupus to take anyone but his mate lightly." Fane grinned at the connotations they were using to keep from having to actually say making love.

Jacquelyn caught that thought. "Nope, it's called not taking it lightly. Deal with it."

Fane laughed out loud at her embarrassment, which caused everyone in the room to look at him. He couldn't help himself. She was such a joy to his heart. He didn't care if she never called it what it was so long as she would be his.

"Are you two ready to share the conversation with the rest of us now, or would you like to take this in another room?" Jen asked sarcastically.

"Nope, no need to leave, we are just all one big happy family … sharing, talking, and getting all the gory details of life as a werewolf. Just another typical Wednesday night," Jacquelyn rambled on nervously.

"Are you ready for me to continue, my Luna?" Fane asked her.

"Bring it on," Jacquelyn told him.

"The Blood Rites ceremony is performed by the Alpha of the pack you are joining through your mate, so it will be performed by my father. In some ways, it is much like a human wedding. There are usually only a few witnesses—family and close friends. We will exchange vows." Fane took a breath because he knew what he was going to say next she would not like. "And then we do the Blood Rites," he finished vaguely. He knew she wouldn't let him off that easy, but, he thought, it didn't hurt to try.

"Fane, sweetie, what exactly are the Blood Rites?" Jacquelyn asked him with syrupiness in her voice he knew better than to believe.

"Understand, Jacquelyn, we are not human. There are some things our wolf nature demands, and one of those things is a blood rite. A male *Canis lupus* wants the world to know his mate is his. There are several ways this happens. His mate takes on markings that match those on his body and would fit like a puzzle piece. The markings on *Canis lupus* reveal their place in the pack. For instance, I am a dominant so my markings are on the right side of my body. They are also very elaborate, and they go to the front of my chest as well, indicating that I am an Alpha. My father explained to me that when *Canis lupus* finds his mate, he will develop new markings visible even with clothes on, like on the neck, and this tells all *Canis lupus* he is mated.

Fane paused to give her a chance to ask questions, and then just to humor her, he turned and looked at Jen, who responded with, "Oh, I'm good. Carry on, this is great stuff."

Fane winked at her and grinned.

To his and her surprise, Jacquelyn reached over and slapped his arm. "Quit winking at my friends. Jen's gonna hyperventilate, and Sally's gonna pass out. Get on with this whole Blood Rites thing." She growled at him.

"You're a violent little thing, aren't you?" Fane teased.

She gave him a look as if to say, "I'm waiting."

"That is one way the male's mate is marked."

Sally raised her hand like she was in school.

Jen rolled her eyes and said, "Put your hand down you dork and just ask."

"How do the markings identify her to other werewolves if no one can see them unless she wears a low-back shirt like Jacque did tonight?" Sally asked.

Fane growled and that earned him another slap on the arm from Jacquelyn.

"Don't growl at my friends either."

"I wasn't growling at them, love. I was growling at the idea of another seeing your markings. The markings on the female are meant only for her mate to see. If another male sees them, he is looking at something he is not supposed to. The markings are precious to the rightful male mate because it is the first thing that indicates the she-wolf is his. It was very difficult for me tonight with yours showing. It helped that your hair covered up most of them," he told her.

"So, it's kind of like some guy looking in her lingerie drawer and seeing all her hot little outfits, huh?" Jen stated with a grin.

"Only you would come up with that analogy. You know that, right?" Sally asked her.

"I'm just clarifying things, you know, breaking it down, making it chewable," Jen responded.

"Jen, Sally, I love you guys, but zip it, okay?" Jacquelyn asked them in exasperation.

Both girls ran their fingers across their lips as if to close a zipper and gave her a thumbs up. Jacquelyn nodded her thanks.

147

"Another way a male *Canis lupus* shows he found his mate is the ability to speak to her through their thoughts. I cannot speak to anyone else nor hear anyone else's thoughts but yours. Just as you can only speak to me and hear my thoughts," Fane continued to explain. He noticed the look Jacquelyn was giving him was less than pleased, and he asked her, "Does that bother you, Luna?"

"Well, there are some things I don't want you to know," Jacquelyn told him shyly.

"Oooh, like that time we snuck out and went skin—" Jen started but was quickly interrupted by Sally.

"JEN," Sally hollered. "Let's get that popcorn now. I think you need something to keep your mouth occupied, or we are going to shove your foot in it, okay?" she finished sweetly.

"Once again my parade is saturated in the downpour of hurricane Sally," Jen retorted.

Jacquelyn watched as her two best friends walked to the kitchen, and then she turned and looked at Fane.

"Are there any other ways a male marks his mate?" she asked him.

"I think you would be more comfortable if we talk about it privately."

Jacquelyn's eyebrows rose in apprehension. "That bad, huh?" she asked him.

In response, Fane simply took her hand, pulled her up from the couch, turned to Lilly and Sorin, and told them, "I think the rest of this conversation needs to be only between me and my mate."

"I can understand that," Lilly responded.

Sorin simply nodded his understanding.

Fane looked at Jacquelyn and said, "Lead the way, Luna."

CHAPTER 10

*J*acque continued to hold Fane's hand as she led him up the stairs to her bedroom. Before they reached the top, Jacque heard her mom yell, "Jacque, leave your door open, please. Mated or not, you are still living under my rules."

Jacque laughed, so thankful for something that made her feel like she was just a girl with a boy, hanging out. Not a *Canis lupus*, not a mate, just teenagers.

"You got it, Mom," Jacque hollered back.

As they entered her room, Jacque let go of Fane's hand and stepped away, putting some distance between them. She was beginning to feel just a tad claustrophobic and needed space.

"You can sit in that chair or the window seat," she said indicating both places.

Jacque suddenly felt very nervous. Being in her room alone with him felt so intimate, yet she couldn't deny she was very relieved that whatever he had to tell her was not going to be broadcast to everyone downstairs.

"So, what is this other thing that marks the female as a

mate? I'm assuming it has to do with the Blood Rites?" she asked him.

"You are correct. It is about the Blood Rites. The reason I wanted to speak with you alone about it is because it is the only part of the ceremony done in private," Fane explained.

"Whoa, whoa, whoa, back up. I thought you said there was no *taking it lightly* stuff in this ceremony," Jacque said a little frantically.

"Luna, I'm going to lay this out plainly for you. There will be no lies, half-truths, or bush beating. I'm going to say it bluntly," Fane told her firmly.

Jacque tried, she really did, but she couldn't contain the laughter.

"*Meu inimă*, my heart, would you please share with me what you find to be so funny?" Fane asked her patiently.

"It's called beating around the bush, prince of wolves, not bush beating," she told him, still giggling despite her efforts not to.

"Oh, well, my mistake. There will be no beating around the bush any longer. We are going to call it what it is, so if you turn a lovely shade of red, I will try hard not to find it adorable."

"Fine, spit it out already," Jacque answered, irritated by his little sermon.

She planted herself on her bed, legs Indian-style, back straight, and her hands folded in her lap. She was trying desperately not to be anxious, but she was quite unsuccessful. Finally, Fane began to explain the Blood Rites, and he was right, what he told her made her blush so badly she felt the heat of it in her face.

"What I told you is true about the bonding ceremony. We do not have to consummate—or make love—whichever you prefer to call it, to be fully mated. We do, however, have to exchange blood."

Jacque cringed at that. "That's gross. You do realize that, don't you? I mean surely that can't be good for a person."

Fane gave her an "I'm not finished" look which made her abruptly stop talking.

"There is no eloquent way to put this. It just is what it is. I will mark you and take your blood by biting you." Fane paused waiting for her reaction, she did not disappoint.

"YOU ARE GOING TO WHAT ME?" She was completely caught off guard by his revelation. I mean, when he said exchange blood, I was thinking a finger prick, a little embarrassment because I'd have to suck on his finger and vice versa, but biting me, that is in a whole other category of embarrassment.

Fane walked over to her bed and knelt in front of her. He placed his hands over hers, and she instantly felt reassurance flow through her. She closed her eyes and let herself soak it up, embracing the comfort he was providing her.

When she opened her eyes, she was staring into glowing, crystal blue eyes. "How did you do that?" she asked him.

"For wolves, touch is a very powerful thing. It provides comfort and reassurance to them, so it is with *Canis lupus*. Like other things, it is even more potent between mates. You needed my comfort, and I could do nothing else but provide it for you. When you need something, your inner wolf calls to me, I can feel it, my wolf can feel it, and we are obligated to do what we can to provide that for you."

Jacque tried not to think about that. But call her crazy, which at this point she was bound to be, she could just picture herself craving a Snickers ice cream bar in the middle of the night while a raging thunderstorm wreaked havoc outside, here came Fane knocking on her window, soaking wet, with a Snickers in hand. That could be kinda handy.

Fane had apparently caught all of her little daydream because he chuckled at her.

151

"You do think the oddest things. You know that, right?" Fane asked her.

"Let's stay on track, wolf boy. Bite me where exactly? Since this has to be done in private, I'm a little leery of the answer," she told him.

"Relax, Luna, I'm not going to bite you anywhere you might one day like," Fane said.

Jacque knew he was just trying to get a reaction out of her, and much to her chagrin, it worked like a charm.

"You just stop that thought right there. There will be no discussing of the future likes and dislikes of our maybe-one-day physical relationship, got it?" Jacque told him with finality.

"I will humor you for now," Fane told her with a grin. "Moving along, love, I will bite you on your neck. Rest assured, Luna, I am a werewolf, but at least I'm not a vampire. My bite will not last so long as to drain you of your blood, only as long as it takes for enough blood to flow, so I can swallow some and leave my mark on you."

Jacque was quiet for a moment. She took a deep breath, let it out slowly. What do you mean *leave your mark on me?* I get that when you bite me you will get blood in your mouth and yadda, yadda, but how are you going to leave a mark on me?" Jacque asked.

"I'm not sure how I leave a mark on you. I think it's just a part of the whole supernatural aspect of bonding. The mark I leave is the visual symbol that you are mated," he explained. "The final warning to other males that you have been bonded is smell."

"I'm going to smell? Please tell me I'm not going to stink, 'cause I don't do stinky, okay?" Jacque implored him.

"No Luna, you are not going to stink. To other *Canis lupus,* you will smell like me because you will have taken my blood, and I will smell like you when I have taken your blood. Once we have consummated our mating, the smells will intensify greatly," Fane explained.

"You just had to throw that last curveball in there, didn't you? Well, don't get your hopes up 'cause I'm not going to swing at it," Jacque told him. "This whole biting thing is done in private. Why?" she asked.

"Would you like me to bite you on the neck in front of your mom?" Fane asked.

"Point to you. You're right. There is no way that mouth of yours is coming near my neck in front of anyone—not my mom and especially not your parents," Jacque said.

Oh crap. I have to meet his parents. She felt panicky at the thought yet she didn't know why. Jacque hadn't been nervous when she met Trent's parents. She heard Fane growl as he caught the thought of Trent passing through her mind.

"Oh, shut up already, you over-possessive, royal Romanian pain in the proverbial backside. It's not like I'm thinking about him biting my neck," Jacque said sarcastically. Once again, she just couldn't help it. She became a sarcastic witch when she was nervous.

Fane stood up and sat down next to her on the bed. He leaned closer to her and swept her hair away, revealing the markings on her shoulders and neck. Fane traced the marks with his fingers and let out a low growl. Jacque shivered at his touch and found she couldn't quite keep her breathing even. She felt like she might pass out at any moment. What came next almost sealed her fate.

Fane leaned even closer and whispered in her ear. "I would hope you were not thinking of him biting your neck. I assure you that once I do, you will never need to think of another again." And then he gently placed his lips on her neck. Jacque didn't even try to suppress the small moan that came out of her tightly closed lips. But Fane could not leave well enough alone. After he kissed her neck, he playfully nipped her neck with his teeth while pulling his lips away.

Jacque jumped and turned to look at him breathlessly, putting her hands up as if to ward him off. She told him, "I, um..." She shook her head and rubbed her face with both hands as she struggled to get her thoughts and words to cooperate with her mouth. "I understand now why that part is done in private. Thank you for demonstrating."

Fane grinned at her wickedly. "I could demonstrate again. It is proven that people are most likely to remember things when done three times."

"Nice try, Don Juan, but it's people remembering things they are told three times, not things they do," she countered.

"We could test out the theory to see if it applies to actions as well. I'm all for scientific study," Fane teased.

"Well you're out of luck because I suck at science and therefore do not enjoy it," she said matter-of-factly.

Fane leaned forward again, and this time Jacque leaned back, but he wasn't deterred. He just grinned and leaned closer.

"You mean to tell me, my *puțin foc*, little fire, you did not enjoy my demonstration? If you did not, then I did not do it correctly, and I would feel obligated to try again."

Closing her eyes, Jacque immediately thought of a wall shielding her mind, and then she came up with a plan. Evasion was not working, so it was time to move on to plan B: If you can't beat 'em, join 'em. *Let me see if I can give him a taste of his own medicine, and just maybe it will throw him off his game so I can retreat. You know what Jen would call you, right? Yeah, yeah, I'm a chicken s** t, so be it.*

Her plan of attack decided, Jacque stopped leaning back and pressed into him. This confused him and made him back up a tad. Encouraged by the little victory, she got a little bolder and scooted her body closer to his. Fane's brow furrowed, and she could tell he was wondering what was going on. But he did not move. He just sat very still. Jacque decided the angle she was currently in was all wrong for her scheme, so she got up on her knees and scooted around until she was directly behind him, sitting on her knees with her feet behind her. She placed her hands on his shoulders and leaned her face close until her mouth was right beside his left ear.

Fane shuddered and it made her grin. *Take that, you little seducing hound.* She let her breath flow over his ear as she told him, "How do you like them apples, wolf boy?"

Fane leaned forward to get away from her mouth, and she could see the quick rise and fall of his back from breathing quickly. She found herself rather intrigued by his behavior. She could not think of a time that Trent had responded to her like that … oops, she had let her wall down during that thought.

Fane stood up so abruptly that Jacque fell forward and had to catch herself on her hands to keep from falling on her face. She looked up and saw Fane pacing her room quickly in obvious agitation.

"Fane, I'm sorry. I didn't mean for you to hear that. I wasn't trying to think about the physical part of my relationship with Trent. I was merely comparing your reactions." Jacque tried to explain, hoping to calm the wolf currently wearing a hole in her carpet from his frantic steps.

"Jacquelyn, you are not helping," he told her with a growl. "I realize you do not understand the intensity of my feelings for you, but I cannot change my nature. In the wild, wolves mate for life, and a male wolf will kill any other who tries to take his mate. It is the same with my species. I realize this *Trent*," Fane said his name in obvious repugnance "was a part of your life and you can't change that, and it's not that I dislike him as a person. It's just that I am jealous of the

155

obvious affection you felt and still feel, for him. I don't like the fact that you were intimate with him when that is my right alone." Fane closed his eyes and took slow deep breaths, pressing his fingers to the bridge of his nose.

When he looked up at Jacque, she could see the struggle going on inside him. She could tell he wanted to both give her space and give in to his desire to hold on to her tightly.

Jacque got up off the bed and walked to him. This time she was not trying to beat him at his own game. She was not trying to seduce him. She only wanted to reassure him. At that moment, she realized she wanted to be his, and she desperately wanted him to be hers and no other's.

She put her arms around his waist and laid her head on his chest. Fane answered her unspoken thought. "I am only yours, my Luna. I was yours from my first breath, and I will be yours until my last."

Jacque closed her eyes as tears ran slowly down her cheeks. She pulled him closer to her as his hands rubbed her back, and he kissed the top of her head. When she pulled back to look up at him, he took his hands from her back and gently held her face. Then he did the sweetest thing Jacque had ever experienced.

Fane kissed her forehead, he kissed her eyes, he kissed her cheeks and her nose, he kissed her chin, and when she thought she couldn't wait any longer, he kissed her lips. It was soft and slow and tender. Jacque let out a soft moan that made Fane growl. He increased the pressure of his lips on hers, and the kiss became much more passionate.

Finally, Fane pulled away and leaned his forehead against hers. To Jacque's relief, he was just as breathless, and it took a moment to compose himself.

"I think it's time for me to say good night, love, or my good intentions of keeping your virtue until we are bonded just might take a backseat to my hormones," he said and, from the look on his face, it was obvious he desired her.

Jacque smiled at him. She didn't want to be separated from him for even a minute, but she knew her mom would never let Fane spend the night, no matter if he was her mate or not.

"Sorin is staying here to help give you and your mom protection. If at any point you feel unsafe, call to me. I realize your mom is not completely comfortable about you and I being mated, but I need you to understand your safety comes first, and I will not leave you unprotected just to acquiesce to your mom. Do you understand this?" Fane asked her earnestly.

Jacque knew her mom would want her safe even if that meant Fane being at their house every day, and that idea suited her just fine.

"Are you always this bossy?" Jacque asked him, ignoring his question.

"When it comes to your safety, yes. I retain the right to be bossy," Fane told her. He hugged her close one more time and then let her go. Jacque immediately felt lonely without his touch. It shocked her because she felt close to tears over him leaving. *Good grief, Jacque. Get a grip. He's just going across the street."*

"That is part of the bond, love. It is hard for mates to be apart for very long and for them not to share their thoughts. A mate's soul is not complete without the other, and mates need that closeness—they crave it," he explained to her.

"What am I supposed to do while we are apart? I mean, goodness, Fane, you haven't left yet, and I'm sad over the mere idea of you gone," she told him desperately.

Fane placed his hand on her neck, on the very spot his lips had been earlier. "I will come to you the instant you ask for me. If I have to sleep on the floor right outside your door, I will do it if that's what you need."

Then Fane said the one thing Jacque did not expect to hear.

"I love you, my Luna. I was made to love you, to protect, and provide for you. Never hesitate to tell me or ask me for what you need."

Jacque stood up on her toes and kissed Fane firmly on the lips. She pulled away quickly and said, "You better go now before I beg you to stay." She turned him toward her bedroom door and pushed him out.

She didn't want to watch him walk away from her, as silly as that might be. Instead of using words, she sent him a picture from her mind. It was of him holding her close. She was tilting her head to the side like wolves do to show submission, and like a female would do for her mate to fulfill the Blood Rites. She had no idea where the thought came from. Maybe it was her subconscious letting him know she would submit to the Blood Rites ceremony. *That's news to me.*

In her mind, she heard Fane growl in response to the thought, but all he said was, *"Soon, my love, very, very soon."*

Jacque shivered at his words. *"Oh goody,"* she responded sarcastically.

Hey, what else would he expect from her? Sarcasm was her specialty.

Jacque went over to her window and sat in the seat, staring out at the street. She was waiting for Fane to leave her house, so she could watch him walk back to the Henrys'. Yep, she had it bad. She saw Sorin step out and then Fane after him. Sorin hugged Fane again. *Man, they are a touchy bunch, aren't they?* Then they talked for a few minutes. When they finally parted, Sorin positioned himself directly in front of Fane, put his hand over his heart, bowed slightly, and turned his head to expose his neck. The only response from

Fane to acknowledge Sorin's obvious submission was a curt nod. Then Sorin turned and walked back into Jacque's house.

Before Fane turned away to walk back to the Henrys' house he looked up at her window. At first, Jacque wanted to duck away, embarrassed at being caught watching him … again. Then she figured what the hey. How often did she get to hanker after hot Romanians?

"I would hope you don't hanker after any other … Romanian, hot, or otherwise. Luna, what does that even mean?" Fane sent her his thoughts.

"You're really going to have to invest in a good dictionary and thesaurus. You know that, right?"

She watched as he blew her a kiss, and she couldn't help thinking how much she would have rather her lips been on the receiving end of that kiss instead of his hand. Her neck tingled at the thought of his lips, and she was telling herself to get a grip when she realized she had missed something earlier. Jacque jerked her window up and leaned out.

"Fane, you conveniently forgot to tell me how *I* take your blood," Jacque told him.

"I didn't forget. I thought that would be obvious, love," Fane replied. "You get to bite me back." Fane winked at her, grinned, then turned to walk back to the Henrys'.

"If you don't want to bite him, I will."

Jacque turned to see Sally and Jen standing in her doorway. Sally lifted her right hand, which held a coffee mug. "Hot chocolate?" she asked.

"You better believe it," Jacque said.

FANE SMILED to himself as he walked across the street toward his host family's house. He hadn't forgotten to tell Jacquelyn she would have to bite him. He had just been waiting for the right moment because he was quickly learning his Luna was unpredictable. He didn't know if she would be happy about getting revenge for him biting her, or if the idea of having to bite him hard enough to draw blood would be the final shove that pushed her over the edge. To his relief, she didn't freak out … yet. She simply looked confused, and he figured it would sink in shortly and she would contact him later tonight.

Halfway up the stairs to his room, he ran into Brian. "How was the date?" Brian asked waggling his eyebrows.

"It was good. Jacquelyn is a wonderful girl," Fane answered.

"You gonna take her out again?"

"I hope so. I didn't ask her tonight. You know, didn't want to come across as obsessive or anything," Fane told him and chuckled to himself. He knew he was beyond obsessed, but then again, she wasn't just a girl he liked. She wasn't just a crush. So honestly, he was being pretty reasonable about the whole situation. *Yeah, keep telling yourself that.*

"Oh, you had a phone call while you were out," Brian told him.

"A phone call? Was it from my parents?" Fane asked.

"No, it was from Steven, the salesman from the dealership. He asked that you call him back tonight and that it was very important. I wrote his number down and taped it to your door."

"Okay, thank you," Fane replied absentmindedly as he continued up the stairs past Brian.

"I'll see you in the morning," Brian called to him.

"Yeah, see you."

As Fane walked into his bedroom, he pulled the paper off the door.

For a moment, he just stared at the piece of paper, not sure if he should call his Alpha first or return Steve's call. He decided to call Steve first because then he could relay the conversation to his father afterward.

Fane picked up the phone and dialed the number Brian had written on the paper. He listened to it ring four times before someone finally answered.

"Hello," the voice said.

"I'm calling to speak with Steve, please," Fane said politely.

"Hold, please."

Fane waited for several minutes before another voice came on the line. He tried not to think about all the scenarios that could play out under the circumstances and, unfortunately, each was no better than the other.

"Is this the pup from Romania?" a deep voice asked.

"If by *pup* you mean the Romanian prince of the *Canis lupus*, then you are correct," Fane responded, already wanting to growl. "To whom do I have the displeasure of speaking?" Fane asked.

"My name is Lucas Steele. I am the Alpha of the Coldspring pack. I'm calling to find out why you are still in my territory when you have not been sanctioned to be here. Not only that, but why are staying across the street from the female I have claimed as my own?" Lucas asked, his voice becoming a growl the longer he spoke.

Fane's eyes began to glow, he felt his canines lengthen, and he closed his eyes to gain composure. This mutt had dared to claim Jacquelyn as his, and if he came near his mate, Fane would rip the man's throat out. Once he was calm and able to speak, Fane responded, "There is no record of your pack. Therefore, I do not have to seek permission to be here. As for the female you are referring to, unless you can prove that she is indeed your mate, then you have no claim on her."

Fane heard a low growl on the other end of the phone. He waited for Lucas to respond and for a moment thought the other wolf was no longer there, but then he heard him speak. "Are you trying to say that you can prove she is *your* mate?" Lucas asked.

"*Da*, yes."

Lucas then said the very thing Fane had been hoping to avoid. "Then I challenge you for the bonding ceremony."

Fane was silent.

"You know how this works, correct?" Lucas asked. "Regardless, let me refresh your memory. Even if she does carry your marks, she is not bonded to you, and therefore, I have the right to challenge you for the bonding ceremony. If I win, this means you die, then I will take the female as my mate, and she will be bonded with me. If you win, well, the outcome is obvious," Lucas explained.

Fane took a deep breath. His Alpha was going to be livid. This was not how Fane had expected to start his senior year in high school.

He needed to get Jacque and her mother away from this lunatic. There was nothing else for it. He was just going to have to take them back home to Romania. It was sure Jacque wouldn't take it well. He didn't know how Lilly would react. She at least understood how dangerous *Canis lupus* could be.

Fane had to buy himself some time in order to get Jacquelyn and her mother out of the country, which meant she would have to go without him. He didn't like that idea, but he would do whatever he could to keep her safe.

"I can do nothing else but accept. However, I have the right to request my Alpha be present at the challenge to ensure a fair fight, and because he is in Romania, it will take two days for him to get here," Fane told him.

"I know the rules. You may call your Alpha to come and witness. But during those two days, Jacquelyn ...," Lucas paused when Fane snapped his teeth and growled, but then continued without showing in any way he had noticed Fane's reaction. "... will be under house arrest just in case you were planning on trying to smuggle her away while we await your Alpha. I will be coming by to inform her of my intentions. I will keep two guards at her house, and you will not be permitted to see her during this time," Lucas explained.

Fane was quickly losing control of his composure, and Lucas Steele finally pushed him over the edge. Fane's nails grew and sharpened. His face began to lose its human shape as the wolf tried to push himself out. His mate was in danger—another male was attempting to take her from him—and it wanted blood.

"Fane, are you alright? What's wrong? Something's wrong so don't try to tell me it's not 'cause I will kick your butt if you lie to me after that whole 'there will be no half-truths and lies and blah, blah, blah,' so spit it out." Fane heard Jacquelyn in his thoughts, and her voice calmed the wolf immediately. Fane realized at that moment how precious having a mate was, for only she could tame his wolf.

"*Something* is *wrong, but I cannot tell you what right now. Please trust me. Give me a few minutes, and I will explain.*" He knew he was going to have to tell her everything, especially since this Lucas Steele was going to her house. At least Sorin was there and would protect her with his life. She is to be Fane's queen one day, and she is to be valued above Sorin's life.

"Fine, five minutes. Then I want you at my front door to talk to me face to face," Jacquelyn demanded.

"I will be there," Fane answered.

Fane hadn't realized that Lucas was asking him a question since he had been distracted by his mate's thoughts.

"Do you understand the terms I have laid out for you regarding the bonding ceremony challenge?"

"I do," Fane said.

"Then I expect to receive a phone call the minute your

Alpha is here. My wolves will be at her house in one hour. You have until then to see her. I would advise you to not let my wolves catch you touching her. As you know, while the challenge stands, you cannot attempt to bond with her or you forfeit." Then the line went dead.

Fane paced around his room pulling the wolf back. His nails returned to their normal length, his canines receded, and when he looked in the mirror, he saw that, although his face had gone back to normal, his eyes still glowed ice blue. *Well," I think that's the best I can do.* He felt his wolf stir as if to tell him he was lucky all that was left of the phase were glowing eyes.

Fane's wolf had never been that angry before. He and his wolf were in agreement that the idea of this other Alpha anywhere near their mate was infuriating. Fane was not sure how he was going to manage refraining from crossing the street and tearing Lucas Steele into pieces. Fane looked at the clock and realized it had been four minutes since he had heard from Jacquelyn and, because he wouldn't put it beyond her to march across the street if he didn't show up, he decided he'd better get over there.

For the sake of expediency, and to keep from bothering Brian and Sara, Fane decided to take the window. Two stories might have been a challenge for a human, but for a Grey, jumping is second nature. He leaped to the ground, then set off at a jog to Jacquelyn's door.

When he got there, she was already standing on the porch with a robe wrapped around her, foot tapping, and wearing a look that would make even an Alpha Grey stop in his tracks. She looked adorable.

"What the hell was that? Do you make it a habit to jump out of two-story structures? Were you thinking, 'Hey, the front door is such a typical way to leave a place why not mix it up a bit, ya know, throw some vava in the voom and fall out of the window instead'?" Jacquelyn asked sarcastically while trying to catch her breath from her little rant.

"Relax, Luna, I didn't fall. I jumped. Jumping is second nature to me, and I chose it because I didn't want to bother Brian or Sara. How are you?"

"How do you think I am? Here I am, sitting and drinking my hot chocolate, explaining to my two best friends that I have to bite some guy, you know, the usual, and BAM." Jacquelyn clapped her hands together to emphasize her words. "I'm nearly knocked over by a wave of emotion or something," she finished, sounding less aggressive and wearier than she had when she had started.

Fane took her hand in his, brought it to his lips, and kissed it gently. She shuddered in response. He hated that he was causing her distress, especially since it was about to get worse. Knowing the wolves would be there soon, Fane didn't have much time to waste.

"I need you to get your mom, love. I will get Sorin," Fane told her.

"Why? What's wrong, Fane?"

"Let's get inside, gather everyone, and I will explain. Bring Jen and Sally also, please," Fane said as he led her in the house.

"Sorin is in the room down the hall from the kitchen," Jacquelyn told him.

Fane liked that there was distance between the other wolf and his mate, but the logical part of his brain that was not yet affected by his possessive streak worried it was too far for him to be able to protect her effectively.

Fane headed toward Sorin's room as Jacquelyn went to get her friends and mother.

Before Fane could even turn the corner to go down the hall toward Sorin's room, his guard was there. Sorin exposed his neck in submission to his Prince and then asked, "Have you called your father yet?"

"Not yet. I want to talk to Jacquelyn and her mother first and let them know what is going on. The wolf claiming to be Alpha of this territory is sending Greys over here to watch Jacquelyn's house. I don't think he is aware you are here, and we need to keep it that way," Fane told him.

Fane and Sorin made their way back to the living room and saw all four ladies seated on the couch. Fane wanted to have Jacquelyn sit by him, but he relinquished the idea, knowing she needed to be close to the people she trusted most.

I trust you, Fane. He heard Jacquelyn's thought in his mind, and as she said it, she stood up and came to him. He took her hand and led her to the loveseat. That small act made Fane's heart swell with love for his mate.

Lilly looked a little sad when she saw her daughter sitting next to Fane, but she quickly shook it off. "Fane, tell us, please," Lilly said.

"There is a pack of Greys here in Coldspring, and the Alpha, Lucas Steele, contacted me. He is claiming Jacquelyn as his mate." Fane couldn't help the growl that came out as he said this last part.

"The hell I am!" Jacquelyn yelled, abruptly standing up. "I don't even know this crackpot." She looked at her mom. "Do I?" she asked, sounding less confident.

"No, Jacque," Lilly answered. "I don't know him either. Fane, have you seen him?"

"No, I have not met him in person." Fane turned to Jacquelyn. "You will know him soon enough, *meu inimă*, my heart. He is planning on coming here tomorrow to tell you himself."

"Just who the hell does this guy think he is? He can't just march his furry butt up in Jacque's house, and if he thinks he can, he has obviously underestimated my ability to go all kung fu on his hide," Jen ranted.

Fane smiled at her, appreciating her loyalty to his mate.

"Will you be with me?" Jacquelyn asked him, sounding like she already knew the answer.

"No, love, I will not be able to. Lucas has challenged me for the bonding ceremony. I cannot be with you until after the fight. He is allowed to see you one time to let you know of his intentions, and then he is not allowed to see you either," Fane explained.

"What do you mean he challenged you for the bonding ceremony? What fight?" Jacquelyn asked.

Fane took her hand and pulled her down next to him on the loveseat. "Because we are not bonded, any male has the right to challenge me to be your mate, even if they are not your true mate. I have no choice but to accept the challenge. What that means, Jacquelyn, is that Lucas and I will fight in our wolf forms. The one left standing will be your mate."

"When you say, 'the one left standing,' you're saying the one left alive, aren't you?" she asked him.

"Yes, love, the fight is to the death," he answered.

Jacquelyn sat quietly for a few moments. Her head was down so he could not see what her eyes would tell him.

"Are you alright?" Fane asked through his thoughts as he placed a hand under her chin and pulled her face up to look at him.

"No, Fane, I am most definitely not alright. I'm freaking out at the moment if you must know. The idea of bonding, or whatever, with you, was crazy. The idea of bonding with a total stranger, a stranger that happens to be a werewolf, mind you, is beyond my ability to remain reasonable," Jacquelyn told him.

"I second that motion," Sally said.

"I third it," Jen put in.

"You can't third something, you dork. You just say 'aye' to show you are in agreement," Sally told her.

Jen just stuck her tongue out at Sally and ignored her comment.

"You aren't going to be bonding with anyone but me!" He growled.

"Yeah, yeah, beat your chest if you need to while you're at it, Tarzan," Jacquelyn said sarcastically.

"I will request my Alpha be present at the fight, but it will take two days for him to arrive. I was going to try and have Sorin smuggle you and your mom out of the country, but Lucas suspected as much and is putting your house under watch by his wolves. However, he is not aware that Sorin is staying here, so that is to our benefit. Should I lose—"

"You will NOT lose!" Jacquelyn said firmly.

Fane continued as if she had not spoken. "Sorin will get you and your mom to safety. You must promise me, Luna, that you will go with him and allow my pack to keep you and your mother safe."

"I will make no such promise because nothing, and I mean absolutely nothing, is going to happen to you. If you get as much as a scratch on your handsome face, I'm going to kick your werewolf a—"

Before Jacquelyn could finish, Fane had his mouth on hers, kissing her firmly.

"Finally, I get some action!" Jen exclaimed.

When Fane finally pulled back from Jacquelyn, she looked a little dazed. She quickly recovered, however. "You just kissed me," she said.

"I did, love," Fane responded with a sly grin.

"In front of my mom," Jacquelyn said, clearly embarrassed.

"And Sorin and your friends as well," Fane pointed out, sounding smug.

"Don't be a smart-ass," Jacquelyn told him.

Fane stood up and looked at his watch. He only had ten minutes left with his mate. It infuriated him that he had to obey the rules of the challenge, but if he did not, he could wind up having to forfeit and lose her. The thought made his heart hurt. He tugged her up off the loveseat, not caring about their audience, and kissed her like it might be their last. He held her face tenderly in his hands and tried to memorize her features ... how soft her skin was. He pulled back abruptly and turned away, overwhelmed with such strong emotions he didn't know what to do. Fane wanted to crush something. He wanted blood—the blood of the one who dared to take his mate. He was breathing hard, and his eyes were glowing when Jacquelyn spoke.

"You kissed me again!" she said, stomping her foot like a child. "Is PDA a big thing with your pack, 'cause that could be a problem," she continued but stopped as soon as Fane turned to face her, and she saw his eyes.

CHAPTER 11

*J*acque's breath caught when Fane turned toward her and she saw his eyes glowing, like when you see an animal at night and light hits their eyes. *Freaky.* She realized once she got over the shock of his eyes, that Fane was on the verge of losing control. She was not sure what might happen if he did, and she could tell he was fighting for it as hard as he could. She didn't know what to do or how to help him.

Jacque was too busy staring at Fane to realize Jen had walked up beside her. "He needs you to tame the beast that is roaring inside him to kill something. Go to him," Jen whispered and then pushed Jacque toward Fane. Jacque looked at Jen and then at Sally. She couldn't believe something so profound had come out of Jen's mouth.

Sally shrugged. "Who knew?" she said answering Jacque's unspoken question.

Jacque turned her attention back to Fane as she walked to him. She was close enough she could feel his breath on her face. She reached up and laid her hand on his cheek. His eyes closed, and he leaned into her hand like a dog begging to be petted. Jacque smiled, but then she felt his anger, fear, and jealousy flow through her. Fane's eyes snapped open, and he stared into her eyes.

"I have not meant to scare you. I would say that my wolf is the one out of control, but that would be a lie. The man is just as out of control as the wolf right now, and that makes me very dangerous." Fane shared his thoughts with her.

You would never hurt me," Jacque told him in complete confidence.

"No, it is impossible for a Grey to harm his mate. Others, however, innocent or not, cannot have that guarantee. I have to go, Jacquelyn. Lucas' wolves will be here any minute, and in the state, I am in I cannot guarantee I will be civilized with them," Fane told her.

Jacque shook her head before he even finished speaking. "I don't want you to go," she whispered.

Fane pulled her to the side and turned so his back was facing the others and she was shielded from their sight. He moved her hair away from her neck and kissed her in the same spot he had before, the spot where he would leave his mark. *It better be his mark.*

"I love you, Luna," Fane told her.

"What does Luna mean?" she asked him.

"I will tell you soon, but now is not the time. I must go before the other wolves get here." He held her a moment more then stepped away.

Jacque snatched his hand before he could get much further and pulled him to her. She looked him in the eyes, still seeing the wolf glowing there.

"I love you, but if you let this Alpha take me as his mate, I will die just so I can come kick your royal, Romanian butt. Got it?" Jacque asked him.

"Say it again," Fane told her.

"Say that I will kick your royal Romanian butt?"

171

"No, love, say the first part.".

It dawned on Jacque what he was talking about, and it made her smile. She leaned in and whispered, "I love you."

"Thank you," Fane said so softly she almost missed it. He kissed her on the forehead and turned back to the others. He looked at Sorin, who stepped forward and bared his neck again.

"You will protect her with your life, or you forfeit it," Fane told him in a voice Jacque had never heard him use.

Sorin sank to his knees, and it didn't look like he meant to. It was like someone had forced him there. She heard a whine come from Sorin, and then Fane walked to him and laid his hand on his head. He said something in Romanian then walked to the front door.

Jacque rushed to follow him. Just as she stepped out, a car stopped in front of her house and two men got out. Jacque grabbed Fane's arm, not in fear of herself but fear for him. Fane instinctively took her hand without thinking about the fact that Lucas had said he didn't want his wolves to see Fane touching her.

As soon as he touched her the other wolves growled, baring their teeth, their eyes glowing. Jacque's breathing increased, and her hand tightened on Fane's.

Fane turned to her. "You have to let go, love. They are growling because I'm touching you."

"I don't give a flying sack of crap that they don't like you touching me. I will touch who I want. I will bond with who I want, and I will not have mangy mutts growling at me in my own yard," Jacque yelled. She let go of Fane's hand and walked toward the other wolves.

Fane was so surprised he'd barely reached her when she got in the face of one of the men. She had her finger in his face and was yelling every expletive known to man, and some not known, for that matter. Jacque had never felt so angry. How dare this Lucas whoever try to tell her what to do, dictate who could touch her, or challenge her mate?

The wolf she was yelling at was leaning back as far as he could to keep from touching her. She was no longer aware of her surroundings. She had tunnel vision, and the only thing she could see was this wolf in front of her who dared to come in her territory. She didn't pause at that moment to think about the fact she had just called her yard her territory. She would file that away for later.

Jacque felt something touch her arm. She saw the face of the werewolf in front of her and heard him growl ferociously. She turned to see who had touched her. It was Fane. He was saying her name and trying to pull her back from the other wolf. Jacque realized they had an audience since everyone in her house had now come outside. She didn't bother to stop and look around to see if any of the neighbors were watching.

Jen was marching down the walkway and right into the other wolf's face. She put her hands on her hips and glared at him. "You think I'm scared of you, hairball?" she asked sarcastically. "I'm your worst nightmare. Just remember we all gotta sleep sometime, so I hope you can sleep with one eye open." She winked at him and then turned to walk back to the house.

Jacque finally let Fane pull her away from the car then he stepped away from her, and though she tried not to let it hurt her, she couldn't stop the stab of rejection she felt.

"I'm not rejecting you, meu inimă, my heart. Please believe that. I'm trying to protect you," Fane told her through his thoughts.

She looked at him and nodded her head in acknowledgment as she watched him face the other wolves. He walked past them, and when he made it to the street, he turned and told them, "If either of you touches her, I will kill you and use your pelt as a rug."

Jacque watched him the entire way until the door to the Henrys' was closed. One of the wolves standing in her yard walked up to her and bared his neck to her.

"Do you think it wise to bare your throat to the one who would rather see it torn out?" Jacque asked, surprising herself for sounding so confident and in control, despite the emptiness she felt without Fane by her side.

"I bare my throat in acknowledgment of my Alpha's mate," the wolf told her.

"Then you bare it in vain because I am NOT your Alpha's mate. If he kills every wolf on this earth, I will still not be his mate." Jacque growled.

"Go inside, my Luna. I can feel how tired you are," she heard Fane tell her.

"I am just fine, thank you very much. I will go inside, but not because you told me to. I'm just tired of standing out here with these buttheads," Jacque responded.

She heard Fane laugh. She felt his joy and that made her smile, which made the wolf in front of her cock his head to the side like a dog looking quizzical. Jacque blew a breath out in exasperation and turned to go into the house. Before she could make it in the front door, one of the wolves spoke. "Lucas said to tell you he will be here at 9:00 a.m."

When Jacque walked in the living room, everyone was seated, each with a mug of what she presumed was hot chocolate. Jen grinned a knowing look at her and winked. She saw Sorin sitting in the ugly chair and realized he had not been outside. *What's up with that?*

"Why did you not come out to defend your prince?" she asked him, sounding a little more accusatory than she meant to.

"The wolves do not know there is a Grey in the house. If I

had gone out, they would have scented me immediately. We do not want to provoke them any more than we need to until we are a little more matched in numbers," Sorin explained.

The man was unflappable and it frustrated Jacque. "Yeah, yeah, I get it," she said.

Despite what Jacque told Fane, she was very tired. She didn't know what time it was, and frankly, she didn't care. She suddenly just wanted to lie down and sleep. Sally and Jen must have picked up on this because they got up and took their mugs to the kitchen then came back and led Jacque upstairs. They helped her lie down and cover her with a blanket. Jacque watched them blearily as they sat on the floor. She could see the worried looks on their faces.

"I know she's tough, but I think this is wearing her out," Sally said.

"Well, duh!" Jen responded. "Wouldn't it wear you out if you just met the man of your dreams then it turns out he's a werewolf, then turns out you're his mate or whatever, then it turns out there's this other pack of wolves with a psycho, werewolf leader who wants you as his mate, then it turns out..." Jen paused. "You get the picture."

"When you put it like that, it is a lot to take in," Sally agreed.

Jacque didn't have the energy to respond. Instead, she slowly drifted off into a fitful sleep.

JACQUE WOKE up to the sound of Fane's voice, and for a moment she thought he was there in her room but quickly realized he was talking to her through his thoughts.

"Luna, wake up please," Fane said.

"Haven't we talked about this whole waking-me-up-way-too-early-could-be-hazardous-to-your-health thing?" Jacque said.

"I'm sorry to wake you, love, but I wanted to talk with you before Lucas arrives."

"Ugh! I was hoping this was all a bad dream," she moaned. "Well, not you, but I mean the part about this Lucas dude and the challenge."

"I'm sorry, Jacquelyn," Fane told her sadly.

"Ah well, that's how it goes. I'm too irresistible for my own good," Jacque teased, trying to lighten the mood.

"That you are, Luna," Fane replied.

Jacque picked up her phone to look at the time and saw that it was eight-thirty. Crap, she needed to get up and get dressed. *What do you wear to talk to a crazy, Alpha werewolf?*

"As much clothing as possible," Fane answered her thought.

"I was thinking maybe I should wear that bikini you like so much," she teased him.

"That would be a very poor choice, Luna. I want your marks covered completely," Fane replied.

"I think a please is in order," Jacque told him.

Fane growled but then relinquished. *"Please, love."*

"Oh, alright, since you're not being all jealous or possessive," Jacque smarted off.

Jacque got up and tiptoed around her two best friends. She wondered if their parents knew they were at her house. Jacque figured they must know or the National Guard would be out looking for them. She stepped into her closet and flipped through the shirts hanging there. She honestly hadn't realized how many T-shirts she had with smart-ass sayings on them. *Go figure.*

The one she finally settled on made her smile. It was a black, baby-tee that had a picture of Edward from *Twilight* on the front, and "Team Edward" on the back. That made her laugh out loud. "Take that, you mangy werewolf."

"You're just too pleased with yourself, aren't you?" she heard Fane say.

"Hey, get out of my head, you perv. I'm trying to get dressed." Jacque feigned outrage.

"Sorry, love, I was just curious to see what you would pick. Your sense of humor is one of the things I love most about you. Please be safe, don't provoke Lucas, oh, and maybe it would be wise to keep Jen away from him," Fane told her.

"Good idea. I feel like I should say bye, or talk to you later, but that's just weird," Jacque told him.

"How about I just tell you I love you?" Fane asked her.

Jacque smiled. "I love you, wolfman."

The last thing Jacque heard was Fane's deep chuckle. She could feel him pull away from her thoughts, and she felt bereft. Jacque took a deep breath, started going through her jeans, and picked out a low-rise pair of cargo pants.

She walked back through her room, past Sally and Jen, out her door, and to the bathroom to dress and throw her hair up in a ponytail. Jacque realized once her hair was up that the marks on her neck came up above the collar of her shirt.

"Hells bells." She huffed and pulled her hair back down. She pulled the front out of her face and secured it back with bobby pins. "That's as good as it's gonna get," Jacque told her reflection in the mirror.

When she walked back into her room Sally and Jen were both up, stretching and yawning. They took one look at her shirt and cracked up laughing.

"You are my hero," Jen told her.

"Kill 'em with sarcasm. I always knew that was your motto," Sally told her, still laughing.

"I'm sorry I crashed on y'all like that last night. I was just so tired. I don't think I have ever been that tired," Jacque told them.

"Well, it's not like you're under any stress or anything," Jen said sarcastically.

Jacque grabbed a pair of flip-flops from under her bed and slipped them on. As she reached for her phone, she heard Jen's phone start playing the *Jaws* theme song. Sally and Jacque looked at her. "It's my mom's ring tone."

"Nice," Sally and Jacque said at the same time.

Jen answered her phone and stepped out in the hall to talk to her mom.

"Do your parents know you are still here?" Jacque asked Sally.

"Yeah, I called them last night. Your mom talked to both my parents and Jen's," Sally answered.

"She did? What did she tell them?" Jacque asked.

"She asked them if they minded if we stayed the rest of the week for a final vacation before school starts. Just the girls, doing girl things like facials and pedicures and whatnot. They totally bought it and thought it was so nice of your mom to let us all get one final week of relaxation before our stressful senior year starts," Sally said as she put the back of her hand on her forehead and swooned.

"My mom totally rocks," Jacque said.

"I totally do, don't I?" Lilly said, standing in Jacque's doorway.

"Hey, Mom, what's up?" Jacque asked her.

Lilly looked at her daughter's shirt and gave her thumbs up. "Nice job on the shirt."

Jen scooted in past Lilly and plopped back down on the floor. "My mom just wanted to know if she could bring anything over for us, brownies, nail polish ... ya know, girly stuff. I told her we had it covered. She said to tell you thank you again, Lilly."

"Your mom wouldn't thank me if she knew the big, bad wolf was coming over to play," Lilly said. "Speaking of big, bad wolves, Lucas Steele is here."

Jacque's mouth dropped open. "*Here*, here? As in, in this house here?"

"Yes, Jacque, he is *here*, here," Lilly answered. "He is asking to speak with you in private."

Without even thinking about it, Jacque reached for Fane's mind. *"He's here."*

"I know, love. I saw his car drive up. Are you okay?" Fane asked her.

"I'm okay. I'm about to go talk to him. Be with me."

"Always."

Jacque asked Sally and Jen to wait in her room. She didn't want them brought to Lucas' attention.

As Jacque walked into the living room, she saw him sitting on the couch, arms spread out wide over the back, looking quite relaxed. *Smug little furball.* She was pleasantly surprised to hear Fane's chuckle in her mind.

"Are you comfortable?" Jacque asked Lucas as she walked into the living room.

When he turned to look at her, Jacque was caught off guard by his eyes, which were two different colors. His right eye was crystal blue, and his left eye was as green as ivy. He had brown, wavy hair that he wore messily, but she could tell it was a carefully placed messiness. He had a five o'clock shadow across a strong jawline, and when he smiled at her, a dimple appeared on both cheeks.

"I am. Thanks for asking," he responded.

He had a deep voice, but not quite as deep as Fane's. She had to admit he was an attractive guy. She heard Fane growl. *"Chillax, wolfman. I only have eyes for you,"* she told Fane.

"Jacque." The sound of her name brought her attention back to her living room, and she realized Lucas was now

179

standing in front of her. She had to look up to see his face. He was at least six feet, maybe a little taller. "My name is Lucas Steele. I'm sure Fane told you that I am the Alpha of the Coldspring pack."

"Yeah, he told me. He also told me you are under some sort of delusion that I am going to be your mate," Jacque retorted.

"I distinctly remember advising you not to provoke him, Luna. Do you remember that?" Jacque heard Fane's voice in her mind.

"I don't know. Some things seem kind of hazy at the moment," she responded vaguely. Fane growled again.

I have a feeling he's going to be doing a lot of that being mated to me.

"I claimed you before he even knew you existed. You should be mine," Lucas told her calmly.

Jacque was staring at him intently trying to get a lock on how old he was. She could tell he was older than her, but she couldn't quite tell how much older.

"How old are you?" she finally asked.

He looked a little surprised by her question. That's good, keep him on his toes.

"I'm twenty-two," he answered.

"You do realize that I am not eighteen yet, so that makes me jailbait?" Jacque pointed out.

"Human laws do not matter to our kind. Besides, I'm not saying we have to consummate our relationship, just that you will bond with me," Lucas told her.

"You so did not just say that. I mean, good freaking grief man. Is that all you wolves talk about?" Jacque asked, obviously annoyed.

Lucas looked a little confused then caught on. "Are all human females this silly?" he asked her.

"I am not silly," Jacque said indignantly. His eyes

wandered down to the front of her shirt, and she realized he had noticed the vampire depicted there. She smiled and then turned around to show him the back, without thinking about it beforehand, she pulled her hair up so he could read the words.

At first, he was silent as he read it, but then she heard a deep, feral growl.

Jacque dropped her hair back down and turned slowly. Lucas' eyes were glowing, and his teeth had grown quite long. His breathing was fast, and she could tell he was struggling to keep his wolf under control.

"He wasn't lying when he said he could prove you were his mate," Lucas said, his words a little difficult to understand because of the length of his teeth.

Jacque's eyes got big as she realized he had seen her marks. Just then she heard a ferocious snarl and realized Fane had caught that last thought.

"I'm sorry, Fane. I didn't mean to show him the marks. I accidentally lifted my hair and—"

"Pay attention to Lucas, Jacquelyn. Look at him, and let me see his face," Fane instructed her.

Jacque pictured Lucas in her mind just as she was seeing him.

"Jacque, you must be careful. He is not in control of his wolf," Fane told her.

"Yeah, ya think," Jacque accidentally said aloud.

Lucas snarled and his eyes narrowed. "Are you able to speak through each other's thoughts? Are you speaking to him now?" he asked her.

"Umm, maybe and not your business," she answered.

Lucas lunged at her, grabbing her by the arms. Jacque slammed the wall down in her mind so Fane could not see what Lucas was doing. She had no idea how Fane would react to Lucas' actions, but she guessed it wouldn't be good.

She couldn't risk him barreling through the front door and murdering the man right in her living room. Jacque was quite certain pre-challenge murder was against the contest rules.

"Do not play games with me. I am an Alpha, and you will answer me truthfully, mate." He growled in her face.

Jacque jerked her arms free and stepped back from him.

"Listen carefully, Lucas Steele, because I will only say this once. I am NOT your mate, I will never be your mate, and if you ever put your hands on me again, I will cut them off along with other body parts you might want to use one day. Got it?" Jacque told him with as much force as she could put behind her words.

"That's a shame too because you're kind of cute. But it happens to the best of them," Jen said as she sauntered into the living room with Sally right behind her.

"And the worst of them," Sally finished for her.

Both girls stood on either side of Jacque with their arms crossed, an obvious wall of solidarity against Lucas.

Lilly walked into the living room and took in the scene. She looked at Jacque and saw the red marks now appearing on her arms from were Lucas had grabbed her daughter and Lilly's mouth tightened in anger.

"I think it's time for you to go now, Mr. Steele," Lilly told him in forced politeness.

Lucas turned his gaze on Lilly, who took an involuntary step back. He took a deep breath, obviously trying to compose himself, then looked at Jacque, "I have challenged Fane for the bonding ceremony. If I win, you will be mine. Nothing and no one will keep you from me." And with that, he turned to walk out the front door.

All four of them followed him, and when they got out the door, they saw Fane jump from his second-story window, take two bounding steps, and land right in front of Lucas.

Three men climbed out of Lucas' waiting vehicle and surrounded Fane and Lucas.

"Oh, S@#T! Jen hollered

"I second that," Sally said

"I third it," Jacque said, eyes so wide they threatened to pop out of her head.

FANE SAW Lucas lunge for Jacquelyn before she could put the wall up between their minds, and the rage he felt called his wolf to the surface. Fane was nearly completely phased when he heard Sara chattering downstairs. That was enough to pull him back so he could keep from becoming a huge, black, snarling wolf in his bedroom. It wasn't enough, however, to keep him from growling like a dog with rabies. The anger he was feeling was so tangible it was making it hard for him to breathe.

Lucas had touched his mate. He had put his hands on her in a threatening way, and by doing so, he had violated the challenge rules. That meant Fane would be allowed to see Jacquelyn for the duration of the two days they had to wait until his father arrived. Because he was Jacquelyn's true mate, challenge rules say he can protect her if the challenger causes physical harm to the female.

Before the thought was even complete in his mind, and without any thought to who might see him, he leaped out his window into the front yard. He took two giant steps and jumped, landing right in front of Lucas Steele. He was dimly aware of other men exiting Lucas' car and surrounding him, but he paid them no heed. He'd rip all their throats out if need be.

Lucas crouched low immediately, growling. "If you touch me you forfeit the challenge."

"Ai rănit ceea ce este al meu, you harmed what is mine." Fane snarled.

"Oh crap, he's talking in Romanian and that means he's pissed, doesn't it? They always talk in their native tongue in the movies when they're fixing to kick somebody's a—" Jen tried to finish but Jacquelyn slapped her hand over Jen's mouth and shook her head from side to side.

"Let me translate for her," Sally said. "Shut the #@$% up, Jen!"

"My bad," Jen whispered once Jacquelyn had uncovered her mouth.

Fane could not remember a time when he had been so angry. He could feel his wolf pushing to come out, to defend their mate. *"Ați încălcat regulile de provocare*, you violated the challenge rules," Fane growled.

He knew he needed to calm down, but when Fane glanced over and saw the red marks on Jacquelyn's arms, his wolf won. He phased in the blink of an eye, and had Sorin not lunged in front of him, Fane would have torn out Lucas Steele's throat.

Instead, Fane collided with Sorin and fell backward, grunting as he hit the ground. In an instant, he was back on all four feet, head low, eyes narrowed, and teeth bared. He took slow, calculating steps and placed himself in between Lucas and his mate. Jacquelyn stepped back when Fane approached and it hurt to know she was afraid of him in his wolf form.

He continued to move forward, pushing Lucas farther away, and prepared to lunge again when he heard Sorin yell, *"Nu-l atinge, prinț*! Do not touch him, Prince!"

Fane stopped in his tracks. He did not move closer, but he continued to growl and glare at Lucas.

"As Fane has said, you violated the challenge rules by causing harm to Fane's mate. Therefore, it is Fane's right to stay with her while we await the arrival of his Alpha and the time of the challenge," Sorin informed the wolf.

"Who the hell are you?" Lucas snarled.

"I am the prince's bodyguard. It is my right to be here as a witness to the proceedings."

Lucas narrowed his eyes. Had Fane been thinking rationally, he would have understood Lucas was searching his mind for a loophole. Apparently, he found none. "Regardless, I did not harm the female!" Lucas spat.

"Hey, fleabag, the female has a name!" Jen yelled.

"Jen, now is not the time, hon. Keep your trap closed," Sally said through pursed lips.

"Oh, right, sorry. I just get so carried away. I'm good. Carry on."

Sally and Jacquelyn rolled their eyes.

Lucas must have decided during that little interlude he needed to be more diplomatic because when he spoke the second time it was quite a bit nicer.

"I did not mean to cause Jacquelyn harm. I do not think red marks on her arm constitute a so-called violated challenge," he told Sorin.

"What you think does not factor into what simply is. It is time for you to take your pack and leave. Our Alpha is on the way. You will be notified immediately when he arrives."

Lucas and his men didn't move. It looked as if he was about to say more when Sorin stepped toward him and spoke again. This time his voice was calm and low. "I will regard any further refusal to leave as a direct challenge to the authority of Vasile Lupei, Alpha of the Romanian Grey Wolves? Do you really want to pit your rogue pack against the Romanians? We will descend upon you in a fury that you feeble whelps can't begin to comprehend."

Lucas's jaw clenched and unclenched as he stared at Sorin. Fane's mouth slavered as he looked up at the man.

Fane was ready to attack. He would take Lucas first, then the one to his right. Fane knew Sorin would understand to take the two on the left. They'd spent enough hours training together back home to understand perfectly each other's battle techniques.

Fane could tell Lucas was fighting with everything he had not to bare his neck to Sorin. The bodyguard's words had been an outright challenge to the rogue Alpha's authority. Lucas would now submit or attack. Fane didn't care which. The cur had touched his mate. He was already a dead man walking. The other three wolves tilted their heads in spite of themselves. Slowly, without speaking, Lucas backed away and got into his car. The other wolves followed suit. The car peeled away in a squeal of tires.

"*Cu respect, prinţul meu, vă rog să veniţi*, With respect my prince, please come."

Fane gave the retreating vehicle one more snarl for good measure then trotted over to where Jacquelyn stood. He put his head against her thigh and nudged her backward.

"You gotta be kidding me. You're even bossy when you are in your wolf form," Jacquelyn told him rolling her eyes. He nudged her again a little harder. Finally relenting, she turned to go back toward the house.

"Come on girls, show's over ... for now, anyway," she told them.

Once in the house, everyone filed into the living room which was quickly becoming the meeting room. Jacquelyn knelt in front of Fane and ran a finger down the center of his muzzle. Fane closed his eyes, and a low hum came out of his throat.

"You were great out there, you know?" she whispered to him.

Fane opened his eyes, and they just stared at each other for a minute. Then Fane licked Jacquelyn smack on the face.

"EWWWW! You have GOT to stop kissing me in public. It's getting out of hand," Jacquelyn told him, wiping her face. Fane simply looked at her with his tongue hanging out the side of his mouth in a goofy grin.

"Fane, I think we need you back in your human form, please," Sorin told him respectfully. "Let me get you some clothes." Sorin walked down the hall and reappeared a few seconds later with a pair of jeans and a shirt and handed them to Jacquelyn.

"Uh, what am I supposed to do with these?" she asked Sorin.

"What do you think, my *puțin foc*, little fire. Bring them." Fane said in her mind.

"Wait, hold on," Jen said holding her hands up, "this is obviously a job for a woman who appreciates a fine-looking specimen like wolfman."

Jen tried to take the clothes from Jacque, who stepped back and held the clothing out of Jen's reach.

Fane took a few steps up the stairs and looked back to Jacque. *Coming?*

Jacquelyn huffed out a breath and headed up the stairs after him. Fane heard Jen and Sally let out catcalls. He giggled inwardly at how red his Luna's face was.

"There are doors up there that close perfectly. No admiring of naked werewolves in this household. I don't care whose mate you are, young lady," Lilly called after Jacque.

"You go in first," said Jacque when they reached her bedroom door. He padded in and she threw the clothes in after him. Then she quickly shut the door, waiting out in the hall.

"Sure you don't want to join?" he asked through their bond.

"Quite," she replied.

"How long does this take anyway?" she asked, waiting on the other side of the door.

"How long does what take?"

"You know, the whole changing back into a human thing?"

"I've already told you, I don't change. I phase. It's much different. But it only takes seconds."

Fane heard her knock very gently on the bedroom door.

"Come on in."

He couldn't help but chuckle as she gasped at him, exactly the response Fane had wanted as he stood there with a blanket wrapped around his waist. Jacque stammered and stuttered and began to retreat. She squealed as he grabbed her wrist and pulled her against him.

"Sorry, love, didn't mean to pull you quite that hard," he told her with a sly grin.

"Uh-huh, sure you didn't," Jacquelyn said as she twisted her wrist to get free from his grasp. Fane let go easily but did not step away from her. He was still grinning as she backed up a few paces.

"What are you doing? Don't you think you need..." Jacquelyn stopped mid-sentence when her eyes wandered over Fane's torso. Fane realized she was looking at his markings, and it made his wolf happy that she noticed them.

"What do you think?" he asked her, noticing the reservations flee from her eyes.

She walked around him, circling him like a predator seeking out its prey. Her eyes narrowed as she followed the lines of the marks. A couple of times her hand reached out like she wanted to trace the marks, and it took all of Fane's control not to lean into her hand. Like the wolf, he craved her touch.

"They're beautiful. I didn't realize the marks would cover so much of you, but you said they come around to your chest because you're Alpha, right?" Jacquelyn asked, still completely mesmerized by the marks.

"That is correct. I have more marks than others." Fane

reached out and ran a finger across Jacquelyn's neck as he said this. She slapped his hand away. "No touching while you're standing in nothing but a blanket," she told him, trying to sound firm but not able to wipe the smile off her face.

When she finally stopped and just stared at him, he couldn't help but tease her. "Have you looked your fill, or do you need a few more minutes? I'd be happy to let you study them if you'd like," Fane told her with a wink.

"Yeah, I bet you'd like that, wouldn't you?"

"Well, if you are not going to take advantage of me while I am so vulnerable, I suppose I should get dressed," Fane told her grinning.

Surprisingly, she didn't respond or turn to leave. Fane decided to shock her into action. He started to unwrap his blanket. "Of course, if you want to watch me dress, you are welcome to, seeing as how you are my mate. You could even help if you'd like."

That worked. Jacquelyn turned bright red then abruptly spun around to face the door. Fane dressed quickly and tried to keep his mind out of hers, although he was very curious about what she was thinking.

"Okay, love, all done." He was slipping his shirt over his head as she turned around.

"You know you're beautiful, don't you?" Jacquelyn asked him.

"What do you mean?"

"I mean *you*, all of you. Your skin is beautiful, you're all buff and built, and your eyes are incredible. You're just beautiful," she explained.

"Well, nobody has ever told me that, so no, I did not know I was beautiful. Thank you," he said placing his hand over his heart and bowing his head. "You are exquisite. Did you know that?" he asked her.

"I wouldn't say exquisite. I mean, I don't think I'm a movie star or anything, but I suppose I don't break the mirror," she responded.

"No female I have ever seen holds a candle to you, Luna."

They were quiet for a moment. Fane was looking at her face, her beautiful green eyes and endearing freckles. He let his eyes wander down her neck to her shoulders and arms, where the red marks that were quickly becoming bruises caught his eyes. He growled low.

"Come here please, Jacquelyn," Fane told her.

Jacquelyn had stepped back at the sound of the growl.

"I am not growling at you, *meu inimă*, my heart. I merely want to look at the marks that mongrel left on you," he explained.

"It's nothing. They don't even really hurt anymore," Jacquelyn fibbed.

"Jacquelyn, love, don't tell me untruths. I know when you aren't being honest with me."

"Who are you, Santa Claus?" Jacquelyn retorted.

"Just come here, please. Do I need to come over there?" Fane asked with a wicked gleam in his eyes.

"Pipe down, I'll come to you."

Jacquelyn walked over to him, and he gently touched each arm where the bruises were. Jacquelyn flinched. Seeing the movement, realizing the pain that mongrel had caused his mate, almost caused Fane to phase all over again. Instead, he took a steadying breath and leaned down and kissed her arms gently over the bruises, wishing he could heal them with his touch. He had failed to protect her, his mate. She had needed him, and Fane had not been there.

"I'm sorry," he whispered. "I'm sorry I was not there to protect you. I should have been."

"Fane"—Jacquelyn reached up and ran her hand down his cheek—"this was not your fault. You were not allowed to be there, and how was anyone to know that psycho fur ball would hurt his so-called mate? You have nothing to apologize for, so just knock it off. Got it?"

Fane looked into her eyes and could see the sincerity there, no condemnation or anger, and he was so thankful. She was truly amazing, and she was his. Thank the moon she wanted him because he would have hated spending the rest of their lives pining after her.

"I am grateful you do not condemn me. Nonetheless, you are my mate. I should always be there to protect you, which is why you will not be out of my sight until the challenge. I will trust no one to protect you but me," Fane told her.

"I don't think my mother—"

He stopped her with a finger to her lips.

"I will talk to Lilly, but as I said before, I will not put your safety second to her approval."

She stepped forward and kissed him. When she leaned back, Fane looked at her quizzically. "What was that for?"

"Just because I can, and I wanted to," Jacquelyn told him simply.

"Oh, well, in that case…" Fane grabbed her around the waist and tossed her on the bed, covering her body with his. Jacquelyn let out a squeak as she hit the bed. He held his weight off her by supporting himself on one forearm. Then he leaned down and nuzzled her neck with his nose. Jacquelyn began to giggle and push at his chest.

"Stop that, it tickles," she told him laughing. "I'm not kidding, Fido. You're going to make me pee on you."

Fane pulled his head back to look at her. Her eyes were crinkled with laugh lines.

"I'm a wolf, not a dog, love, and if I don't get to pee on you, then you most certainly do not get to pee on me," Fane teased her.

He leaned forward and kissed her gently, and then a little

harder. By the time he pulled away, they were both trying to catch their breath.

"I think we better go downstairs now," Fane told her, still trying to get his breathing under control.

Jacquelyn reached up and stroked his face, gently pulling him closer. "Or not," she said just before she began to kiss him again.

Fane let it go on a moment more before he finally pulled away and stood, dragging her up at the same time.

"As much as I would love to stay right here with you, love, Jen might come looking for us soon and finally get that show she's been waiting for," Fane told her as he winked at her.

"Ugh. Fine, have it your way, but you're the first guy I've ever heard of that has walked away from a willing female," Jacquelyn told him.

Fane pulled her back as she tried to walk past him. "We have plenty of time, *meu inimă*, my heart, and I don't want just a willing female. I want my mate, bonded to me, wearing my mark."

"Good grief, and here I thought I was picky," she teased. "Okay, wolfman, if we're going down, let's go. Oh, and I won't be there when you decide to tell my mom you're staying. I'm going to be conveniently occupied with something that would normally be unimportant but, for some reason and at that exact moment, needs my undivided attention."

Fane ran a finger across the marks on her neck, and Jacquelyn shuddered. "Whatever makes you happy, love."

Jacquelyn rolled her eyes and took his hand as they went to join the others downstairs.

CHAPTER 12

"Seriously Sorin, how old are you?" Jacque heard Jen asking as she and Fane walked into the living room.

"Jen, are you being rude?" Jacque asked her nosy friend.

"Jen rude? Never," Sally said in mock astonishment.

Sorin was just grinning good-naturedly. "No, I don't mind her asking. A hundred and thirty-five."

The girls laughed.

"No, seriously," said Jen. "How old? Twenty-five, thirty?"

Sorin just raised his eyebrows.

"Wait," said Jen. "Is he serious?"

Fane nodded. Everyone was silent for a few heartbeats, shocked, even though Fane had told them *Canis lupus* can live for centuries. Hearing it from the mouth of one that has lived over a century was a little different.

"SHUT UP," Jen hollered. "What have you been doing for a hundred and thirty-five years? Don't you get bored?" she asked him.

"Jen, it is not essential to your livelihood to know everything about everyone. You know that, don't you?" Sally asked her.

"Maybe not, but it does make life more interesting," Jen told her

Sorin sat listening to the girls' banter, and when they were finally quiet, he leaned forward and put his elbows on his knees. "I can't say I have ever gotten bored. Humans are too interesting to ever be bored with them. I have enjoyed my long life and see it as a gift. However, I do envy the males of my species who have found their mates. I have been looking for mine all these years. My wolf grows restless, and if I weren't so close to Fane and my Alpha, I fear I might have a little pent-up aggression."

"What do you mean if you weren't close to them?" Sally asked him.

Jacque was sitting down at one end of the couch, and Fane was sitting on the floor in front of her with his back leaned up against her legs. Sorin looked at Fane as if asking for permission to speak.

Fane spoke instead. "When a wolf lives so many years without his mate he can become volatile and aggressive. The reason the female *Canis lupus* are so precious is because they balance out the male's violent nature. They bring peace to the battle constantly raging inside the wolf, especially the dominant ones. An Alpha helps keep the wolves under control. He can command the wolves in ways others, even dominants, cannot." Fane looked up at Jacque, and the look on his face made her heart ache. She didn't understand what she did for Fane, but she was grateful it was her and not some other girl.

"So am I, meu inimă, my heart," Fane told her through his thoughts.

Jacque winked at him, loving the way he listened to her, and not even minding that he was being nosy.

"Not nosy, just attentive," he told her.

She slapped his arm, "Yeah, keep telling yourself that if it makes your conscience feel better," she teased him aloud.

The whole room turned to look at them, obviously confused by the comment from Jacque that made no sense, as no one else had heard the previous comments.

"My bad," she said sheepishly.

"Must be nice to be able to talk to each other without anyone else listening to your conversation, which, by the way, would so be handy in class," Jen mused.

"Anyway," Fane continued, "that is what Sorin means when he says it helps when he is around me or my father. I am not the Alpha yet, but his wolf recognizes that I am next in line to be Alpha, and so I can control his wolf."

"I'm sorry you haven't found your mate, Sorin. It seems so unfair Fane found me when he is so young," Jacque told him as she absentmindedly traced the marks on Fane's neck.

Finally, after nobody had said anything for several minutes, Lilly stood up and suggested everyone pile in the kitchen and help make breakfast.

"Might as well. Don't want the wolves to get hungry," Jen said laughing.

"You crack yourself up, don't you?" Jacque asked.

"Quite often, actually," Jen responded.

After everyone had eaten breakfast, Fane asked Lilly if he could speak with her. Before her mom could drag her into it, Jacque grabbed her two friends and headed up to her room.

"What was all that about?" Sally asked.

"Fane is going to tell—not ask but tell—my mother he is staying in our home."

"Does he know your mom will chew him up and spit him out, werewolf or not?" Jen asked.

"I told him I would take no part in it, but he said my safety came before him trying to appease her and that he would not trust anyone else to keep me safe other than himself," Jacque explained.

"Well, maybe he's itching for a good fight after not being able to beat the crap out of that psycho wolf today," Sally said.

"Yeah, that or he's just delusional that being a prince or Alpha or whatever is going to have some bearing on what Lilly will allow. HA! Yeah, right," Jen said with a smirk.

Jacque felt a little nervous and began to wonder if she should have stayed with Fane to at least help smooth things over. *Naw, he's a big boy. He can take care of himself.*

"I heard that, Luna," she heard Fane tell her.

Jacque couldn't suppress a giggle. She was always caught off guard when he responded to one of her thoughts, especially when she wasn't thinking it *to* him. She also tried not to think about the fact she had access to his thoughts. It was weird to consider intruding.

"Intrude away, love. I have nothing to hide from you."

"Yeah, wolfman, that's what worries me." She heard him chuckle in her mind in response.

Sally and Jen were lying on Jacque's floor going through her CD's when she heard her mother yell her name.

"The stuff is going to hit the proverbial fan," Sally said.

"If I'm not back in ten minutes, come looking for my body, please," Jacque told them only half joking. Lilly could have a pretty hot temper when she got upset about something or when she was pushed in a direction she was not ready to go.

Jacque found Fane and her mom seated at the table in the dining room.

"So, what's up?" Jacque asked her mom innocently.

"Fane just informed me that he plans to stay here until after the challenge. I wanted to know what you thought about that," Lilly told her.

Jacque was a little surprised by her mom's words, so it took her a moment to formulate an answer.

"You … what … I…" Jacque tried to spit it out, but it just wasn't happening.

"Jacque, are you okay?" her mom asked her.

"I'm just a little confused. I thought you would be mad he wanted to stay here," Jacque explained.

"I want you safe. I may be a stubborn woman, but I am not a stupid one. Are you okay with him staying here?"

Jacque looked at Fane then looked away when he winked at her. She wanted to say *of course* she was okay with it, duh! Who wouldn't be okay with a major hottie with a Romanian accent staying at their house? But she didn't say that.

"I'm okay with it if you are," she answered nonchalantly.

"Alright then, I guess that's settled," Lilly said, then she turned to Fane. "Lay a paw on my little girl, and you will be a three-legged Lassie, got it?"

Fane winced and then asked, "You both do realize I'm a wolf, not a dog, right?"

Lilly shrugged and then stood up and walked over to hug Jacque.

"I have to go to the bookstore and do some work. I'm not sure when I will be home, so you will have to fend for yourselves when it comes to dinner."

"Lilly, please allow Sorin to accompany you. I do not like the idea of you out alone," Fane told her

"I don't want Sorin to have to sit around my bookstore while I work. I will be fine. No one is going to mess with me in such a public place." Lilly answered

"Maybe, maybe not, but I want Sorin to go with you." Fane's tone said the discussion was over. It was weird to hear a seventeen-year-old guy talk with such authority, and yet it seemed so natural coming from Fane.

Sorin appeared in the entryway to the dining room. He

turned his head slightly away from Fane, exposing his neck, and waited for Fane to tell him what he wanted from him.

"Sorin, please accompany Lilly to her bookstore while she works. I don't want her out alone with everything going on. I wouldn't put it past Lucas to do something stupid like snatch Lilly to force Jacquelyn to cooperate," Fane told him.

Jacque hadn't even considered something like that. Man, her life had turned into a movie. She could probably sell it to HBO and make a fortune, and she'd consider that once all this was done.

"HBO? What is that?" Fane asked her.

"You are just as nosy as Jen, aren't you?" Jacque asked him back.

Fane shrugged his shoulders and waited for her to answer his question. Jacque let out a breath and rolled her eyes.

"Oh, good grief, it's a television station. I'm thinking I could make a killing selling my story to them for a miniseries or something," she answered.

Lilly laughed and shook her head as she walked out of the dining room with Sorin on her heels.

Jacque and Fane were left in the dining room staring at each other. After a few moments, Jacque began to feel self-conscious and turned to go back up to her room.

"Hey, where are you going?" Fane asked as he reached for her arm.

"I was going to go back up to my room to see what the girls are doing. Why? Where are you going?"

"I guess I need to come up with something to tell the Henrys as to why I am going to be staying over here all the time," Fane told her.

"You could tell them the truth. You never know. They may take it well."

"I'm not sure what else I can tell them. Nothing really

makes sense as to why I would stay at your house as opposed to theirs," Fane explained.

"Do you want me to come with you?" Jacque asked him.

Fane looked surprised by the question. "You would do that for me?"

"Well, I do have some conditions, of course," Jacque teased.

"Really? And what might those be?" Fane asked her flirtatiously.

"I want Jen and Sally at the bonding ceremony thingy," Jacque blurted out.

"Is that all?" Fane asked surprised.

"Give me time, and I'll think of more, but for now that will do."

"Done," Fane answered.

"Let me run up and tell Jen and Sally we are going to go over to the Henrys'," Jacque told Fane.

Thirty minutes later, Fane and Jacque were sitting in the Henrys' living room on the couch across from Sara and Brian. Both looked a little shell-shocked by what Fane had just told them.

"Sara, Brian," Jacque spoke gently, "are you all okay?"

Sara looked at Jacque as if she just realized she was in the room.

"Are you okay?" Sara turned the question on Jacque. "I mean you're his mate, right? Are you okay with that?"

"I'm great with it. I mean, I'm still a little stunned and it does all seem very surreal, but other than that I'm rosy," Jacque told her.

Brian had still not said anything, and Jacque was beginning to wonder if he was going to be able to process this without freaking out. Then he surprised her by saying, "I knew there was something different, something special about you, Fane. I'm not saying I understand all of this, but I trust you, and I want Jacque and Lilly safe from whatever is going on. So, we believe you and support you."

"I truly appreciate your trust. I am going to try to limit my time here because I don't want to give Lucas a reason to use you against us. Please stay alert for anything odd or out of place," Fane told them.

"We can take care of ourselves. You just worry about what you need to take care of. You said your father is coming to help?" Brian asked.

"Yes, my father is coming and so is my mother, but they will only be here to keep the challenge fair. My father is a very, very strong Alpha, and few would dare to challenge or defy him."

Jacque stood up, went over to Sara, and hugged her then Brian. "Thank you both for being so awesome," she told them.

"Yes, I have to agree with Jacquelyn. You both are very awesome," Fane said shaking Brian's hand and then hugging Sara as well.

Fane, Jacque, Jen, and Sally spent the rest of the day hanging out in Jacque's room. Occasionally they would talk about the whole challenge thing, but mostly they just quizzed Fane on all things Romanian. They asked him what different words were in Romanian. Jen wanted to know how to curse in Romanian. Go figure. He told them about the folklore of werewolves and vampires. Jacque steered the conversation quickly away from that because she didn't want to know if vampires were real. She was just coming to terms with were-wolves, and there was no need to overwhelm her already wavering sanity.

Fane was a good sport, even when Jen tried to ask about Fane's personal dating experience and the like. He just winked at her and politely said, "A prince doesn't kiss and tell, Jen."

Of course, the wink nearly made Jen hyperventilate, and so it was only fair for Jacque to slap Fane on the arm for nearly making her friend pass out because he was so freaking hot.

"I don't understand why you're hitting me, Luna. She is the one who asked about my previous experience with girls," Fane defended.

"I'm hitting you because you flirted with her and nearly killed her. Don't you even realize how drool-worthy you are?" Jacque asked him.

Fane cocked his head to the side and narrowed his eyes. "Drool-worthy? What does this mean?"

"What it means, Romeo, is when you walk into a room, every chick there forgets she is with the guy standing right next to her and wishes she was with you," Sally piped in.

"Exactly. Well put, Watson," Jacque told Sally.

"That's what I'm here for, Sherlock," she retorted.

Jacque looked over at Jen to see if she had recovered from her swooning. Jen was lying on her stomach, propped up on her elbows staring dreamily at Fane. Sally followed Jacquelyn's line of sight and slapped Jen on the butt.

"OW," Jen yelped. "What the hell, *chica?*" she said glaring at Sally.

"I was thinking maybe we should go see what we can round up for dinner," Sally said. "It's already 5:15 p.m., and you know how you get if you go too long without eating, Jen."

"Yeah, yeah, just call it what it is. You want to give Simba and Nala here a little privacy. It's all good," Jen said as she stood up to follow Sally out of earshot. Jacque shouted, "He's a wolf, you nymphomaniac freak, not a lion." Jacque heard Sally and Jen laugh as they descended the stairs.

∼

FANE LOOKED over at Jacquelyn who was lying on her bed. She was still grinning over Jen's *Lion King* reference. Fane was so thankful she had friends with such great senses of humor. Laughing could get you through a lot.

"How are you doing, Luna?" Fane asked her.

Jacque looked at him and smiled sweetly. "I'm doing. How are you?"

"I'd be better if you were closer to me," Fane replied.

"Where did all this boldness come from?"

"When I realized I could lose you at any moment, I decided I wouldn't waste any time I have with you. And seeing as how I love being close to you, touching you, I feel it's a major waste when you aren't next to me."

"Oh, well, in that case…" Jacquelyn paused as if to think about it. "Nah, I'm too comfortable to move."

Fane laughed, caught off guard once again. He went over and sat on the bed next to her. He placed his hand on her back and rubbed circles, just enjoying her nearness.

"Keep that up, and I'm gonna be sound asleep," Jacquelyn told him with a sigh.

"I will rub your back for you every night if you like, my Luna," Fane told her.

"What does Luna mean?" Jacquelyn asked not for the first time.

"It means moon in Romanian," Fane answered.

"And why exactly do you have a pet name for me that refers to a big, round space crater?" Jacquelyn asked skeptically.

"It is an honor to be called Luna, and only an Alpha female earns that title."

"There's just a small problem with that, you know, just a minor little thing really." Jacquelyn paused. "I'm not an Alpha female, Fane."

"Awe love, but you will be once we are bonded," Fane pointed out.

She didn't respond. He rubbed her back and listened to the hum of the fan motor. He was trying very hard not to intrude on her thoughts. He wanted her to share with him without him having to fish it out of her brain.

"So, why is it an honor to be called Luna?" she finally asked.

"Because the moon influences many things on this earth. For instance, the moon controls when the tide rises and falls. And you, as the Alpha female, will have great influence with your mate and with the pack. No other female has the influence you will have. When I call you Luna, I am telling you I recognize how important you are to me and our pack."

Jacquelyn just stared at Fane for a few breaths. "Wow, I was thinking you were gonna say something about how like the moon I light up the darkness in your life, yadda, yadda. You know, something sappy."

"I could say something sappy if you want," Fane told her.

"No, no, I'm good with what you gave me. I don't see how I could possibly be all that influential, but we'll cross that bridge when we get there," Jacquelyn told him.

"You will see, one day, and probably sooner than you think, how the Alpha female is like the moon," Fane said as he continued to rub her back.

After a while, Fane decided sitting up was no longer comfortable and laid down next to Jacquelyn. He folded his arms in front of him and laid his head on them so he was looking right at Jacquelyn's face. She had fallen asleep during their silence, and Fane was content watching her sleep. He hadn't realized how tired he was from worrying about Jacquelyn all night and found himself drifting off as well.

Fane woke with a start. He blinked rapidly to clear his sleepy eyes, he realized the room was dark. He pulled his phone out of his pocket to see what time it was, 8:00 p.m. He looked over to where Jacquelyn laid, but she was gone. He put his hand on the spot where she had been and felt it was still a little warm, so she had not been up long. He drew on his wolf hearing to listen to the house, which was silent.

No reason to panic…even though a house that is supposed to contain three teenage girls is totally quiet. His mind reflexively sought out Jacquelyn.

"You do have a good reason as to why you are not in this house, right, Luna?"

Fane could feel her blocking him from her thoughts, which meant she was up to no good. Why was he not surprised?

"Why on earth would you think I was up to no good?"

Fane grinned to himself at her false innocence.

"Where are you love, and what mischief have you and your sidekicks gotten into?" Fane asked her.

Fane could tell by her silence he wasn't going to like what they were up to.

"We were bored so we climbed up on the roof to look at the stars. See, it's not that bad, is it?" Jacquelyn responded.

Fane let out a slow breath, trying to control the strong protective instincts that were a part of his genetic makeup. He knew she was fine, but what if she slipped and fell? What would he do if something happened to her? *Get a grip, Fane. You can't put her in a bubble.*

"No, you can't put me in a bubble, but because I know it would make you feel better, I will come in from the roof. See, I can be reasonable … but don't always count on it," Jacquelyn teased him.

"Thank you, Jacquelyn, you are right. It will make me feel much better if you come back in." Fane was so thankful his mate cared about his feelings and concerns. She didn't know it yet, but those qualities would be a treasure to an Alpha who

would often feel as if he were bearing the weight of the world on his shoulders.

Fane got up and headed downstairs to see if he could find something to eat. He was hungry, and his wolf was hungrier. Fane found some bread and lunch meat and put together a decent sandwich. Suddenly, he heard an ear-splitting scream.

Fane dropped his sandwich and took off. He threw open the front door open and was instantly hit with the unmistakable smell of *Canis lupus*. His lips pulled back in a snarl as a low growl began to build in his throat. Fane's wolf pushed to be let out. His mate was in danger and he wanted blood.

"Jacquelyn, where are you? Are you alright?"

For a moment, there was no response, and it was enough to cause Fane's hold on his wolf to waiver and his eyes phased. He could feel the rest of his body shaking with the need to phase.

"I'm okay, just in shock. We're in the backyard. Please come," Jacquelyn told him.

Even though she said she was okay, he could tell she was scared. Fane ran around the side of the house and came to an abrupt stop. Fane understood now why they had screamed. About ten feet from Jacquelyn's back door were four dead animals. Fane walked to where the three girls stood. He stepped in front of Jacquelyn, placed his hands on either side of her face, and made her look at him.

"Are you alright? Did you see anyone?" he asked her.

"There was no one out here. We had climbed down from the roof and were fixing to go into the house when we noticed a shadow on the ground. When we came over to investigate, we saw those," she said, pointing at the four still bodies on the ground.

Fane looked over at Sally and Jen and saw they were both just staring at the animals. "Are you two okay?" he asked them.

Jen slowly turned her head to look at him. "Is it just me," she asked, "or are there four carcasses in Jacque's backyard? And if so, is this Lucas's way of threatening her?"

Fane stepped away from Jacquelyn and went over to inspect the four animals. He noticed right away there were no bullet wounds or arrow piercings. There were, however, tears in the animals' jugulars. These four had been killed by wolves, they were all clean kills, and there was no damage to the rest of their bodies. He also noted they were laid out in order of size, smallest to largest. The first was a rabbit, next a fox, then a small doe, and last a large buck deer. Fane let out a low growl. Jacquelyn walked up to him and placed her hand on his arm, and it was enough to calm him.

"This is no threat. It is an offering and a demonstration," he answered.

"Offering for what and to demonstrate what exactly?" Sally asked.

"Lucas is offering Jacquelyn kills from his hunt, a peace offering of sorts. He is also demonstrating his ability to provide for her and the pack. He wants her to know he can take care of her should she become his mate. It is a wolf thing, so to speak," Fane explained.

"Okay, first of all, EWW!" Jacquelyn started. "Second, why in Sam Hill would I want four carcasses laying in my backyard, and three, what the hell am I supposed to do with them?"

"I'm thinking bonfire," Jen said.

"Uh-uh, nope, that would stink," Sally retorted.

Fane pulled out his phone and dialed Sorin's number. Sorin picked up on the first ring.

"*Da*," Sorin said.

"*Am ceva ce am nevoie să faci.* I have something I need you to do," Fane told him.

A few moments later, Fane put his phone back in his

pocket. He had explained to Sorin that he wanted him to take the four animals over to the car dealership where he had purchased his motorcycle and put them out front. After a brief silence, Fane pulled his phone out of his pocket again and dialed another number.

"*Da?*" Fane heard, as his Alpha answered the phone.

"*Unde eşti tu?* Where are you?" Fane asked him.

"Your mother and I have just landed in Newark and are boarding the plane for Houston. It's a little less than four hours from here to there. How far is Coldspring from Houston?" his father asked.

"A little less than an hour," Fane answered.

"We should arrive at Jacquelyn's between 1:30 a.m. and 2:00 a.m. What has happened?" Fane's father asked with concern lacing his tone.

"The Alpha, Lucas Steele, broke the challenge rules by harming Jacquelyn. Sorin stopped me from killing him, and now he has left four dead animals in Jacquelyn's yard."

Fane heard his father growl. "How did he harm your mate?"

"I wasn't there to protect her." Fane tried to swallow down the shame he was feeling. "He saw the markings on Jacquelyn's back and neck, got angry, and grabbed her arms hard enough to leave bruises. *Îmi pare rău că te-am părăsit, tată.* I am sorry I failed you, father.

"*Tăcere,* Silence. You have not failed me, son. You had no choice but to honor the rules of the challenge. You don't have time to sulk over what happened. Do you hear me?"

Fane took a deep breath. He knew this is what he needed to hear, and he was thankful that he had decided to call his father.

"I hear you, Alpha," Fane answered.

"You have a fight to prepare for and a mate to protect. What happened is past. Take the anger you have over this and use it to fuel you during the challenge, but do not dwell on it."

"Thank you, *Tată*, father. I will see you soon."

Fane took Jacquelyn's hand and led her toward the house. "Ladies, I don't think our furry friends need an audience any longer," he told them as he held the back door open for them.

Without saying anything to each other, and without any conscious choice, they all went and sat in the living room. Jen and Sally each took an end of the couch while Jacquelyn and Fane sat on the loveseat. Fane was absently tracing the markings on Jacquelyn's neck when Sally finally broke the silence.

"What now?" She asked Fane.

Fane was staring at Jacquelyn and had to make himself pull his gaze away to look at Sally.

"My father and mother will be here around 1:30 or 2:00 a.m. Tomorrow he will call Lucas to make him aware of his arrival, and then they will set the time and place for the challenge," Fane explained.

"Are you nervous?" Jen asked him.

Fane felt Jacquelyn tense at the question.

"*Inima mea, va rog sa nu faceti griji*," Fane thought to her.

"I have no idea what you just said, but I have a feeling you are telling me to chill out. Am I right?" she asked him.

"I didn't exactly put it like that. What I said was, my heart, please do not worry."

Turning to look at Fane, Jacquelyn said, "How can you tell me that? You are going to fight another wolf to the death, and you tell me not to worry. Yeah, I'll get right on that."

"Jacquelyn, I am not without defenses. I am from a strong bloodline, I am a dominant, and I stand to be Alpha to the largest pack of Greys in the world. All of these things make me stronger, and I have found my mate. Please, love, I don't want you to be upset," Fane implored her.

Jacquelyn didn't say anything. She just stood with her back to Fane, head down, looking utterly defeated, and the pain coming from his mate broke Fane's heart.

"I think a hot bath is in order. What do you think, Sal? Hot bath for the wolf princess?" Jen asked Sally with a look that said get up off your butt.

Sally was a quick study. "Yep, most definitely. A hot bath is just what the doctor ordered ... or something like that."

Fane watched helplessly as the two girls took his defeated and worried mate upstairs, away from him. His wolf was protesting, and so was the man. *We should be the one comforting her. She is ours to protect and love.* Fane began to step toward them but stopped abruptly when Jen pierced him with a stare and gave a short nod of her head that was most definitely a command for him to back off. He couldn't help the growl he let out.

"Don't you growl at me, White Fang. I'll have you neutered and declawed so fast you won't know what hit you," Jen retorted.

Fane cocked his head to the side, looking at her, and then shrugged his shoulders. "At least you got the species right."

Fane let the girls go without further protest and sat back down on the loveseat. He let out a deep breath and laid his head back. He was tired and, to his chagrin, he was worried. Not worried about winning the challenge. He felt confident he could beat Lucas so he wasn't worried about that. He was worried about Jacquelyn wanting to watch. The fight was going to be violent and messy. Fane could only imagine how scary it would be for her. He was learning when his Luna was angry, she tended to be impulsive in her reactions. His only consolation was that his mother would be there to keep Jacquelyn from doing anything that would put her in harm's way. The thought of something happening to her caused him to be short of breath like he was having a panic attack. *Okay, Fane, get a grip.*

After several deep breaths, he started to calm down. He closed his eyes and tried very hard not to slip into Jacquelyn's mind to see if she was okay. It took all the manners his mother had beat into him not to listen to her thoughts. Instead, he laid there humming a tune from one of his favorite artists. Believe it or not, Fane, a Romanian, was a country music fan. Who knew? It was a song he wanted to share with Jacquelyn because it described so well how he felt. *Soon, but not tonight.* Tonight, she didn't want to be with him, but soon.

CHAPTER 13

*J*acque lay in the tub her two best friends had filled with hot water and bubble bath. She felt bad for walking out on Fane, but she was hurting, scared, and anxious. No amount of him telling her she shouldn't worry was going to make it better. Tears ran down her cheeks as she imagined all the horrific possibilities of what could happen at the challenge. *He expects me not to worry —as if.*

She stayed in the tub until the water cooled. As she got dressed and combed through her curls, Jacque pondered whether she should go to Fane or just go to bed. If she were honest with herself, she would do what every bit of her was craving to do: crawl up in his lap and let him hold her and spend as much time with him as possible. It truly was a no-brainer. As much as she loved Jen and Sally, a hot Romanian prince and, as fate would have it, her soul mate was waiting for her. She knew what Jen would say, something along the lines of "If you don't go to him, you better believe I will." Yep, mm-mm that's what she would say. Okay, decision made.

She winked at herself in the mirror as she turned to leave the bathroom.

Before she went down to Fane, Jacque stuck her head in the door of her bedroom to thank Sally and Jen and let them know she would be downstairs. But before she could even open her mouth to speak, they were already answering her unspoken thoughts.

"You're welcome, we love you, you love us, we're the best friends ever, and all that sap," Jen said without looking up from the magazine she was flipping through.

"Yes, we're okay if you go down to Fane, no it won't hurt our feelings, and we all know if you don't, then Jen will," Sally said with a wink.

"True dat," Jen threw in for good measure.

"Okay, you two are the best friends ever. I mean that. I'll be back in a little while," Jacque started.

"Don't hurry on our account. You know we will want details, and if you come back up here with nothing juicy, I might just throw you out the window. Any questions?" Jen said without looking up.

"You haven't looked into that medicine we've talked about, have you?" Sally asked her sarcastically.

"Details, okay, got it," Jacque said as she turned to go.

Just as she started to head down the stairs, she heard Jen yell, "Don't think I won't know if you're lying. I know how many bases you've been on, you redheaded puritan. I will be able to tell fact from fiction."

"Oh, shut up already," Sally scolded.

Jacque laughed and shook her head. Jen was just trying to lighten the mood. Jen knew how hotheaded Jacque could be, and if she went to Fane already upset it would be hard for her to calm down and be reasonable. Reasonability wasn't one of her stronger attributes, much to her frustration.

As she walked into the living room, she saw Fane sitting

on the loveseat. His arms were stretched out on the back of the seat on either side, and his head was resting backward. His eyes were closed and, because his breathing was so slow and even, it was hard to tell if he was awake.

"I like the smell of your shampoo," Fane said suddenly.

Startled by his unexpected words, Jacque tried, without success, to suppress the squeak that escaped. Fane had not moved, nor had he opened his eyes. He just continued to sit there calm and collected. Jacque rolled her eyes and went around to the couch.

Fane slowly raised his head and pinned Jacque with those piercing blue eyes, her heartbeat sped, and her breathing got a tad bit shallower. She had to look away from him before she made a fool of herself by drooling. "Yeah, that would be so cute," Jacque snorted to herself.

"Does being near me repulse you, Luna?" Fane asked her

Jacque knew she must look confused, because, frankly, she was. How could he possibly think he repulsed her? If anything, he should be the one repulsed.

"Why would you ask me that?" she asked him.

"I know no other reason why my mate would choose to sit away from me instead of by my side," Fane told her, sounding so formal and old fashioned.

"Throw me a bone, Fane," Jacque said in obvious exasperation. "Did it occur to you that maybe I just needed some space because it's hard for me to think when I get close to you?"

Fane grinned, obviously pleased with her comment, then stood up slowly, rising to his full height so Jacque had to tilt her head back to look up at him. He walked around the coffee table separating the two couches and sat down close to her.

"Are you having a hard time thinking now?" he asked her softly.

With a shuddering breath, all Jacque could do was nod her head.

"Why did you come back down here, *meu inimă*, my heart? I didn't think you wanted to be around me," Fane told her.

Jacque tried to scoot a little bit away from him, but it was in vain because he just scooted with her. Dang stubborn werewolf.

"At first I didn't want to be around you." His head lowered at her words, so Jacque quickly went on. "I didn't want to be around you because I didn't want to hear you tell me not to worry or that it is going to be okay. Then I realized none of that really matters. What matters is being with you, spending time with you. I hate it when we are apart. I'm sorry if that sounds so desperate, but it's the truth."

Fane wrapped his arms around her and pulled her close to him.

"Thank you, Jacquelyn. You have no idea how hard it was to sit here on this couch and not come to you, and even harder not to seek out your thoughts. I love you. I'm sorry if my words upset you. I'm here if you want to worry, not worry, or anything else."

Jacque closed her eyes, soaking up the feel of him against her, the safety she felt with his arms around her, and the warmth pouring through her from his words. She didn't know how she had been blessed to be Fane's mate, but she was thankful beyond words.

"*As am I.*" She heard Fane's thoughts in response to her own, and it made Jacque grin.

They sat there in silence for quite a while. Every now and then Jacque would hear Fane humming a tune she couldn't place. Eventually, Jacque curled her feet up on the couch and leaned her head down onto Fane's chest. Fane grabbed the blanket thrown across the back of the couch and covered her.

"This is how I want to spend my nights for the rest of my life," Jacque told Fane.

"I guess that's a good thing since I intend to keep you for the rest of your life," Fane said, only half teasing.

"It's late, love. Why don't you go to bed? I don't want you to be tired tomorrow."

Jacque looked up at him and kissed him gently on the lips.

"I don't want to sleep in my bed tonight," she told him.

"Just where were you planning on sleeping, Luna?" he asked her.

"Well, this is a wide couch. I imagine two people of reasonable size could sleep on it together," she said, trying to suppress a grin.

"What do you think the mom of one of the reasonably sized persons would say when she found her with another reasonably sized person of the opposite sex laying on a couch together?"

"Don't know. Want to find out?"

Fane laughed at her silliness and, much to her surprise, he shrugged his shoulders and said, "Only live once. If I'm going to die, I would rather die lying in the arms of the woman I love, even if it is by said woman's mother."

Fane kicked off his shoes and stretched out his long body on the couch. Jacque laid next to him. Fane put his arm over her waist and pulled her close against his chest. Jacque giggled when she heard him make a purring sound.

"What are you laughing at?" he asked her.

"Did you just purr? 'Cause I didn't think wolves purred."

"I didn't purr. I rumbled," Fane said with as much dignity as he could muster.

"You rumbled? Seriously? Pray tell, what does that mean?" Jacque asked him, trying hard not to laugh.

"When wolves are content, they often make a rumbling

sound that comes from their chest. I guess you could say it's equivalent to a cat's purr," he explained.

"It's cute," Jacque said.

Fane began humming again and periodically kissing Jacque's hair. The last thought Jacque had before falling asleep was that she didn't have any details Jen would think were good, and that made her smile.

FANE DIDN'T WANT to sleep for fear of missing a moment of Jacquelyn in his arms. He figured it wouldn't last much longer because once her mom got home, she would probably make Fane sleep on the porch. Still, he would sleep in an igloo if it meant he could spend this night holding his mate, his Luna. He took a deep breath, taking in her smell—cotton candy and snow—and pulled her even tighter against him. *Mine.* Fane's wolf was restless to complete the bonding and the Blood Rites. *First, we must fight—for her, for the future of our pack. We must fight.*

He hadn't realized he had fallen asleep until he felt something nudging his arm and a voice telling him to wake up. Fane opened his eyes, blinking several times to clear his vision. He looked down at Jacquelyn and saw she was still asleep. She must have been really tired to sleep through three Romanians speaking ninety to nothing in their native tongue. With that thought, he realized his mother and father were here conversing with Sorin.

"Shhh," Fane told them, pointing at Jacquelyn. "She needs to sleep. Can we take this to the dining room, please?"

Fane slowly crawled over Jacquelyn, trying not to jostle her too much. Once up, he straightened the blanket covering her and leaned down to kiss her forehead.

"Sorin, did Lilly come home with you?" Fane asked his guard.

"Yes, she went straight to her room when we got home. Although, as she walked through the living room past a certain couch where two bodies lay, she did mumble something about a stinking, grubby-pawed werewolf. It was difficult to hear her, and there might have been an expletive or two." Sorin was obviously taking great pleasure in sharing this information, especially in front of Fane's parents.

Fane chose not to take the bait but turned to his father instead. "You brought some of the pack with you?" Fane had just realized he could smell other Greys in the house. He tensed at this and suddenly wanted to be back in the living room with Jacquelyn. Although she was his mate, they weren't bonded, and an un-bonded mated male *Canis lupus* was the most dangerous kind. As if on cue, he heard a slapping sound then Jacquelyn yelling, "Get your nose out of my face, you trespassing hairball!"

Fane moved before she finished her sentence, and he had his packmate by the throat and on the ground.

"What are you doing with your nose near my mate, Boian, and why should I not snap your neck for being so near her?" Fane asked the wolf.

"I meant no disrespect," Boian answered.

"I knew we were missing something. Didn't I tell you, Sally? I said, 'Hey Sally I think something's going on downstairs.' And what did you say? You said, 'No, it's just your imagination.'" Everyone turned to see Jen and Sally coming down the stairs. "Okay, Fane, we're here. You can continue strangling whoever this fine piece of meat is."

Fane slowly let the other wolf up and stepped in front of Jacquelyn, not taking his eyes off Boian or relaxing his stance.

"Would someone like to clue me in as to what in tarnation is going on?" Jacquelyn asked, trying to look around at the people in the room but unable to do so because Fane was right in front of her. "Fane, seriously dude, you have a great backside, but I don't think this is the time for me to admire it. Could you please get your royal butt out of my face?"

The other wolves in the room all tried to disguise their laughs with coughs, obviously finding it amusing that a little human would talk to the Prince of their pack in such a way.

"You can park your royal butt in front of me, Fane. I don't mind," Jen told him with a wink, which only made the other wolves laugh harder.

Fane growled but acquiesced to Jacquelyn's wishes, moving to the side but remaining standing. It was not wise to sit in front of other dominant wolves. It made you look like prey.

"Jacquelyn, Jen, and Sally, I would like you to meet my father, Vasil Lupei, and my mother, Alina Lupei." Fane then turned to three other new additions to the room, one of them being the wolf he had disciplined. "And this is Boian, Skender, and Decebel. They are upper members of the pack."

Jacquelyn stood up, attempting to straighten out her shirt. She started to fix her hair but quickly abandoned the attempt. She walked over to Fane's parents and extended a hand. Fane could see the nervousness in her eyes.

"I'm Jacquelyn, Fane's, um, well his, you know, um..." Jacquelyn tried to spit it out, but it just wouldn't leave her lips.

"My mate," Fane finished for her.

"Yeah, what he said," she agreed. "It's so nice to meet you. I'm sorry you're seeing me all sleepified and stuff."

"She cleans up real nice," Jen threw out there.

"Thanks for that, Jen," Jacquelyn retorted.

Fane walked over and put his arm around her waist. She

was beautiful to him, even with her hair a mess and sleepy eyes.

"*Tata, Mama, Nu este uimitoare?* Isn't she stunning?" Fane asked his parents.

"*Într-adevăr este.* Truly she is," Alina answered.

"Would you care to share what exactly y'all are talking about?" Jacquelyn asked Fane through her thoughts

"I told them you were stunning, and they agreed," Fane answered.

Alina stepped forward, pushed Fane away from Jacquelyn, and embraced her. "Jacquelyn, it is so wonderful to meet you. I am so thankful Fane found you."

"Thank you," Jacquelyn said simply.

Then it was Vasile's turn. He embraced her as well, but when he spoke to her it was in Romanian, "*Esti jumătatea fiului meu, mica lui lumină. Prin moartea sau viaţa lui vei fi protejat de pachet.* You are my son's other half, his little light. By his death or life, you will be protected by the pack."

After he said this, every wolf in the room responded, "*După cum o vei face, Alpha, se va face.* As you will it, Alpha, it will be done."

"What exactly just happened? 'Cause we all know there was some sort of pack voodoo going on," Jen said looking at Fane.

It was Fane's father who spoke instead.

"That is something Fane can discuss with you later. Right now, we have more pressing matters. Jacquelyn, I hate to ask this of you, but I need you to get your mother."

"No need, I'm here. Believe it or not, it's kind of hard to sleep with a pack of wolves in your living room. By the way, I'm Lilly Pierce, Jacque's mother," Lilly said as she strolled into the living room.

Alina walked right up to her and hugged her just as she had Jacquelyn.

"I'm Alina, Fane's mother, and this is my mate, Vasile," she told Lilly.

"It's very nice to meet you both. Please make yourselves at home while you are here. Although I'm not sure how we are going to accommodate all of you," Lilly told them.

"Oh, I talked with the Henrys, and they were more than happy to provide us rooms in their home," Fane explained.

"So, what's this pressing business that needs to be discussed?" Lilly asked Vasile.

Jacquelyn turned to go sit on the couch and started to pull Fane with her, but he did not move, nor did he let her hand go. She looked back at him in question and saw that he was staring at the other wolves in the room.

"Are you just going to stand there through this whole conversation? If so then you're on your own 'cause I'm tired, I'm cranky, and I want to sit down ... now, Fane," Jacquelyn told him glaring daggers at him.

Fane was not going to sit down until the other wolves submitted first. He knew they were being stubborn because there were females in the room, and they wanted to look all big and bad. He also guessed his father was not going to intervene because he wanted to see if Fane could submit other dominates. Only one way to find out. *I've had enough of this.* He turned so that his body was facing each of them directly. He looked at each wolf—First Boian, then Decebel, and last Skender—until each dropped their eyes. Then Fane spoke in the voice they could not disobey.

"*Sta.* Sit." All three sat immediately, eyes still lowered.

Fane turned and bared his neck to his father then pulled Jacquelyn over to sit on the couch.

"You are going to explain that later, right?" Jacquelyn whispered.

"Do I have a choice, Luna?" Fane asked.

"Point to you," she told him.

Alina and Lilly both sat on the loveseat while Jen and Sally sat on the floor in front of the couch. Sorin was in his usual spot, the ugly chair, and the three wolves were all sitting on the floor around Sorin's feet. They did not look happy. Vasile stood at the front of the room staring out at everyone.

Jen looked over at Jacquelyn and whispered, "You know this calls for some hot chocolate, right?"

Jacquelyn nodded in agreement as Sally stood up and said, "I'm on it."

"The challenge is to be tomorrow," Vasile announced. "I will call Lucas Steele in a few hours to discuss the details. One important aspect will be the location. I do not want the challenge to take place in his territory. It needs to happen in a remote location where there is no chance bystanders will happen upon it. Do any of you know such a place?"

Jen and Jacquelyn spoke at the same time. "Field of Dreams."

Jen reached up and fist bumped with Jacquelyn. "Good call, Sherlock," she said.

"All in a day's work, Watson," Jacquelyn responded.

"What's the Field of Dreams?" Fane asked.

"It's just an empty field out in the boondocks," Jacquelyn answered.

"Okay, so why then is it called the Field of Dreams?" he asked again.

"Jacque's just embarrassed to say," Jen told him, "It's called the Field of Dreams because it's where all the couples go on Friday nights, and, ya know, hope their dreams come true, so to speak."

Fane looked at his mate to find her face nearly as red as her hair.

"Do you have personal experience with this field?" he whispered in her ear.

Jacquelyn slapped him on the leg, hard. "No, you possessive caveman, and you already knew that." She growled, forgetting briefly she had an audience.

"She's a feisty little thing, isn't she?" Fane's father commented.

"*Nu ai nici o idee.* You have no idea," Fane answered.

"Will there not be children at this field? Making their dreams come true?" Vasile asked, eyeing Jen.

"Nope, the city recently fenced it off. It's got a locked gate now. So, we would have to do some B & E, if y'all are okay with a little law-breaking, that is," Jen offered.

"What is B & E, love?" Fane asked Jacquelyn.

"Breaking and entering," she answered.

"That's not a problem," Vasile told her. "Okay, good, location is determined. The next thing I need to discuss is the challenge itself and how werewolf law works." He paused as Sally walked back into the living room with mugs of hot chocolate and handed them out. Once she was seated on the floor next to Jen, Vasile started speaking again.

"Jacquelyn, what I'm going to tell you now is not pleasant, but it is our way and our law. It is going to be hard for you to understand and accept, but I tell you now as your Alpha— and yes, I am your Alpha as you are my son's mate—you must abide by these laws and rules. Are we clear?"

Jacquelyn looked at Fane, and he saw the panic in her eyes.

"It is okay, love. He is only trying to keep you safe. Trust me," Fane told her.

She held his hand and turned to look at Vasile. "Crystal."

Vasile nodded his approval and continued. "The rules permit that an Alpha who challenges another wolf may bring his first four wolves, but the rest of his pack must stay away."

"What do you mean by first four?" Sally asked

"A wolf pack is a hierarchy. You have the Alpha and then

you have your dominants and your submissives. From there they are put into order of their rank. Usually, just the first four are acknowledged. An Alpha's first, or Beta, as we call them, is the next in command. He is the next most dominant after the Alpha, and it goes from there to the second, third, and fourth, each one descending in their level of dominance," Vasile explained.

Sally nodded.

"Now, the rules also allow for the challenged to bring his Alpha and first four, which is why I brought three pack members, Sorin makes four. The only others allowed in attendance are the Alpha female, Alina, and the female over which the challenge has been issued. No others will be permitted," Vasile said resolutely. "I realize each of you wants to be there with Jacquelyn, but I must make you understand it would be too dangerous. There are going to be ten wolves in a small area, two of them fighting for the right to take a mate. This will make the others edgy. Women tend to do that to us males. If Fane is not the victor, it will be me and my wolves between Lucas and his wolves. It will be easier to protect Jacquelyn if our attention is not divided."

Fane did not miss the way Jacquelyn's face fell when his father mentioned the possibility of Fane not winning. He realized then this next part of the conversation was going to be bad ... very, very bad.

CHAPTER 14

*J*acque looked away when Vasile mentioned Fane might not win. The thought made her sick to her stomach. She was also scared beyond belief knowing she would not have her friends or her mother there for support. Granted, she would have Alina, and she was thankful for that, but she couldn't help feeling very alone.

"You okay, puțină lumină, little light?" Fane asked her.

"No, wolfman, I'm not," she answered.

"Jacquelyn."

Jacque turned her attention back to Vasile when he called her name.

"I need to make some things clear to you. I imagine my son has kept these from you because of their ugliness. We *Canis lupus* are not human. Some of our traditions follow the way of the animal we carry inside us. When I say this is a fight to the death, that's exactly what I mean. If Lucas gets Fane by the throat and submits him, which is to say that Fane stops fighting, Lucas will still kill him. Some fights are fought until one wolf submits or is killed. This fight is not that way because a wolf will not give up his mate. If another wants an un-bonded, mated female, he must kill her mate to have her." Vasile paused. Jacque simply stared at him.

How am I supposed to just stand there and watch another kill him? Jacque felt like she was about to be sick.

"If Fane loses, you and your mother will have to come to Romania under my protection. Lucas will not give you up. He will expect you to become his mate. The only way to avoid it is to leave. Do you understand that?" Vasile addressed both Lilly and Jacque. Both nodded solemnly.

"I'm sorry to speak of this so bluntly. Please do not mistake it for a lack of care. He is my son, remember. I will have to watch him fight and maybe die, without intervening. Even though I know I could save him, I am not permitted to. Believe me when I tell you I understand your fear and pain. As your Alpha, I must make sure you understand the possible outcomes and results of those outcomes." As Vasile finished there was a small sniffle, and when Jacque turned in the direction of the noise, she saw it was Alina crying. Jacque's heart broke, and her own tears began to spill.

Jacque got up and went to sit by Alina, wrapping her arms around her. Jacque didn't know what to say because she knew there was nothing to be said that would ease the fear. So, she just hugged her and cried with her. The room was silent, other than the soft cries from the two women who loved Fane so much. Tears streaked the face of both Sally and Jen. Lilly's eyes were closed and her body trembled.

Finally, Alina and Jacque pulled themselves together. Fane got up, walked to his mother, and knelt in front of her. He touched her face gently and whispered, *"Te rog, nu plânge, mamă. Îmi frânge inima.* Please do not cry, Mother. It breaks my heart."

Alina kissed Fane on the forehead. "I'm your mother. It's my job to cry. Now comfort your mate before your Alpha begins to think you aren't taking care of her," she teased him, and then she turned to Jacque. "I can see already I am blessed beyond measure to have you as my son's mate."

"Thank you. The feeling is mutual," Jacque responded.

Fane took Jacque by the hand and led her back to the couch.

"Okay, I'm good. Let's keep moving. What else do we need to discuss?" Jacque asked Vasile.

"I think, for now, that is enough. I want Boian, Skender, and Decebel to go over to the Henrys' and get some sleep. I need them at their best at the challenge."

The three wolves were up and moving before Vasile finished speaking, Jacque felt Fane relax as the three walked out the front door. She turned and looked at him questioningly. "Is it really that hard to be around them?" she asked, heedless of those around them.

"We'll talk about it later, Luna," Fane told her gently.

Jacque shrugged. She was tired and, frankly, didn't want to think about the challenge anymore. Alina must have seen this in Jacque's face because she tactfully asked her if she would like to take a walk with her.

"Lilly, you don't mind, do you?" Alina asked Jacque's mother.

"No, not at all. I think it will be good for her to get out of the house and away from all this testosterone," Lilly told her.

"Amen," Jen and Sally said in unison.

Jacque stood up, looked down at her wrinkled clothes, and realized she had slept in yesterday's clothes. *What a wonderful first impression I must have made to Fane's parents.*

"Alina, let me take a quick shower. I feel all grimy," Jacque admitted.

"Go right ahead. Take your time. I would love to visit with your mom as well since we're going to be family," Alina said.

"That sounds like a great idea. Alina, do you like coffee or hot chocolate?" Lilly asked as the two women headed in the direction of the kitchen.

Jacque turned to Fane and told him she'd see him in a little while, but apparently, that wasn't sufficient, because as she walked away, he followed her to the bottom of the stairs.

"Jacquelyn, are you—"

"If you plan on finishing that question with the word 'okay,' I just might save Lucas the trouble and strangle you myself," Jacque growled at him.

Sally and Jen walked past Fane and Jacque and up the stairs.

"Man, Sally, you would think getting to sleep on the couch with her man would have put her in a better mood. Maybe he's not as good as he looks if you know what I mean," Jen said.

"Jen, we really, *really* need to have a conversation about when to keep your mouth shut, and if you don't, then how fast you should run," Sally retorted as she followed her mouthy friend up the stairs.

Jacque shook her head, feeling overwhelmed. She knew she needed to give herself a pep talk or a good kick in the ass, which was even more effective. She was not a "wuss," dammit. She was not a frail, little flower that withered at the slightest show of bad weather. So, what on earth was her problem?

"It's the bond, Jacquelyn. It makes you feel things on a whole different level than a human. I know it's hard to understand because it's all so new to you. You aren't weak, love. Your spirit recognizes that I am your other half, and it rebels against any notion of being separated from me. Just as my spirit rebels against being separated from you, and even worse, I'm constantly fighting to keep my wolf under control because all he sees is that you are our mate, you are in danger, and you need to be bonded to me," Fane explained to her.

Jacque lifted her head and looked into Fane's beautiful blue eyes, eyes that she wanted more than anything to be what she saw every morning when she woke up and every night when she closed her own. Fane was right, she didn't understand. She wanted to, but it's like her brain couldn't keep up with her emotions. She would just have to come to grips with it all and accept it, maybe then it wouldn't be so scary.

"Thank you, Fane. I can imagine it must be frustrating for you because I am so clueless. Crap, it's frustrating for me because I know I must be frustrating you," she admitted to him.

"I am not frustrated, Luna. How could I possibly be frustrated with the one person who gives my existence meaning? If you begin to understand anything at all, I hope it's that you have given me what every male *Canis lupus* longs for, needs, and can never be complete without. You, and only ever you, complete the very core of who I am. No, love, I am not frustrated with you. I am wholly, ardently, unabashedly in love with you."

Jacque put her arms around his waist, holding onto him as if it would keep the storm raging around them from tearing them apart. She laid her head against his chest and listened to his heart, allowing the rhythm to calm her. Fane kissed the top of her head and gently rubbed her back. As he had done before, he whispered words in his language, and they seemed to ease the tension from her mind.

"I love you, wolfman," Jacque whispered, and knew with his wolf's hearing he wouldn't miss it.

She took a deep breath and pulled away from him. He reluctantly let her go but did not take his hand off her hips.

"I'm gonna go now, 'k, so I can spend time with your mom. What are you going to do?" she asked him.

"I'm going to be with my father when he calls Lucas, and then I think I will sleep for a little while. I didn't realize how tired I was until the pack left and I was able to relax," he told her.

"That reminds me... Are you going to tell me what the whole staring contest was about with the guys leaving and you suddenly deflating like a balloon with a hole in it?"

"I will tell you about it, Luna, but not right now. You go take your shower. I know my mother is eager to get to know you, and seeing as how I plan to have you all to myself tonight, she better get her fill during the day," Fane said as he pulled her close one more time and kissed her on the lips.

Jacque pressed closer to him, wrapping her arms around his neck and pushing her lips firmly against his. She loved it when he kissed her. His lips were so soft and gentle. Fane pulled back much too soon for her liking, but she let him go.

"I'll see you later," he told her.

Just like before when he was leaving to go back to the Henrys', Jacque felt an impending sense of doom at the idea of him not being with her. She hated how desperate it made her feel. She was not the desperate type. She never had a problem if she and Trent went several days without talking. At the sound of Fane's growl, she realized her mistake.

"Remember, love, when you are emotional you tend to broadcast your thoughts. I try not to listen, but sometimes it's a little too tempting not to, and when I hear his name in your mind, I can't tune you out," Fane explained. "I know in my mind I don't need to be jealous, but the wolf in me considers you mine even when I didn't know you."

Jacque grinned at him having just realized she would probably be able to get some dirt on him about past girls from Alina.

"I guess I will just need to be more careful about not broadcasting when I'm emotional," she told him innocently.

"That's a thought, or you could just not think about him," Fane told her, his voice getting deeper as they continued the topic.

"That's a thought, too, albeit not a reasonable one, but a thought nonetheless." Jacque winked at him as she turned to climb the stairs.

"See you later, wolfman," she called over her shoulder. Jacque heard him growl and couldn't help but grin. If nothing else made her smile, she could count on aggravating him doing it every time.

"Glad I can amuse you, my love," she heard Fane's voice in her head.

"Me too," she replied, which earned her another growl.

As ALINA and Jacque walked down the sidewalk, Jacque had a hard time not looking back at Sorin, who followed at a distance—their guard, as it were. She was amazed that four days ago she was just Jacque, a small-town teenager, about to be a senior in high school. Then *BAM*, she's the mate to a werewolf prince who is going to have to fight another werewolf to keep her. Seriously, what happened that fate somehow got a wild hair up its butt and decided to throw her a curveball? She was truly baffled by it all.

"Jacquelyn or Jacque? Which would you prefer I call you?" Alina's voice pulled her from her disbelieving thoughts.

"Well, everyone but Fane calls me Jacque. For some reason, he has called me Jacquelyn since we met, and I just haven't bothered to say anything. Then again, he rarely calls me my name. Usually, it's Luna, or love, or some other Romanian word that I have no idea the meaning of," Jacque told her, smiling at how much she liked the different endearments by which Fane referred to her.

"Vasile seldom calls me Alina."

"What does he call you?" Jacque asked and then her manners caught up with her. "I mean if you don't mind me asking."

"I don't mind. He calls me Mina," Alina told her.

"What does it mean?"

"You're going to laugh when I tell you because it just solidifies the fact that werewolves are indeed pushy, bossy, and possessive. It simply means mine. How ridiculous is that?" Alina said laughing.

Jacque couldn't help laughing with her.

"I haven't known werewolves even a week yet, and I still see the significance of that," Jacque told her.

"What has Fane told you about us?" Alina asked Jacque.

"Well obviously, he's told me about the whole werewolf family trait thing, and about y'all being the royal family, so to speak, but other than that, not really anything."

"Fane never has been the talkative type," Alina said. "I suppose, too, all he's been able to think about is keeping you safe. Grey males tend to be obsessive when it comes to their mates and children."

"Yeah, I suppose he has been a little preoccupied with the whole crazy, psycho Alpha trying to get in his Kool-Aid and steal his chick," Jacque said, and then burst out laughing when Alina looked at her like she had grown a third arm.

"Do you always talk like that?" Alina asked

"Unfortunately, it's a side effect of hanging around Jen. She's much, much worse," Jacque told her, shaking her head as she thought about her crazy best friend.

"You care very much for Jen and Sally, and it's obvious they care for you. I'm sorry that they won't be able to be with you tomorrow," Alina told Jacque.

"I would rather my friends be safe. If it's going to be dangerous, then they should stay away. You are right. I do care for them. I love them. They are my best friends, and I honestly don't know what I would do without them."

Alina and Jacque walked a block in silence. Jacque thought about Alina's question. *What has Fane told you about us?* Was Alina simply referring to the bonding and Blood Rites stuff, or was there more that Fane hadn't told her? She would ask him tonight. If there was more, she was hoping it wasn't something like for the good of the pack you must produce a male heir within one year of the bonding because that would suck.

"Fane has explained to you about the bonding ceremony, I hope," Alina said, finally breaking the silence.

"Yeah, he told me about it. Not in great detail but the gist. The Blood Rites thing is a bit different from what we do in our bonding ceremonies," Jacque joked.

Alina laughed, apparently appreciating the good humor Jacque took in everything.

"Because you are female, I know you will break it down a little better. Will you give me a clue as to what to expect?" Jacque asked Alina.

"In the ceremony, Vasile will first bond you and Fane. There are three things that happen for a bond to be made. First, you will say vows. I have a copy of the vows you will say to Fane, and Vasile has a copy of the vows Fane will say to you. After the vows, the male presents the female with an offering, a way to show her he can take care of her and provide for his family," Alina told her before Jacque interrupted.

"He's not going to give me a dead animal, is he?"

Alina laughed. "No that is what a real wolf would give his mate. The symbolism is the same. The offering must be something of value that required him to sacrifice in order to get it. As a wolf sacrifices energy when on the hunt, so must a male *Canis lupus* give up something to provide for his family. Want to know what the catch is? Just as a female wolf can turn away a male wolf's offering, so can we. You don't have to accept what Fane offers to you."

"What did Vasile give to you?" Jacque asked Alina before she could tell her mouth not to say what her brain was thinking.

"Before you hear it, you must first realize that Vasile and I have been mated for over two centuries, so what was in then is most definitely not in now," Alina teased.

Jacque was shocked to hear how long she and Vasile had been together.

"Well, I must say you don't look a day over thirty-five," Jacque told her.

"Now that you know just how long ago it was when we bonded, I will tell you Vasile gave me two things. The first was something I needed. My family was poor, and we didn't have much, so he gave me a horse. She was beautiful."

Jacque watched as Alina's face lit up with the memory of an animal she had obviously loved.

"She was sable with a dark chocolate mane, tall and very elegant. I named her Cosmina, which means beauty. The second thing requires an explanation as well, maybe a small history lesson. In that day and age, wealthy families and nobility all had family crests or signets. Vasile comes from a long line of Alphas, which is our equivalent to royalty, and so his family has a signet. The signet was used to identify the family you were from, the social class you were in, and in our case, the pack you were in. Different families carried their signets in different ways. Vasile's was a ring." Alina held out her hand to show Jacque the gold ring.

It had an oval-shaped face, and on that face was a grid of four diamonds. In each diamond, there was a symbol. The top left was a crown, the top right was a wolf, the bottom left, a sword, and the bottom right a full moon.

"The crown represents the royal lineage, the wolf distinguishes we are werewolves, the sword testifies that as the Alpha family we are the sword of justice keeping the discipline among the pack, and the moon acknowledges the importance of the females in the pack," Alina explained.

"What was the significance of giving you the ring?" Jacque asked.

"It was his way of offering me a place in the royal line. He was telling me that no matter my lineage, if I bonded with him, I would be accepted as the Alpha of the female pack members. In essence, he was offering me unconditional acceptance," Alina answered.

"I take it that was a significant offering," Jacque said.

"Yes, it was."

"And what is the last thing for the bonding?" Jacque asked.

"Since you are human, this final act might seem very weird. The third thing is the Blood Rites where you will exchange blood, and Fane will put a visible mark on you for others to know you are his."

"Okay, you're right. It is quite freaky-deeky to me because we don't go around biting each other, but I'm trying to keep an open mind. Does it hurt?" Jacque asked, sounding very nervous.

"Well, I'm not sure how it is going to be for a half-human. It does cause some discomfort—it is a bite after all—but some find it pleasurable because it is so significant to the bonding. It's the way you complete becoming one with your mate," Alina said, making it sound so normal, even though it was so not normal.

"Well, I'm not going to say I'm not nervous because that

would be the understatement of the year. I am trying very hard to keep an open mind," Jacque told Alina.

"I think Fane is very blessed to have you as his mate. I know it is going to be a big change for you, especially once you move to Romania, but—"

"Wait, wait, throw it in reverse. What do you mean move to Romania? Fane has not said a single thing about moving to Romania!"

"That's what I was afraid of. Fane is next in line to be Alpha of the Romanian pack. He must be there to learn what that entails. You also need to be educated about what it means to be Alpha to the females. It is going to be hard for some of the females to submit to one who is half-human. You are going to have to learn to hold your own," Alina told her.

"What about my senior year? What about my friends, my mom? What the crap, man?" Jacque said.

"The plan is to get you and Fane private tutors for your senior year. When you are not studying, you will be learning about the pack and traditions and how to be an Alpha. As for your mom, she is welcome to come with us, and, if she doesn't, the pack will pay to fly her out any time you want. Your friends are welcome to visit, too. The tutor would work with them as well if, by chance, they came for an extended visit or some kind of exchange program. We realize we are asking you to give up a lot, and we will do everything we can to make it easier on you."

Jacque just stood there staring at Alina in total disbelief. She felt completely blindsided. Why hadn't Fane said anything to her? How could she possibly leave her life here? Would her friends' parents even consider allowing them to go with her?

"Fane is so busted," Jacque said aloud, although only saying it to herself.

"Is everything okay, Luna?" she heard Fane ask.

"You have been holding out on me, and just to prepare you, it might be wise of you to get anything I could use as a weapon as far from me as possible," Jacque told him.

Fane did not respond. She was already getting angrier because she knew he wasn't going to argue with her, that he would surrender. She wanted a good argument. She needed to vent her frustrations at the injustice of it all.

"Jacque, are you okay?" Alina asked her.

"Not sure just yet, but I'm not going to have a meltdown or anything," she answered.

"I think we should head back now. It's nearing lunchtime, and I'm sure Fane is probably edgy with you not in his sight," Alina told her.

"Right now, it might be a good thing that I'm not in his sight," Jacque muttered under her breath.

CHAPTER 15

*F*ane knew he was in trouble for not telling Jacquelyn she would need to move to Romania after the bonding, but there were so many changes happening all at once, he hadn't wanted to throw more at her. Obviously, he had been wrong not to tell her. This whole mate thing was difficult. Even if they were meant to be together, that apparently did not mean things would be smooth. Although he would still rather have her, even if she was mad at him, than not have her at all. She was actually pretty cute when she was mad. Hopefully, he could smooth things out when they talked tonight.

Fane's father had spoken to Lucas Steele and set up the time and location for the challenge. Lucas had asked several times if Jacquelyn was going to be there, and that had set Fane and his wolf on edge. Lucas also had the nerve to ask if she had received his offering, which had caused Fane to let out a ferocious growl for which his Alpha chastised him. "You never lose control. It gives the other wolf the upper hand," he told Fane.

Fane stepped outside to calm down, and his father had

followed him out. At first, his Alpha didn't say anything to him, he just let him wrestle with his emotions, but then he spoke.

"You must realize some of the intensity of your emotions is because the bond is not complete. Once it is, you will have much more control. Until then, you are going to have to rein it in. Tomorrow during the challenge, if you lose control, you will not be able to think clearly. The rage will fog your brain, and that will slow your movements. You have to separate your emotions from your fighting. Do you understand what I'm telling you?" Vasile asked.

"Yes, but it's easier said than done." Fane lowered his head, and in a very soft voice, he told his father, "I'm afraid. Does that make me weak?"

Vasile went to his son and wrapped him in a tight hug as he used to when Fane was a pup.

"That you can admit your fears shows how strong you are. Only a fool pretends not to fear difficult and frightening things. I am Alpha of the Romanian pack, the largest *Canis lupus* pack in the world, and yet I am afraid too. All will be well, Fane. You are strong and able, you have trained all your life to fight in both of your forms, you will win, you will be bonded with Jacquelyn, and one day you will be Alpha." He sounded completely confident. Fane wished he shared his father's assurance.

Fane took in the comfort that came from having his Alpha hug him, pouring his power over him. For wolves, touch was a major part of their comfort, and he appreciated his father's willingness to give him such a gift.

After Vasile pulled away from Fane, they turned toward the sound of a door opening and then closing.

"Sounds like your mother and Jacquelyn are back. Let's go fill them in on what is planned for tomorrow," Vasile told him.

Fane hesitated. He couldn't believe it, but he was nervous about seeing Jacquelyn. He knew she was upset with him, and he felt ashamed he had withheld information ... okay, very important information, from her.

"Is something wrong, Fane?" his father asked him.

"While Jacquelyn and Mom were out, she learned about having to move to Romania," Fane explained.

"Ahh," Vasile said in understanding. "You did not tell her yourself, and now she is upset with you. Rightfully so, I might add. You know there should be no secrets between mates."

"I was trying to spare her any further stress—at least until the challenge is over. I wasn't trying to be deceitful, but I see now I should have put more faith in her ability to handle difficulties," Fane admitted.

"You will learn, Son. Granted, you may fail a lot in the process and even spend nights in, as the Americans say, the doghouse, but nonetheless, you will learn," his father told him, patting him on the back. "Come, let's go face the wrath of your little fire. Once she gets it out of her system, she will be better."

Fane walked cautiously into the living room feeling like prey, which was weird since he was a predator. He didn't like it at all. Jacquelyn was seated in the ugly chair, as he had heard her think of it. That placement, combined with her posture, told him she didn't want him sitting by her. He couldn't help but grin. As if she felt his presence, she looked up directly into his eyes, and that look pierced him to his soul. She was his ... and she was angry. In fact, if it were possible, he imagined steam would be coming off those red curls. Before he could go to her, Jen walked right into his line of vision. She didn't look too happy either.

"A word, furball," Jen said before walking into the dining room. She obviously expected him to follow, which he did.

She turned and pinned him with a stare equal to the one Jacquelyn had already given him.

"I'm going to say this one time, and only once. It would be very wise of you to listen up. If there is anything, and I mean anything, even if it's something like you have an extra toe or whatever, anything at all you are not telling Jacque, you had better come clean. What you did was so, so, so not cool. Do you get that? You have walked into her world and pulled the proverbial rug out from underneath her feet. She deserves to know the truth about everything. If there is some weird mating ritual, then I'm giving you fair warning, 'cause in case you haven't noticed, she's a little touchy about the whole physical part of a relationship. If you don't tell her now, you're liable to end up as a rug in front of her fireplace. Are we clear, Cujo?" Jen asked.

"Very, very clear. I didn't mean to—," Fane started to say.

Jen held her hand up to silence him. "Save it, fleabag. I'm not the one you have to convince. You make Jacque happy, that makes Sally and me happy."

"Jen, are you done laying down the law with my mate yet?" they heard Jacquelyn ask.

"I suppose I'm finished," Jen said. But before she was out of the dining room, she added, "For now."

Fane watched Jen walk out of the room, thankful she had not lived up to her reputation of inflicting pain. When she was no longer in sight, he went back to Jacquelyn. She was leaning against the wall with her arms folded across her chest. Her glare wasn't quite as harsh as when she was sitting in the chair, but it was still a glare, nonetheless.

"Jacquelyn…" Fane started, but Jacquelyn started shaking her head.

"I don't want to talk about it right now. I just want to get something to eat. I want to get away from those wolves that just came into my living room, and then I want to go lie in my bed and brood. Whatever you have on the tip of your tongue, just save it."

Fane had been so engrossed in his conversation—well, his scolding rather—with Jen that he had not heard or smelled the other wolves come in. He growled as his eyes phased to his wolf sight.

"I understand," Fane said. Again, Jacquelyn tried to silence him, but this time he would not submit. "No, Jacquelyn, you are going to listen to what I have to say." Jacquelyn's head snapped up at the tone in Fane's voice. He tried to soften it, but by the look on her face, he was unsuccessful. "I understand you are mad at me, and rightfully so, but for the moment I need you to please trust me and do as I say. We are going to go to the kitchen and get something to eat, and then we are going to go up to your room. If you don't want me in the room with you, that is fine. I will sit in the hall. As long as the other wolves are in the house, you will be close to me," he finished with a low growl.

Jacquelyn took in a sharp breath when she finally noticed his eyes had phased. She walked over to him and took his hand and placed it against her cheek. She closed her eyes, pressing her face against the palm of his hand and whispered, "Yours."

Fane leaned down and blew warm air on her neck, putting his scent on her. Then he kissed her lips softly. "I love you," he told her gently.

"I know," Jacquelyn said in reply.

Fane pulled his hand away from her face and took her hand. He led her into the kitchen and deftly made two sandwiches. He grabbed a bag of chips and two bottles of water from the fridge, then, turning to Jacquelyn, he told her, "I want you to walk in front of me, please."

Jacquelyn acquiesced to his wishes without argument. They walked through the living room, and as they did, she could feel the eyes of the other wolves on her. Fane snarled at them, and Jacquelyn saw them all drop their gazes immediately. Fane was holding it together by a thread. He needed to bond with his mate, or he was likely going to wind up killing one of these wolves.

Once in Jacquelyn's bedroom, he eased up a little. Knowing she was safe and with him helped calm him and his wolf. They both sat down on the floor, and Fane spread their makeshift picnic in front of them.

"Do you want me to sit out in the hall?" he asked her.

"No, you dork, I'm not going to make you sit in the hall even though I'm not very pleased with you," Jacquelyn told him. "I don't want to talk about that right now. Tell me about these other wolves. Why did you go all postal on Boian when he got in my face, even though he wasn't doing anything?"

Fane took slow breaths, calming himself. Jacquelyn didn't realize how valuable she was to a Grey male. He had to help her understand, but to do that, he had to stay calm.

"You are a female."

"Spot on there, wolfman. Any more bright revelations to share?"

"You didn't let me finish, Luna."

"Oh, my bad, please do continue," Jacquelyn said.

"You are a half *Canis lupus* female, able to mate with a male. The female to male ratio for werewolves is somewhere around thirty males to one female. To put it simply, you're in very high demand. Now, yes, you have found your mate, but the catch is, you are not bonded to your mate. No Blood Rites have been performed, no mating has taken place, and to unmated males, that makes you fair game. Naturally, around other unmated males, I'm just a little territorial when it comes to you. I can never show weakness to another dominant wolf. For them to see weakness in me means I'm vulnerable. And vulnerability to a wolf means easy prey," Fane explained.

"Is that why you would not sit down until they did?" Jacquelyn asked.

"That's correct. A more dominant wolf's head is never lower than the less dominants. As for why I took Boian to the floor, he was closer to you than he should have been, and he scared you. For those reasons, he needed to be disciplined. He now knows not to go near you, or I will kill him," Fane said matter-of-factly.

"Isn't that a little over-the-top?" she asked him.

"Not when it comes to *Canis lupus*. Unmated males can be volatile and unpredictable. Giving them boundaries helps them keep their wolf in check. The other reason is a mated female is not to be touched by another male unless her mate says it is okay. That is just another way to prevent fights. I know it doesn't make sense to you and seems archaic, but there is an animal that lives inside us, and that animal has to be kept under control. The human part of me is what kept me from tearing Boian to shreds. The wolf would not have shown mercy, which is what sets us apart from full-blooded wolves," he answered.

Jacquelyn didn't say anything. She just took bites of her sandwich and chewed slowly, obviously in thought. Fane ate his sandwich as well and let her think about what he had told her. He knew it was a lot to take in, but he also knew she had a right to know everything.

"So, did I freak you out?" he asked her.

"Fane, sweetie, I'm way past freaked out, but I'm dealing," she answered.

Fane finished his sandwich and then stretched out on her bedroom floor, arms behind his head. He let out a big yawn and closed his eyes.

"I'm gonna take a nap if you don't mind. Could you please

stay up here until the other Greys leave?" he asked her, trying very hard to not sound like he was ordering her around. *See? I'm learning.*

"Since you asked rather than demanded, I will stay. I'm kind of tired too."

Jacquelyn stood up and stretched, then kicked off her shoes and climbed up onto her bed. She laughed when Fane turned and propped himself up on an elbow, looking at her questioningly.

"You're just gonna let me sleep on the floor, Luna?" he asked her incredulously.

"Well, you are a wolf. I don't think it's a good idea to start the habit of you sleeping in the bed, you know, with all the shedding and whatnot," Jacquelyn teased.

Fane stood up, unfolded his tall form, and stalked forward, eyes squinted, looking every bit the predator. Jacquelyn squealed and started to get up off the bed, but before she could, Fane wrapped his arm around her and pulled her back down. They were both laughing and breathless when Fane looked down into Jacquelyn's eyes. He kissed her on the forehead, settled in next to her, and pulled her close to him. Once again, he started humming his favorite country song until they drifted off to sleep.

"Should we wake them up?" Sally asked Jen.

"Yeah, but first we should draw on their faces. We could put paw prints on Jacque's face and claw marks on Fane's," Jen said laughing. "Get it? Paws, ya know 'cause he's a wolf."

Sally was looking at her like she had grown an ear on her forehead.

"Oh, never mind," Jen said as she batted her hand at Sally.

"You are one disturbed little girl, you know that, right?" Sally asked her sarcastically.

Jen gave Sally a "go to hell" look and then said, "Just wake them up already. Fane's dad said he needed to talk to all of us, and I'm guessing that means the prince and princess here."

"There's no need to wake us up, you dip. Nobody could possibly sleep with Thelma and Louise standing over them gabbing. And if you had drawn anything on our faces, I would personally make sure the entire school knew you had a third nipple," Jacque told her crankily.

"Who has a third nipple?" Fane perked up.

"Oh, bring up the word nipple and you're all ears, furball. And you," Jen said, pointing her finger at Jacque, "know I don't have a third nipple, so how can you possibly tell people that?"

"I know that, but do they? And how exactly would you disprove me? Flash the school at a pep rally?" Jacque asked, sounding victorious.

Sally laughed and Fane grinned.

"Man, she so got you pinned, sista, ha!" Sally pointed at Jen and gave Jacque a fist bump.

"Okay, fine, whatever. Both of you get your royal arses up. Fane, your dad wants to talk to everyone down in the living room," Jen told them. Then she grabbed Sally by the arm and pulled her out the door, muttering as they went, "What the hell? You're supposed to be on my side now that Jacque has to side with her furball all the time."

"Hey, I side with the victor, Thelma. So next time, win and I will be in your corner," Sally told her with a wink.

"Why do I have to be Thelma? I'm more of a Louise personality," Jen whined.

"Seriously, do you want to argue about what movie characters we are going to be?" Sally asked her in amazement.

"I'm just saying," Jen retorted, holding her hands up in surrender.

Jacque stood up and lifted her arms in the air, stretching. She looked down and saw that Fane was watching her intently.

"What are you looking at, oh prince of wolves?" Jacque asked him.

"I'm looking at my beautiful mate, and are the nicknames ever going to stop?" Fane asked her.

"Hmmm, well I guess I could... Nope, sorry, there are just too many possibilities, and I like to explore my creative side," Jacque said in mock seriousness.

Fane stood up, wrapped his arms around her, and kissed her hair. Jacque leaned into him, loving the way he felt against her and the way he smelled. She noticed the clock on her dresser said 6:30 p.m. and her stomach tightened. They had slept the day away, and every minute that went by brought them closer to the challenge. She closed her eyes and squeezed Fane tighter, wishing she could just whisk them away to somewhere safe with just a thought. *Geez, you would think with all this werewolf stuff there would be some way to tele-port or something, but nooooo, that would be too weird—not like werewolves weren't weird or anything.*

"Guess we better head downstairs," Fane said.

She pulled away from him, put on her best smile, and nodded her head. Fane took her hand and they went down-stairs. Everyone was seated already, and oddly enough, they were all in the exact spots they had been that morning. The other Greys were sitting on the floor. Fane didn't hesitate to sit down on the couch.

"What did you need to talk with us about, *Tata*, Father?" Fane asked.

"Just some finalizations of the plans for tomorrow. First, I want Jacquelyn to shower over at the Henrys' in the morning."

Fane put his hand on Jacque's knee before she could protest. "It's so you won't have my scent on you. It will provoke Lucas and his wolves much more if you smell like me," Fane explained.

"Oh, alright then," Jacque said out loud. Everyone looked at her. "Dang, I always do that, and then I look like a crazy person talking to myself."

"I take it you explained why I want her to do that?" Vasile asked Fane.

"Yes, I explained she didn't need to have my scent on her. What about clothes?" Fane asked.

"I've got that taken care of," Lilly said. "I bought her brand-new things and took them to the Henrys'."

"Oooh, did you get her a shirt that says, 'Team Fane' on it, 'cause that would so rock," Jen said grinning.

All eyes turned to Jen, Sally slapped her on the arm, and Jacque just rolled her eyes. Vasile cleared his throat, which brought everyone's attention back to him.

"Second, the challenge starts at 10:00 p.m. Fane, I want you and the rest of the pack there at 8:30 p.m. I want you to know your battlefield, so to speak. You need to look at the ground, check for soft spots, any holes, or sharp objects. Knowing your battlefield can give you an advantage over your opponent. I want you to check it in both forms, wolf and man, understand?" his father asked.

"As you say," Fane responded.

"Lastly, Mina and Lilly, I need you to prepare for the bonding ceremony. I thought about waiting to bond them until we get to Romania, but after seeing Fane's reactions, and especially after the challenge, I think it would be best for all involved if they are bonded as quickly as possible. The evening after the challenge, Fane and Jacquelyn will be bonded," he announced.

Jacque had started having difficulty breathing as soon as she heard Vasile say that her mother and Alina were to prepare for the bonding ceremony. Now Jacque was coughing and trying to suck in air through her closing windpipe. Jen jumped up and began pounding on Jacque's back hollering, "Cough it up."

"She wasn't eating anything, you dip weed. Quit hitting her," Sally told Jen as she jerked her arm and pulled her back down.

Finally, Jacque was able to get enough air to speak. "Don't I get a say in when the bonding thingy happens?"

Vasile looked at her like she had grown horns out of her head. "No."

"NO? What do you mean no? I mean, cripes, I'm the one bonding my life to a wolf for all eternity, I'm the one getting bitten, and I'm the one being hauled off to a third-world country, so NO is not good enough!" Jacque stood up and stomped her foot.

"*Ea doar stomp piciorul ei?* Did she just stomp her foot?" Decebel asked.

Fane growled at him, and that caused the wolf to lower his head in submission. Then Fane turned to Jacque. "It's not a real good idea to yell at an Alpha, Luna," he said as gently as he could. The look on her face made it clear to everyone he should have just kept his mouth shut.

"Oh, this is fixin' to get good," Jen whispered to Sally, who promptly shushed her.

Before Jacque could completely blow her top, Vasile spoke, and there was a push to his words that made everyone, including Jacque, shut up and listen.

"I am Alpha. I know what is best for my pack. Fane is a ticking bomb right now, and I will not have him kill one opponent who is in competition for you only to have him face five more. If you do not want to bond with him, then I will not have him risk his life tomorrow. We will just move you and your mother somewhere out of Lucas' reach. If you do want to bond with him, then you will do it when I tell you to. I'm not asking you to jump in bed with him." Jacque flushed at his words. All the while Fane was growling and trying not to glare at his Alpha. "I am asking you to calm the beast that is raging in Fane. You are his other half, Jacquelyn. You and only you can complete him. Are we clear?" Vasile asked after his speech.

Jacque had tears streaming down her cheeks. *Good grief. When did I become such a cry baby?* The thought of Fane gone, not with her, took her breath away. She did want to bond with him. It was just a shock, that's all. She was ashamed at her outburst, realizing it had come across that she was rejecting Fane. She turned to look at him, and he stared back at her, stark honesty written all over his face. Fane wanted her. He wanted her for however long they had together. How could anyone turn down unconditional love?

"I'm sorry," she began. Fane surged to his feet and roared, storming out the front door. The other wolves whined and cowered, and Alina hung her head, shoulders shaking with silent sobs. Jacque was a little confused, then the lightbulb hit. Naturally, Jen was a step ahead of her.

"He thought you were saying you were sorry that you didn't want him, genius," Jen told her, sounding very put out.

Jacque jumped up and ran after Fane. She made it out the front door and saw he was nearly across the street, striding toward the Henrys'.

"Fane! Wait," Jacque called as she ran after him. "I wasn't..." *Huff, huff, pant, pant.,* "... saying I didn't want you," Jacque told him breathlessly. "Please, how..." Jacque took another deep breath. "Crap. Hold on. I can't breathe," she told him. Once she caught her breath she continued, "How could you possibly think I don't want you?"

Fane had his back to her, his head bent, shoulders slumped in defeat. He didn't answer.

"Dammit, answer me!" Jacque yelled at him as she grabbed his arm and jerked it to turn him toward her. Tears filled his eyes but hadn't spilled over yet. It hurt her to know she was the cause of those tears.

"Do you want me?" Fane asked her.

"Yes," Jacque answered without hesitation.

Fane stepped forward, towering over her, and she took an involuntary step back.

"Then why do you have a problem bonding with me in two days?"

"It's not that I have a problem with it, Fane, I was just taken by surprise. You were raised knowing that one day you would bond with someone in a way that is so far beyond what humans do. I was not. It's just a lot to swallow. But I'm good. I'm okay. I had my little fit and, yes, I stomped my foot, but I'm ready to move forward," Jacque told him.

Fane grabbed her hand and brought it to his lips. He didn't take his eyes off her as he kissed her hand. Jacque's breathing sped just a bit as she noticed the predatory gleam in his eyes.

"So, we are good, yes?" Fane asked her.

"Nope, babe, we are great," she answered and stood on her tiptoes to kiss his lips. Fane growled and pulled her close. Jacque giggled and batted her hand at him.

"Stop that, wolfman. We've gotta go explain to the others that I wasn't rejecting you. Your mother was having a break-down," Jacque told him.

Fane took her hand and pulled her quickly back toward her house. As they entered the living room, Jacque saw that Alina hadn't moved, but Vasile was now sitting next to her with his arm around her. At the sight of Fane, Vasile stood and stepped away from Alina. Jacque rushed to Alina and knelt in front of her.

"Alina, please, I wasn't rejecting Fane. I didn't get to finish what I was saying before he jumped up and took off. I was apologizing for the little two-year-old fit I threw. Apparently, I didn't get them all out of my system as a child. I want to bond with Fane. I will bond with him right now," Jacque said, but then Alina's head snapped up and she put her hands on either side of Jacque's face.

"You can't bond with him yet, child. Once you are bonded, your fates are tied to one another. If Fane is killed in the challenge, you will die as well," Alina explained.

"Hells bells, I forgot about that. Well, I intend to mate with him." Jacque paused when Alina tried to cover a laugh with a cough and Fane rumbled low in his chest. "What did I say?"

"Well, Sherlock, you sort of threw out there you were planning on doing the horizontal mamba with fur ball here," Jen said pointing her thumb at Fane.

"The horiz..." Jacque started to say, sounding confused, then it hit her what she had said. She had said mate, not bond. *Crap.*

"I wasn't talking... I mean I wasn't... That is to say I..." Jacque was trying hard to correct her mistake, but she was thoroughly embarrassed at this point.

Fane walked up behind her and put his arms around her waist, pulling her against him. He leaned down to whisper in her ear. "And here I thought you were so shy," he teased her.

Jacque pulled away quickly and put her hand on his chest as if to hold him back. "Uh-uh, buddy, you back up and keep those paws to yourself. I meant to say I will bond with you once the challenge is over. Bond as in b-o-n-d. Clear?" she asked him.

And repeating what she had said to his father, he answered with a very sly, very suggestive grin. "Crystal." Then to seal it, he winked at her.

"Holy crap, is it hot in here, or is it just the freaking fine Romanian prince? Cuz I am so, so burning up! I mean, did anybody else see that wink and that smile? He wasn't even doing it to me, and I'm all hot and bothered. I mean geez, man!" Jen said fanning herself.

The three wolves on the floor were trying hard not to laugh, but it just wasn't working. Vasile didn't even disguise his laughter, Alina was beaming, and even Lilly was laughing.

Well great. Everyone saw her man make a pass at her, and she couldn't even enjoy it with all these buttheads laughing. The grin on Fane's face meant he was listening to her thoughts, which made her laugh too.

CHAPTER 16

*F*ane pulled Jacquelyn closer to him as he held her in her bed. The night had gone so quickly, and he refused to close his eyes knowing in the morning she would leave and he would not be able to hold her again until after the challenge. Her scent swirled in the air around him, and her heart beat in rhythm to his own. "Mine," his wolf told him. *Yes,* his wolf agreed, *she is ours.* Not realizing it, Fane began humming the same song he had been humming for the past two days.

"What song is that?" Jacquelyn asked.

"You're going to laugh at me if I tell you," he told her, grinning to himself

"Why would I laugh at you?"

"It's a song sung by Willie Nelson and Kimmie Rhodes. Yes, I'm Romanian, I'm a werewolf, and I like Willie Nelson," Fane said, sounding forlorn.

"Well, admitting it is half the battle," Jacquelyn teased.

"It's a song that makes me think of you, of us."

"Will you sing it to me?"

"Only if you don't laugh."

Jacquelyn didn't say anything in response, so Fane took that as his cue. He began to sing to her.

WHILE FANE SANG, Jacquelyn rolled over to face him and watched him with tears streaming down her face.

"That was beautiful. Your voice is beautiful. Thank you," she blubbered and then cried even harder.

Fane pulled her tightly to him. He kissed her forehead, and in between kisses, he whispered to her, "*una prețioasă*, precious one, *iubirea mea*, my love, *te rog nu plânge*, please do not cry."

But Jacquelyn continued to cry, and it just seemed to get harder. "It isn't supposed to happen like this. You're not supposed to meet the love of your life only to have them be forced to fight some delusional werewolf, with the possibility of dying. Dammit, it's not supposed to happen like this." She sobbed and sobbed.

Fane felt the tears that had been hiding in his eyes finally spill over. The wetness ran down his cheeks. He didn't know what to say. Fane was clueless about how to fix it or make her feel better. So, he decided to just be honest.

"I'm scared," he whispered. "I'm so scared. What if I lose? What if the other wolves attack and my father and the pack aren't able to protect you? What if I lose you? I can't lose you. It would kill me. I don't want you there tomorrow because at least if you aren't there, they can't hurt you," Fane told her as he let the tears fall, completely unashamed. This was his mate. He had only just found her, and he loved her, he treasured her, and he would do anything to protect her.

Jacquelyn looked up at him. She took her hand and wiped away his tears, and then she leaned forward and kissed each eye. For a moment they just looked at each other, as if to memorize each other's faces.

"I'm scared too," Jacquelyn told him. "If I could fight Lucas for you, I would. I don't want to see you hurt. I can't even begin to think of seeing you die. How am I going to do this tomorrow, Fane? I'm so scared we won't have a future together."

At those words, images ran through his thoughts, and he heard Jacquelyn weep as she watched them in her mind.

Fane and her at the bonding ceremony, with their family all around them. Then the picture jumped to Fane and her in a room alone, one of his hands cradling her head, the other resting on her waist, him leaning down and biting her neck to complete the Blood Rites.

Jacquelyn shook with sobs as she continued to see his thoughts. She and Fane walking through a beautiful house, hand in hand, then they were wrapped in each other's arms, tangled in bedsheets with passion in their eyes, then Jacquelyn was in a bed that looked like it was in a hospital. Fane was holding her hand, and her belly was swollen with child. Next, she saw Fane rocking a baby to sleep as Jacquelyn sat watching. Then, once again, they were wrapped in each other's arms, laughing, kissing, touching, loving.

Fane's shoulders shook as he wept, crying over what might never come.

"I'm sorry, Luna. I shouldn't have let you see all that. When you mentioned thinking of our future, it made me think of the things I too have dreamt about with you."

The next thing Fane heard was a whisper so soft he almost missed it.

"Fane, make love to me," Jacquelyn said, almost too soft for even wolf ears to hear.

Fane froze. This was the rock and a hard place no man wants to get into with a woman. If he said no, then he's rejecting her, and she will be embarrassed. If he said yes, then he's a jerk because he's taking advantage of her vulnerability.

Jacquelyn would not have asked this if it were just another night, and he would not make love to her until she asked him when there was no threat to any lives and nothing was creating a passion that might not be as fervent as it seemed at that moment. Now how exactly do you word that to a seventeen-year-old female who already has modesty issues? *Good luck with that, Fane.*

"Jacquelyn, look at me," Fane told her. "I want to make love to you. are we clear on that part?" he asked her.

"Yes, we're clear. There's a but coming on, isn't there?" she asked.

"We are both emotional right now. I don't want you to do something you will regret tomorrow night after the challenge. If I win, and I plan to, you will be sad we didn't wait. I want the first time to be special and perfect for both of us. Please don't think I'm rejecting you because you have no idea how hard it is to say no to you," he told her honestly.

"Wow, I'm impressed," Jacquelyn said, wiping away what was left of the tears on her cheeks.

"Are you mad at me?"

"No, I'm not. I'm a little embarrassed 'cause you know how awkward I am when it comes to the whole physical aspect of a relationship," she told him.

"Why are you embarrassed by it? You do realize that it will be fun, right?" Fane asked her with a wide grin on his face.

"Why do you like to say stuff like that knowing it's going to make me blush?"

"Because it's cute. I won't make love to you Luna, but since we are both awake, I will most definitely take advantage of your beautiful lips," Fane said just before he wrapped an arm around her and flipped her onto her back. Jacquelyn squealed and laughed as Fane leaned over her. He bent down and gently kissed her lips. Jacquelyn wrapped her arms around his neck and pulled him toward her. He rumbled in his chest at her boldness. Fane's left hand was cradling Jacquelyn's head while his right hand was gradually rubbing her thigh and moving slowly up to her waist. Fane was quite proud of himself for telling Jacquelyn he would not consummate their relationship, but as he lay there in her arms, feeling her lips on his, their bodies pressed close, he hoped she wouldn't make him wait too long after the bonding. *She will probably want a human wedding first.* It was probably going to be a while before they mated. In that case, he better slow down. He eased off her just a bit and pulled back from her lips. They were both breathing hard.

"Is something wrong?" Jacquelyn asked him, looking very worried.

"No, everything is very right. I just need to slow down a little. My honor only goes so far. Wolf or not, I'm still a guy, and you are a very fine girl," Fane told her with no shame.

"Oh, I see. You were getting all worked up, only to realize all worked up is all there is. Am I right?"

"Yes, Luna, you are brutally right. Can I be brutally blunt?" he asked her.

"By all means," she answered.

"At what point do you plan to make the same offer?"

Jacquelyn laughed at that. "You're worried about how long it's going to be before we do the deed?"

"Well, since you put it so eloquently, yes, that is what I'm asking," Fane answered.

"I want to be married first." Jacquelyn held up her hand to keep Fane from saying whatever it was that was fixing to leave his lips. "Married in the traditional way, not just the werewolf bonding thingy," she explained.

"You do realize our werewolf bonding thingy is more binding than your human marriage, right?" Fane told her smugly.

"That may be, my little furball, but I still want our relationship recognized in the eyes of normal people as legit. Got it?"

Fane grinned at her. "As you wish, Luna."

"That's what I like to hear, wolfman," Jacquelyn told him as she yawned.

"Try to get some sleep, love. It's going to be a long day tomorrow," Fane told her and kissed her on the head.

He began to hum the song he sang to her earlier, and even though he so desperately wanted to stay awake, his wolf knew they both needed rest and helped push him into a deep sleep.

FROM THE MINUTE Jacque woke up, things were a blur. Fane kissed her sweetly, held her close, then finally let her go and watched her walk across the street to the Henrys' house. She showered and put on the new clothes her mom had bought, and they weren't too bad. A pair of cute jeans and a simple, green, fitted, V-neck top. She was proud of her mom for not taking the opportunity to put her in a ridiculous outfit that made her look twelve. *Points to you, Mom.*

By the time she got downstairs, Jen and Sally had arrived, and that put a big smile on Jacque's face.

"What are you two doing here?" she asked, and before she could give them a chance to answer, she added, "And don't y'all smell like the wolves?"

"Nope, we went home, showered, and put on clothes that had not been at your house. So, we are werewolf-smell free," Jen told her.

"Awesome, so instead of fretting by myself, I get to make y'all miserable by fretting with you," Jacque said.

"Shut up! Do you honestly think we would let you spend

this day, of all days, alone? Sorry, *chica*, no such luck," Sally told her.

Jacque was so thankful she wasn't going to be left to her own thoughts. They were already beginning to feel over-whelming, but Jen took charge, and before Jacque knew it, it was 8:00 p.m. She went to the Henrys' front window and looked across the street at her house. Sure enough, she saw Sorin and Fane coming out of the front door. Her heartbeat sped when he turned and looked back at her. It reminded her of the night he arrived, which had only been five days ago. Could it be possible it had been a mere five days since she first laid eyes on him? She felt like she had known him all her life, like he had always been there with her. He grinned at her and winked.

"I love you, Luna. More than I ever thought possible, I love you," Jacque heard him tell her through his thoughts. A single tear ran down her face, and she hastily wiped it away. She was not going to be weak. Jen and Sally had moved beside her and were looking out the window as well.

"That is one fine meat specimen," Jen said with a sly grin plastered on her face.

"Why am I not surprised that is what you would be thinking about at a time like this?" Sally asked her.

"Hey, there is never a time to not appreciate a fine-looking man. Am I right, Jacque? You know I am."

"Well, when it's one as fine as Fane, then yes, you are right," Jacque said with a smile. She knew Jen was just trying to lighten the mood, and she was grateful.

The next hour seemed to drag. Jacque spent most of it pacing the Henrys' living room and mumbling things under her breath. She so desperately wanted to seek out Fane's thoughts, or hear him in her mind, but his father had made it very clear Fane needed to concentrate on the challenge only, so Jacque refrained from sending him any thoughts.

Jacque jumped when she heard a knock on the Henrys' front door. Jen looked out the front window to check if it was friend or foe.

"It's Fane's mom. Guess it's that time," Jen told them.

Jen opened the door and Alina stepped in. She was dressed in black cargo, military-style pants, a black T-shirt, and black boots. Her long hair was pulled back in a ponytail. She looked so badass.

"You look like you are planning on doing more than just watching," Sally told her.

"It's always best to be prepared. I'm trained in all sorts of fighting styles, so if a full-out battle ensues, someone will have to stay in human form to take care of Jacque, and I can protect her even though I will not be in my wolf form," Alina explained.

"Is there any way we could maybe take a vehicle and just be parked close to the field as a backup, like if y'all need a quick getaway? What do ya think?" Sally asked, and it took everyone by surprise.

"Who are you, and where is my little safe Sally who won't even go over the speed limit?" Jacque teased her.

Alina hadn't said anything yet, and when Jacque looked at her, she could tell Alina was considering Sally's plan.

"You do realize that if I allow this, I will be disobeying my husband's orders?" Alina asked them.

"Don't you have to do what he orders, like the other wolves? When he gives them an order, sometimes they have to obey whether they want to or not, right?" Jen asked her.

"No, I am an Alpha female, and I am his mate. He cannot really give me orders. I like to think of them as firm suggestions," Alina told them with a wink.

"Nice," Jen said giving Sally and Jacque fist bumps. "What do you say?" Jen asked Alina.

"I think it is a good idea. However, you must be surreptitious. If the other wolves smell you, there will be an all-out war. Do you understand?" Alina asked sternly.

"We hear you loud and clear. We are good at sneaking. We aren't going to go into how we got so good at it, but rest assured it's almost a specialty of ours," Jen told her.

Jacque was shaking her head, clearly not in agreement with the things transpiring.

"Wait just one darn minute! I can't let you guys do this. Don't you realize how dangerous this is? If anything happened to y'all because of me I would never be able to live with myself." Jacque was on the verge of having one of her two-year-old moments.

Sally and Jen both wrapped their arms around Jacque and squeezed her tight.

"I hate to break it to you, Watson, but Jen and I tend to do what we want even when you tell us not to. When we are smiling and nodding at you, we're just humoring you, not agreeing. Surely you know this?" Sally told her in a sweet tone of voice.

"You two drive me crazy," Jacque exclaimed.

"Whoa, back up wolf chick. What would you do if you were in our shoes? You cannot tell me for a minute you would sit at home and wait on us. So, you just take your little safety speech and shove it," Jen said as she let go of Jacque, backed up, and put her hands on her hips.

"Well, Jen, how 'bout you tell me how you really feel?" Jacque said sarcastically.

Jacque knew they were right. There was no way she would let them go off to something so dangerous while she sat at home. How could she possibly ask them to do the same?

"You're right. I wouldn't stay away. Please promise me you will be so careful!"

"Sweet!" Jen said giving Sally a high five. "We are so going on a stakeout. This so rocks."

Jacque took a deep breath and tried not to give in to the panic threatening to overtake her.

"Jacque, it's time," Alina said gently.

Alina turned and once more told Jen and Sally to make sure they were not seen and to stay downwind so their scent would not reach the wolves. Alina then turned and walked out the front door without a glance back. Jacque knew Alina trusted she would follow, but Alina was also giving Jacque a moment in private with her friends.

"I love you two. Please be careful," Jacque told them as she hugged them both.

"Don't worry 'bout us, Sherlock. You focus on your task, and we will focus on ours," Sally told her.

Jacque didn't linger. She didn't want to turn on the water-works, and she knew they would come if she didn't leave quickly. She waved one last time and rushed out the front door. She saw Alina had pulled the rental car to the curb. Jacque climbed into the passenger seat, and they started off on what proved to be the longest ride of her life, even though the Field of Dreams was only fifteen minutes from her house. They were both silent on the way there, both absorbed in their thoughts, coming to the realization the man they both loved was going to be in the fight of his life tonight, and they both would be watching, whatever the outcome.

Once again Jacque was trying to reconcile the fact that no one could help Fane, not even his own Alpha and father. *How crappy is that?* Alina reached over and touched Jacque's hand, startling her out of her thoughts.

"We are here. There are some things I need to explain quickly. First, I know you've already been warned, but I will warn you again. Do not seek out Fane's thoughts. The images you will see there while he is in battle are images you would never forget. Also, it would distract him. Second, we don't want to draw any unnecessary attention to you so stay close to me and keep quiet. Lastly, should the worst happen, you will turn tail and run as hard as you can to the rendezvous point where the girls are waiting. You will go straight to the airport and board the jet we have chartered. You will not wait for us. Do you understand? We have wolves in position to pick you up at the necessary places. Your friends and mother are to accompany you. There will be no argument."

Jacque's brain was in overdrive. This just couldn't be happening. *Seriously, how had it all come to this?* Jacque shook her head to clear it of the negative thoughts. She needed to be focused. *Just accept it, Jacque. "This is the way it is, and you are just going to have to suck it up and deal. Okay, deep breath. "*I understand," Jacque told Alina, looking her straight in the eyes. Alina simply nodded her head, accepting Jacque's answer. Jacque glanced up for the first time, looking out at the Field of Dreams, seeing it in a whole new light. It was nothing special, and because no one was coming here anymore, the grass had grown tall. There was a path that had been made by a vehicle driving over the tall grass, flattening all in its way. She couldn't see very far because the path took a sudden sharp curve to the right, and the grass left standing blocked her sight. She decided that was a good thing. Just in case someone came by, they wouldn't see anything.

Alina opened her door, and Jacque took this as her cue to get out of the car. As they walked down the man-made path, she did not hear anything at first, but the farther they walked, she began to hear growling and deep voices. After rounding a sharp right curve, the area opened up suddenly into a perfect circle. All the grass in the circle had been completely mown. Someone had set up lights that were attached to chargers all around the circle. Jacque thought this must be something the wolves have had to do many times, and she shuddered at the thought.

As soon as she and Alina stepped into the clearing, everyone froze, except for Vasile. He just continued speaking to Sorin. Alina grabbed Jacque's hand and began to walk toward her husband. A man Jacque had never seen stepped in front of them and fell down on one knee. He turned his neck to the side, exposing it to Jacque. She looked to Alina, not sure what to do, but Alina was not looking at Jacque. She was staring daggers at the man on the ground, and to Jacque's surprise, Alina was growling as well.

"She is not your Luna," Alina said in a very calm but very scary voice. "Move out of our way, or I will break your neck." The coolness of her voice caused Jacque to shiver.

The guy, or wolf rather, ignored Alina completely. Taking a page from Alina's book, Jacque pulled her shoulders back, stood as tall as she could, and in the firmest voice she could muster said, "Go back to your Alpha now."

The wolf whined but stood up, and with eyes on the ground, he turned and walked away. Jacque took a deep breath, closed her eyes to regroup, and then began moving forward with Alina again. She still had not seen Fane or Lucas for that matter. She saw Vasile's other pack members were here, and as soon as Alina and Jacque reached Vasile, those wolves flanked both Alina and Jacque. Vasile stepped in front of Jacque and looked her in the eyes, and although Jacque was not a full werewolf, she felt the power in that stare and had to drop her eyes.

"I trust you have been told what to do in any outcome?" Vasile asked her very softly.

Jacque looked to Alina asking with her eyes if Vasile knew about Sally and Jen. Alina gave the tiniest turn of her head, which Jacque took to mean that he did not, so Jacque simply nodded, not trusting herself to speak and blurt out their whole plan.

"Good, now my wolves will stay around you and Alina for the duration. I want you all to back up about five paces and do not move." Vasile said those last three words with his eyes once again locked on Jacque.

Am I really that bad at following orders? Then she mentally nodded. Yeah, I most definitely am.

They collectively stepped back five paces and stopped. Jacque realized Alina still had her hand. When Jacque saw Fane come out from a curve in the circle, she was glad Alina was there because Jacque took an involuntary step toward him. Several things happened all at once. Every wolf around her put a hand on her to pull her back. Fane's head turned and looked straight at her just as all the hands were descending. Fane let out a snarl and his course of direction changed, coming toward Jacque. A huge growl came from Fane's left and caused him to stop.

"You know, Prince, that if you so much as speak to her before the challenge begins you will forfeit, and I will be able to kill you without a fight, right?"

Jacque realized Lucas had let out the huge growl and was talking now.

Fane growled back, then he looked back to Jacque. He did not take another step toward her, nor did he speak to her. Instead, he looked to the other wolves and his mother.

"Restrain her if need be for her safety, but there is to be no mark left on her body, not a single scratch or bruise," Fane told them. The other wolves, in turn, lowered their eyes and nodded once in recognition of Fane's orders.

Jacque looked at Alina and whispered, "Sorry, that was so my fault."

"It's alright. The wolves are tense. Anything will set them off, so let's just be as still as possible," Alina whispered back.

Jacque nodded and turned back to look at what was happening in the circle. Vasile was standing in the center, and Jacque could feel power coming off him in waves. All of a sudden, every wolf fell to their knees. Jacque looked all around and shrugged her shoulders. *Huh, that's different.*

CHAPTER 17

*J*acque turned and saw Alina still standing, as well as Vasile, and that's when she realized Vasile must have done his Alpha voodoo, as Jen would say.

"I stand Alpha over this challenge," Vasile began. "All rules will be followed. The penalty for any not followed is death at my hands." Vasile paused and looked around the circle at each wolf that was kneeling. None met his eyes. None so much as moved. Jacque could tell some wanted to fight the orders Vasile was giving, but he was more dominant and he was Alpha, so they had no choice but to obey.

"Lucas Steele, come forward," Vasile said looking straight at him. "Fane Lupei, come forward."

Both men came to stand in front of Vasile. Neither looked him in the face. Both appeared to stare over his shoulder at something in the far distance.

"Lucas, you challenge Fane for the bonding ceremony to his mate, Jacquelyn Pierce. Is that correct?" Vasile asked the Alpha.

"Yes," Lucas growled, still apparently under Vasile's control and not liking it.

"Fane, you accepted this challenge understanding that it is to the death?"

"Yes." Fane's voice was steady, no growl, no sign of weakness. It made Jacque want to scream at how unfair this all was. She had only just found him. She shook it off and tried to focus.

"You will fight in wolf form. You will receive no help from your pack. The fight is to the death. Neither of you can choose to submit. If you submit, your opponent will still kill you. Do each of you understand the rules as I have laid them out in the presence of these witnesses?" Vasile asked them.

Both wolves spoke at the same time.

"I understand the rules as you have laid them out. I understand that should I choose to defy your orders, I will be put to death by your hands. Let it be as you have said, Alpha."

Vasile nodded and then turned to walk toward the edge of the circle. He turned and gave the wolves a look. It must have meant something because they stepped apart, and in a matter of a few breaths, where men had been now stood wolves.

The first thing Jacque noticed was that Fane was the larger wolf. But Fane was a large guy, so it would only fit that he be a large wolf. Fane's fur was pitch black while Lucas's was a deep brown. They were both beautiful, and they were both snarling. Their hackles were raised, heads low toward the ground. The picture they made was terrifying.

"Begin," Vasile said, and her heart felt like it had moved into her throat.

For a few moments, all they did was circle one another, and every so often one would take a step forward causing the other to snarl and snap their teeth. Alina still held Jacque's hand, and Jacque was squeezing it so tight she hoped she wasn't hurting her. Suddenly Jacque heard a sound to the left of her.

"Come on, Alpha, he's just a pup," one of Lucas's wolves yelled. In an instant, he was on the ground whining as if in pain. Jacque turned to Vasile. Sure enough, the Alpha was looking straight at the wolf, and power was once again radiating from him. All the other wolves took steps back when they realized the Romanian Alpha was not playing.

Jacque heard a snarl. Turning back to the fight, she saw Lucas had taken advantage of the distraction and lunged at Fane. But Fane was ready and moved before Lucas could get near him. As Lucas turned to get Fane back in his sights, Fane circled around and snapped at Lucas's back leg. The bark that came from Lucas made it clear Fane had hit his mark. Fane backed up quickly before Lucas could react. Jacque watched them circle and lunge, nip and bark. It looked almost like a dance.

She started feeling lightheaded, and Jacque realized she was holding her breath. She took a couple of good deep breaths and tried to relax her stance. *Yeah, fat chance of that.*

Suddenly, Lucas was on Fane. He had managed, somehow in their dance, to get close enough to get a solid grip on Fane's rear right leg. Fane snarled and turned hard, trying to bite at Lucas. Lucas hung on with a death grip. Fane shook his leg violently. When that didn't work, he began to roll his body, twisting his leg at the same time. Jacque froze. If he kept that up, he was going to break his leg. Jacque felt Alina tense. When she glanced at Fane's mother's face, she could tell Alina realized the same thing. Jacque started to say something, but Alina growled, so Jacque put her hand over her mouth as a physical barrier to keep quiet. But just as soon as she covered her mouth, she wanted to cover her ears because the snarls and whines coming from Fane were breaking her heart. Finally, she heard a crack and a whine mixed with a growl. When she looked up, she saw that Fane had managed to get free of Lucas, but he had done it at the price of his leg. He was now fighting with his right rear leg held limply off the ground.

Despite the injury, Fane was still fierce and quick as lightning, Fane lunged forward and had half of Lucas' face in his mouth. Fane made a tearing motion as if he was ripping meat from a bone and jerked his head to the side. Jacque saw fur and flesh sling out of Fane's mouth and heard Lucas howl in pain. Lucas was shaking his head erratically and desperately trying to keep an eye on Fane as he attempted to recover from the attack. As they circled again, Jacque saw that Fane had nearly ripped Lucas' right eye out. There was blood all over his face, and there was no way he could see from that eye. Fane had just evened the playing field.

Okay, wolfman, let's finish this.

Lucas took a running leap and landed on Fane's back. It was far from over. Lucas didn't stay on his back, but instead, he bit into Fane, tore his fur, and then jumped back. Lucas did this over and over, and within a matter of minutes, Fane was bleeding all over, his fur matted. Blood covered the ground. Jacque shook from the effort it took not to scream, not to beg someone to stop this. Tears streamed down her face, and her lips trembled behind her hand. This could not be happening. She squeezed her eyes tight and then opened them again.

She saw Lucas lunge again and bite into Fane's right side. Fane stumbled. He snapped as Lucas jumped back but only got the air. Blood poured from the bite in his side, and she saw Fane fall on his front paws. That was all she could stand.

"STOP! STOP THIS," Jacque yelled as she fought against the grip the other wolves had on her.

"Jacque, be still," Alina said.

Jacque swung around and glared at Alina. "I WILL NOT

BE STILL, DAMMIT! LOOK AT WHAT HE IS DOING TO YOUR SON. DO YOU NOT SEE?" Tears poured out of Jacque's eyes. She didn't care. She was broken inside, and she couldn't stand it any longer.

Fane struggled but finally stood up, and the two wolves continued to circle. Fane got a couple of good bites in, and at least now Lucas was bleeding and his fur was coated in blood as well. Both wolves stopped and were very still, just staring at each other. Jacque cried and fought the grip Vasile's wolves had on her. And just as quickly as the stillness had come, it was gone. Lucas moved in low this time, grabbing Fane under his muzzle on his throat. As Lucas grabbed Fane, Lucas slid and pulled Fane up and over him so that Fane landed on his side. There was a tremendous thud, a low growl, and a high whine. Everyone was still, almost like someone had pushed the pause button on a movie, and then someone hit play. Fane lay still beneath Lucas's jaws. Lucas's wolves growled and howled. Alina stood next to Jacque, still as a statue. No tears streaked her face yet. Jacque lost it. She screamed and cried and pulled against the wolves.

"FANE, GET UP! GET UP NOW! DON'T YOU DARE LEAVE ME! DON'T YOU DARE." Jacque shook with her sobs. The wolves holding her got distracted for a moment, and it was her window. She tore loose from their grip and ran as hard as she could. She plowed into Lucas, pushing with all her might. "GET OFF HIM LUCAS! GET OFF MY MATE, OR SO HELP ME I WILL RIP YOUR THROAT OUT WITH MY BARE HANDS!" Jacque yelled and pushed to no avail. Lucas did not budge. Jacque was vaguely aware of someone wrapping an iron-strong arm around her waist and jerking her back hard. Jacque frantically grabbed at anything she could get her hands on, which happened to be Lucas's fur. She struggled against whoever was trying to pull her away. Instead of being able to hold on, Jacque just ripped out

handfuls of hair from Lucas and, under different circumstances, she would have found it gratifying, but at the
moment all Jacque could see was Fane. Fane on his side,
blood pooling around him. Fane not moving, Fane under the
other wolf whose teeth were still sunk into his neck.

"Please." Jacque sobbed. "Vasile, get him off Fane. God,
how can you let him die? I'm begging you. Please don't let
him die!"

"Get her out of here." Vasile turned and growled at the
wolves holding Jacque. When they didn't move, he snarled.
"NOW! Get her out of here, now!"

"NOOOOOO! I won't leave him. Fane, please, please,
GET UP!" As the wolves began to drag Jacque away, which
they had to do because of her struggles, her pleading got
softer but lost none of the desperation.

"Fane, I love you. Do you hear me? I love you. I don't
want a life without you. Please, love, don't leave me." Jacque's
tears stained her face and shirt from where they poured off
her face. It was no use. Jacque was not strong enough to fight
the wolves. She gave up struggling and instead turned
inward to her pain. She began to cry so hard she started
throwing up, and when she had nothing left in her stomach,
she simply retched up air over and over. The wolves must
have gotten close to where Jen and Sally were parked
because in between sobs and retching, she heard Jen's voice.

"Jacque," Jen shouted as she came plowing toward her.
"Get the hell off her, you mangy mutts!" Jen began yelling at
the wolves all around her. In turn, the wolves growled. "Oh,
hell no, you did not just growl at me. I will castrate you while
you sleep and then hang them on your car antenna, so BACK
THE HELL UP!"

The wolves must have decided Jen was crazy enough to
act on her words because they backed up, hands in the air in
surrender.

"We will not leave her, but we will let you take her into your care," Decebel told them.

"Yeah, yeah, whatever. Now, what happened. Where is Fane?" Sally asked.

The wolves all bowed their heads, and their shoulders slumped in defeat. It was Decebel who spoke. "He has fallen."

With those words, overwhelming dread poured over Jacque. She jumped up, turned back toward the circle, and ran. The wolves were there in a flash, once again holding her around the waist, only this time Decebel turned Jacque toward him and held her. It made her think of how Fane had held her just like that when she had been crying in fear, and it only made her cry harder. Jacque pounded her fist on Decebel's chest as the pain seeped out of her into the night air.

"This cannot be happening. It just can't be." Her body shook, and that made Decebel hold her tighter. He spoke to her softly in Romanian, and once again she thought of Fane. She couldn't take it. Her brain was not able to control her emotions, and so it finally just shut down. The last thing on Jacque's mind before she blacked out was Fane's voice saying *"Soon."* She didn't know if it was her imagination or if it was really him. Whatever it was, she clung to it as the darkness took her.

FANE LAY beneath Lucas's jaws, weak from all the blood loss. He heard Jacquelyn's sobs, her pleading. He had seen her run into Lucas in an attempt to push Lucas off of him, and all the while he had had to lie still. If he had moved, his plan would not have worked. He kept his mind separate from Jacquelyn's, making sure he did not give her any sign he was okay. He hated seeing her hurt, but if she knew he wasn't dead, just very close, she would not have struggled so much and it would have tipped off Lucas. As soon as Jacquelyn was out of sight, Lucas gave Fane one final shake and then began to let go of his neck. The fact that Lucas had not bothered to make sure Fane's heart had stopped was the wolf's mistake. Fane had held his breath, which made Lucas think he was dead. *Foolish, cocky.*

Lucas released Fane's throat, and turned his head up toward the moon, and howled. While he was distracted, his vulnerable throat was completely exposed to Fane, and he took full advantage. With all the strength he had left, he lunged up and sank his teeth deep into Lucas's throat. He tasted his blood, and that fueled his anger. Fane gripped even tighter and felt his jaws crush the vocal cords and windpipe, silencing Lucas's howl. Then Fane jerked his head violently to the left, pulling so hard his teeth ripped Lucas's throat wide open, severing arteries. Blood poured like a rushing river from his throat, pooling on the ground. In less than a minute, Lucas collapsed on his side. Fane would not make the same mistake Lucas did. He took a paw and pushed Lucas onto his back, exposing the most vulnerable part of a wolf. He leaned down and once again sank his teeth into the wolf's flesh, tearing through skin and muscle until he finally disemboweled Lucas. That was an injury from which Fane knew Lucas would not rise.

Fane turned to look at his father, who nodded his head once. Then Fane turned his head upward and howled in victory before collapsing.

"Sorin, Alina, get Fane and take him to the Henrys. Get him cleaned up. I will be there as quickly as I can to heal him," Vasile ordered.

"Forgive me, Alpha, but why do you not want us to take him to his mate?" Sorin asked apprehensively.

"Jacquelyn was hysterical when she was dragged out of

here. She is not likely to be any calmer yet, and she does not need to see Fane in his current state," Vasile explained.

Sorin nodded his understanding. With Alina's help, he gathered up Fane.

Vasile turned back to the wolves Lucas had left behind with his death.

"Who of you is Lucas's second?" Vasile asked them.

A tall, bulky man stepped forward. "I am his second," he answered.

"What is your name?" Vasile asked the man.

"Jeff Stone," the wolf answered.

"You are second no longer, Jeff Stone. You stand Alpha of the Coldspring pack. You are to keep a record of your pack as is *Canis lupus* law. I will check on your pack to make sure you are abiding by the laws. If you do not know them,"— Vasile reached into his back pocket and pulled out his wallet, from which he withdrew a card—"here is my contact information. Call me, and I will help you. Are we clear?"

Jeff nodded and then turned his head, exposing his neck in submission to Vasile.

"Good. Now take your former Alpha and give him a proper burial. Let this be a lesson to each of you that you cannot claim women who are not your mates. Lucas would have never found comfort or peace with Jacquelyn because she was not his true mate. He would have eventually resented her for not being able to give him what he so desperately needed," Vasile explained to the wolves. Then he simply said, "Go," and watched as they collected Lucas's body and left.

Vasile took a deep breath, preparing for the task before him: heal his son and somehow explain to his mate they had intentionally planned for Fane to appear dead. *This is not going to be pretty.*

CHAPTER 18

*F*ane moaned as he struggled to sit up. He was back in his human form and as he looked around, he realized he was in his room at the Henrys' house. He started to stand, but he got very dizzy and had to quickly sit back down.

"Take it easy, Son. You've had quite a night," Fane's father said as he came through the bedroom door.

"Where is Jacquelyn?" Fane asked. The question had been burning a hole in his head since he woke up. He had wanted her there with him so he could hold her and reassure her he was fine. She had been so hysterical the last time he saw her he knew she must still be a mess if she did not know he was alive.

"She is at her house. We did not take you there because I wanted you to look somewhat healthier than you did when Lucas was finished with you," Vasile told him.

That makes sense. Fane gingerly tried standing again and was successful this time. He was thankful someone had thought to put boxers on him so he wasn't naked. He walked over to the mirror to survey the damage.

"It's not too bad, after healing you up a bit. You still have some ugly bruising and minor cuts but no broken bones," his father told him.

Vasile was right about the bruising. Fane looked like someone had taken black, grey, and blue paint and splattered it on him. He had deep cuts on his face, neck, back, and legs. Overall, though, it could have been so much worse. Fane was so, so thankful, for her sake, he had been the victor. Jacquelyn came to his mind, and he felt bile rise in his throat at the memory of her sobs. He had to see her. She needed to know he was okay, and then he was going to have to beg her forgiveness.

"I need to see her, *Tata*, father," Fane said.

"I know, but you need to be prepared for…" Before Vasile could finish, Fane's door swung open so hard it hit the wall with a loud bang.

What came through it was the picture of pure, unadulterated rage, otherwise known as Jen. Sally followed, looking every bit as angry, but in a much more controlled way.

"What on… I mean, how in the…. WTF Fane!" Jen finally yelled. "How could you not tell her you were going to go all armadillo on her? Did you not trust her? Did you think she couldn't handle watching you lay there not fighting back? What on earth was going through that pea-sized, canine mush you call a brain?"

Fane looked confused, and he was. He didn't understand.

"Um … Jen, I hear you and you have every right to be angry, but … well, I don't know what you mean by going armadillo."

Jen rolled her eyes. "You do realize when I have to explain my comparisons and insults it takes a lot of the thunder away, right? It's a Texas thing. Armadillos play dead when they feel threatened. They fall on their sides and go all stiff.

They look dead, but they aren't. Are you with me now, fleabag?"

"Yes, okay, now I understand. There are a couple of reasons I didn't tell her. The first is that we didn't decide on that plan until about fifteen minutes before the challenge started. The second was we needed her reaction to be authentic." Fane realized as soon as Jen's face began to turn shades of purple that the last part might not have been necessary.

"Please, please, for the love of all things that are not were-wolves, tell me you did not just say you wanted her reaction to be authentic." Jen sounded so calm, and her calm was scarier than her yelling.

Fane didn't get a word out before a fist connected with the left side of his face. He was truly in shock. He had never been hit by a girl, and although it didn't hurt, he felt really bad she felt his behavior deserved physical violence.

When he turned his head, he looked at Jen only to see she was, in turn, looking at Sally, who was jumping up and down, shaking her hand, and growling out any and all expletives she could think of.

"Holy crap, man! Why is your face so freaking hard?" Sally yelled.

Jen's mouth was wide open in disbelief, and then a sly grin spread across it. "That was so badass! It's about time you recognize *my* way has its advantages."

"Well, other than my hand being broken, it was worth it," Sally told her.

Fane knelt on one knee in front of the two girls, startling them into silence.

He laid his hand across his heart and bowed his head.

"I am truly sorry my actions caused so much pain. It wasn't my intention, and it tore a hole in me to see my love so broken. I beg your forgiveness but understand if you do not give it," Fane told them with all sincerity.

Jen and Sally looked at Fane, then at each other, and then they looked at Vasile who had silently been watching the whole thing.

"Is he for real?" Sally asked Vasile.

"I ordered him to play dead, therefore, he could not disobey. Ultimately, your anger should be at me. And yes, he is for real, as you put it," Vasile explained.

"Fane," Sally began and then used her hand to tilt his head up so he was looking at them, "we know why you did it, and it was an awesome strategy. It's just that we had to watch Jacque sob so hard she puked up her guts, and then she passed out. It was like her brain couldn't handle what her emotions were doing to her body, so it just turned off. It was horrible, so even though we know it was probably the best strategy, we had to defend our girl. Of course, we forgive you. I wish I could tell you how Jacque is going to react when you tell her what you had to do, but it could go either way. She may be so thankful you're alive she doesn't care, or she may be in such shock from the pain she tries to kill you herself. So, good luck with that." And with that, Jen and Sally turned and left him in silence.

"She doesn't know yet?" Fane softly asked his father.

"No, Son, that honor has been left to you. As the two avenging angels who just left said, good luck with that," Vasile told him. "Get dressed. It's time for you to go see your mate."

His father left him, and Fane stood up, feeling very numb. He was so broken at having hurt Jacquelyn. How was he going to face her? Without any thought as to what he was doing, Fane dressed, brushed his hair and teeth, and then headed over to Jacquelyn's. It was the longest walk he'd ever made, and yet it was the shortest as well.

Fane opened the front door to Jacquelyn's house. Everyone, save Jacquelyn, was sitting in the living room, and as he walked in all their eyes turned on him. He took a deep breath and walked in farther. His mother was the first to move. She came over to him and exposed her neck. Fane took a step back, unbelieving of her action.

"I am your mother and your Alpha, but I acknowledge the sacrifice you had to make." She kissed him on the cheek as a tear rolled down her face. Fane reached up and wiped it away.

"I'm sorry I hurt you, Mama," Fane told her.

"Tsk, tsk, you did what needed to be done. That is what an Alpha does. Because of the responsibility you hold, there will be many decisions you make as an Alpha that others will not understand. No offense to the humans, but they cannot begin to comprehend the weight you will carry on your shoulders, nor the weight you carried this night. You did what no one else could have. That, my son, is what the Alpha does, never doubt that." Then everyone in the room, including the humans, to Fane's astonishment, bowed their heads in submission.

"Jacque is in her room, Fane. She isn't awake yet. She apparently passed out at the challenge, and she has been out ever since," Lilly told him.

Fane closed his eyes and squeezed them against the tears threatening to spill. His mate—his love—broken because of him, but not with Lucas. "She is ours," he heard his wolf say. "As our Alpha said, we did what we had to." Fane turned from the crowded living room and walked up the stairs to Jacquelyn's room.

He opened the door and used his wolf vision to see. The room was dark, illuminated only by a single nightlight. He made his way over to her bed and sat down on the edge. She laid there, her hands folded across her stomach, so still. Fane leaned down and kissed her forehead. He took a deep breath and let her scent fill his lungs. He kissed both cheeks, he kissed her nose and her chin, and then he kissed her lips. Tears ran down his face, and he was trembling. He wanted to hold her, but he didn't want to startle her awake. Slowly, he pulled away from her, and as he sat up, he realized her eyes were open, really open, like very wide open.

"AHHHH!" Jacquelyn screamed and threw the covers over her head. "I've finally gone crazy. His death pushed me over the edge where I've been teetering all along, and then BAM, I'm in the middle of crazy ground." Jacquelyn was mumbling to herself, not totally hysterical, but definitely on the verge. Fane thought he'd better catch her quick before she really did lose it.

"LUNA, you're not crazy. I'm really here. I'm not dead, love. It was fake. I was faking it to lure Lucas into a false victory," Jacque heard the hallucination that was Fane say.

She wasn't going to fall for that. Fane would have told her he was going to do something like that so she wouldn't have to go through it. He would never have allowed her to be hurt so deeply.

"Jacquelyn, please, it's really me. I didn't…" He paused and took a deep breath. Jacque was taken off guard by this show of emotion from a hallucination, not that she had much experience with hallucinations, thank goodness. She pulled the covers down just enough to see Fane. His head was bowed, so he didn't know she was looking at him. "I didn't tell you I was going to appear to die because…" His shoulders shook with sobs, and the tears fell and wet his hands.

"Because what?" Jacque couldn't help but ask.

Fane's head snapped up, and then he cried more. "Luna,

I'm so sorry. I didn't mean to hurt you. Please know that it killed me. I didn't tell you because I needed your reaction to be real, so Lucas would believe he had won."

Jacque sat in stunned silence. She couldn't believe it. Her emotions were at war. She was angry, yes. But who gives a flying flip because he's alive. *He's here, and he can hold you.*

Jacque sat up, leaned forward, and kissed him. She wrapped her arms around him and pulled him down. Fane put his arms around Jacque's waist, and when he pulled her tighter, she let out a sharp yelp.

"What's wrong? What's happened?" Fane asked her, running his hands over her. Jacque saw panic in his eyes.

"It's nothing, just a little sore from the against-my-will retreat tonight. I got a few bruises from being restrained, that's all," Jacque told him, playing it off.

When his hands ran across her stomach, she winced even though she tried so hard not to. Fane growled and then slowly raised the hem of her shirt and exposed her stomach. His growl got much, much deeper. "What the hell happened to you, and who the hell did it?" Fane said.

"Fane, it's nothing. It's—" Jacque tried to explain but was cut off when Fane snarled at her.

"It's NOT NOTHING! You have a bruise as dark as night and as wide as a 2x4 across your stomach, Jacquelyn." Fane paused. She could see the wheels in his mind turning. "Whose arm is that, Jacquelyn? Don't argue with me, Luna. Whose arm is it? You can tell me, or I will discipline each wolf down there instead of just the one."

Jacque sat back up and, to Fane's surprise, pushed him. He was caught off guard and fell off the bed onto her floor. Fane looked up at her in shock.

"Listen up. Your pack restrained me so that I would not get killed trying to kick Lucas's ass. I was trying to kick his ass, in case you forgot, because you didn't tell me you weren't dead, only faking it. So, you aren't going to discipline anyone. You are going to accept that I have a bruise across my stomach, my arms, my shoulders, and my shins because YOU chose to keep ME in the dark. Are we clear?" Jacque was breathing hard from her outburst.

Fane lowered his head then looked up at his mate. "Crystal," he told her and grinned.

"Good, now come back up here and show me how sorry you are," Jacque said playfully.

Fane crawled back onto the bed, and he pulled the hem of her shirt up once more exposing her stomach. He suppressed a growl and then kissed the bruise from one end to the other. She could tell he was taking comfort in the feel of her flesh.

"Okay, stop that. It's tickling me." She giggled.

Fane pulled her shirt back down and gently wrapped his arm around her. He laid his head on her chest and listened to her heartbeat and the sound was like the sweetest music he'd ever heard.

"Fane."

"Hmm."

"Why is your leg not broken?"

"My father healed my major injuries. He can use the power he draws from the pack to heal his wolves. I only have bruises and cuts now," he explained.

"Oh, that's nifty."

Fane chuckled. "Yes, it is most definitely nifty."

Fane raised his head and looked into her eyes. Jacque stared back and shuddered at the thought of losing him. It had almost killed her when she thought he had died. She truly had not wanted to go on.

"I'm so sorry my love for doing that to you. I don't deserve you, your forgiveness, or your love," Fane told her through their bond.

"Oh, shut up. What you did, yes, it was horrible for me,

but it was necessary for you to win. I would go through it again if I knew you would be alive in the end. You deserve more than I can give. I just hope you'll take what I can give you, just me," Jacque told him.

"I love you, Jacquelyn Pierce, my mate, my love, *inima mea*, my heart. I want you to be all mine, with no way for anyone to challenge me for you."

Fane leaned down and kissed her. Jacque moaned, which made him growl. Before things could go much further, Jacque remembered the bonding ceremony and Blood Rights.

"Hey, wait," she said pushing at him.

"You do remember you thought I was dead, right? Now I'm not, and now you can have your way with me because, you know, I'm not dead," Fane told her and then began kissing her neck.

Jacque giggled and pushed him away again. "No really, wait. When are we supposed to do the bond thingy and the whole blood sucking?"

"Vampires, not werewolves, suck blood, love. It's tomorrow, which is not right now, and because I am living in the now and not the tomorrow, I want to reconcile with my mate as wolves do," Fane told her leaning down. Once again, he was stopped by her hand.

"Oh, we're reconciled. We're good to go, no problem," Jacque rambled on.

"Jacquelyn?"

"Yes, Fane?" Jacque said in her most innocent voice.

"You want me to say it, don't you?" Fane asked her.

"Yep, out loud, not in my head," she told him

Fane growled but acquiesced. "I don't mean reconcile as in taking things seriously. I mean through touch." He laughed when she squeaked at that.

"I will not touch you anywhere you don't want to be

touched." And then, mischievously, he said, "However, just name the location, and I will comply." He pulled out of her reach when she tried to thump him for his last comment. When she simmered down, he leaned down again and kissed her.

Jacque turned her head, exposing her neck. Fane rumbled in his chest. Jacquelyn called it purring, and he smiled. He kissed her neck, sniffing her skin.

"My mark will be there after the ceremony," he said.

Jacque picked up on his thoughts, seeing how pleased this made him. She added her own creativity to it, and giggled wickedly when she heard Fane whisper in her mind, *"Soon."*

THANK you so much for reading Prince of Wolves! I truly hope you enjoyed it. If you did, would you please consider leaving a review? They are greatly appreciated!

Continue reading for an excerpt from the second book in the Grey Wolves Series, *Blood Rites.*

ABOUT THE AUTHOR

Quinn Loftis is a multi-award-winning author of over thirty novels, including the USA Today Bestseller, Fate and Fury. When she isn't creating exciting worlds filled with romantic werewolves, she works as a pediatric nurse and crafts like there's no tomorrow. She is blessed to be married to her best friend for over twenty years and they have three sons, a crazy French bulldog, and a cat that wants to take over the world.

QUINN'S BOOKSHELF

The Grey Wolves Series

The Gypsy Healer Series

The Elfin Series

The Dream Maker Series

The Clan Hakon Series

Nature Hunters Academy

Sign up for Quinn's newsletter here:

You can also find Quinn writing contemporary romances as her alter ego, Alyson Drake.